Watch Over

By Amy Reece

Watch Over

Limitless Publishing, LLC
Kailua, HI 96734
www.limitlesspublishing.com

Formatting: Limitless Publishing

ISBN-13: 978-1-64034-147-0
ISBN-10: 1-64034-147-1

Dedication

This one is for all my fellow introverts who know how much energy it takes to interact with actual living people. Dogs are so much easier.

Chapter One

Melanie

It was the cat's fault. She certainly never would have gotten involved if it hadn't appeared in her life, much preferring to keep to herself and mind her own business. She wasn't even a cat person, for heaven's sake! She wasn't much of a dog person, either, but now she had one of each, apparently. Fluff had belonged to Aunt Karen, and Melanie had made a deathbed promise to take care of the small white mutt. Who else would understand Fluff needed his food heated for exactly eight seconds in the microwave and would only eat from the Blue Willow dishes? Of course Melanie had promised to continue to care for the elderly little mop. *Sigh.*

As for the cat, she'd seen the paw prints first. She was rinsing her dishes in the sink and noticing how much dust had accumulated on the bay windowsill when she frowned and leaned in for a closer look. There was definitely a trail of small

1

animal prints in the thick dust and what looked like a butt print where something had sat and stared out the kitchen window. *What the ... ?* Melanie glanced across the room at Fluff, curled up in his little bed, and shook her head. "Some guard dog you've turned out to be."

The cat itself showed up the night after Aunt Karen's funeral. It must have come in through the doggy door, but Melanie was too busy crying to notice. She'd held herself together all day long through the funeral and reception at the church, and was finally able to allow her emotions free rein. It scared the crap out of her when the cat jumped on the table and began purring and rubbing its furry little face against hers, as if trying to cheer her up.

She picked up the chair she'd knocked over and sat down to pet the ginger cat, who sat on the kitchen table staring at her. "Where in the world did you come from?" There was no collar. "You look like you've been through the ringer." The cat had a torn ear and rough coat. She found a can of tuna in the pantry and added a small bowl of milk beside it as the cat made short work of the meal before leaping back on the kitchen table to lick its paws.

"Make yourself at home," Melanie muttered as she put the cat's dishes in the dishwasher. "Doesn't this bother you at all? This cat just waltzed into your home and took over." She addressed the words to Fluff, who continued to snore in his little blue bed. "Apparently not."

She put it out before she retired for the night, but it was sleeping on the end of her bed the next morning. It left soon after breakfast, but returned

2

later that night and every night for the next week. She started calling him Cooper, and finally broke down and bought him a blue collar and heart-shaped nametag. She'd made a vet appointment for him too, but they couldn't get him in until next week.

The note was attached to his new collar; she felt it when she pulled him on her lap as they settled in to watch *Wheel of Fortune* the next day. She didn't really care for the game show, but it had become a habit when Aunt Karen was still alive and she'd continued to watch for some reason. "What's this?" She unfolded the small piece of notebook paper, Pat Sajak forgotten for the moment.

Dear Nice Lady,

I love my new collar and ID tag. Thanks for taking such good care of me and giving me a warm place to sleep every night. The nice man two doors down is writing this note for me on account of my not having opposable thumbs. He noticed me leaving your house this morning. He's a pretty nice guy and I've been spending my mornings with him recently. I especially enjoy helping him read his newspaper. I like to lie on it and make sure it doesn't get away, which is a very important job, let me assure you. Every once in a while I take a bite out of one of the pages if I dislike what is written there. This morning I felt compelled to bite the sports page when the man read the score from the Astros/Braves game and said a naughty word. I wanted to express my solidarity with him in his disappointment over the Astros' loss.

It is with some regret that I have to inform you that, while I like the color blue, I am definitely a female and feel the name "Cooper" may be a bit masculine. The nice man calls me CJ. What do you think about it? I like it a lot.

Sincerely,
CJ Catson

"What in the world?" She re-read the note and laughed softly at the way he'd written from the cat's perspective. She bit her lip as she realized who the author must be. Two doors down to the left was an elderly widow, so it had to be the young guy two doors to the right, who'd moved in about six months ago. She'd only seen him from a distance, but she could tell he was good-looking: tall, dark hair, well built. He was a police officer—she'd caught glimpses of him in his uniform and he often parked his police car in his driveway—but he'd been gone for several months. She'd wondered if he moved or something. Actually, her writer's imagination had dreamed up all sorts of scenarios that included him being deep undercover in a drug ring or organized crime syndicate. She'd seen several different young women coming and going when he was still there and figured he must be something of a ladies' man. Should she respond to the note? What could possibly come of this? She shook her head and reached for a piece of stationary. Why should anything come of it? She would simply write back and that would be the end of it. She thought for a few minutes, then wrote quickly and folded it up before she could reconsider.

There. He could respond or not. It was totally up to him.

***

Finn

Finn grinned and set the binoculars aside as he waited for the cat to arrive through the doggy door the previous residents had installed. He'd left it in place, thinking he might someday want a dog of his own. He realized the binoculars bordered on stalkerish, but a guy could only take so much daytime television. He wheeled his chair to the kitchen table and reached for his morning newspaper, pointedly ignoring the prescription pain medication sitting on the wooden lazy Susan. *Tough it out, big guy!* He was desperately afraid of getting hooked, so he only took them when the pain was unbearable. Instead, he popped two Tylenol and gritted his teeth.

"Mrow."

"Morning, CJ." Finn greeted his part-time pet as she leaped to the table and took up her usual position right in the middle of the sports page. "What have you got for me?" He'd watched through the binoculars as the cute girl two doors down had checked the note fastened to the cat's collar before putting her down on the porch. Not that he was interested or anything. He'd simply noticed she was cute. What red-blooded guy wouldn't? Thanks to the accident, he was in no fit state to start anything with anyone, no matter how attractive. Nor was he inclined. Tatiana had seen to that.

He unfolded the small scrap of pink paper and smoothed it on the tabletop.

Dear Nice Man,

The nice lady is shocked. It took her quite a while to even speak to me again. She thought I only visited her and was surprised to hear I spend the day with you. I told her it wasn't at all personal; I just have a big personality and feel I must share it with all my fans. What would you and Nice Lady do without the privilege of feeding and housing me? I hope you both realize how lucky you are.

Now don't be cranky, but Nice Lady doubts your assessment of my gender. She wants to know how you can tell. She also wants to know what CJ stands for.

Sincerely,

Cooper Catson

P.S. Nice Lady hopes you have a nice day.

He chuckled aloud, startling the cat. "Is she as feisty as this note makes her sound?"

The cat stared at him, but didn't answer. She returned to her grooming, licking her paw and wiping it across her torn ear.

"Nothing? Come on! Give a guy a break. She sits in that house all day and I can't tell what she does. I don't see a boyfriend—or a girlfriend, for that matter. What's her story?" He backed his wheelchair away from the kitchen table and found some more notebook paper in his desk. He chewed on the end of his pen while he tried to decide what to write. He heard a key in the front door, but most of his attention was devoted to writing the note.

"Hey, Finn. How are you feeling this morning?" His sister, Cara, leaned down to kiss his head before setting the grocery bags she carried on the counter.

"Like I got hit by a car. Did you remember to get milk?" He didn't look up from the note.

"Hilarious, really. And yes, I got milk. Did you eat anything for breakfast yet? You shouldn't take your pain meds on an empty stomach." She popped two pieces of bread in the toaster as she spoke.

Finn dropped the pen and wheeled away from the table, heading into the living room.

"Where are you going?" Cara called.

"I'm looking for Mom. I hear so much nagging I'm sure she must be around here somewhere."

"Ooh, you're in a sassy mood this morning. Get your busted up ass over here and eat something." She set a plate of toast and a glass of orange juice in front of him as he returned to the table. "Since when do you have a cat?" She scooped the feline into her arms.

"She's just visiting. Thanks for breakfast, sis. And for picking up the groceries."

"No problem. Mom's still freaking out about you being here by yourself. She's sure you're going to starve to death or fall out of your wheelchair. Oh, you're a sweet kitty. Yes, you are," she crooned to the cat in her arms. CJ was lapping it up, rubbing her face against Cara's chin.

"Mom worries too much. I'll be fine. I love her to death, but she was starting to drive me nuts." He'd been staying with his parents since he was released from the rehab center, but had needed to return to his own home for his mental health. His parents were great, but the hovering was starting to get to him. He'd staged a rebellion and insisted on returning to his own house three days ago. His parents and siblings were taking turns stopping by with groceries and to do the various housekeeping chores he wasn't able to manage yet. Well, that's what his mom and sisters did. His dad and brothers were more likely to bring a pizza and a six-pack.

"Whatcha writing?" Cara leaned over his shoulder.

"Nosy much? It's a note to CJ's owner."

She snatched up the note. "CJ? Her tag says Cooper. Nice Lady? You don't know her owner's name?"

Finn sighed and ran his hand over his jaw, realizing he badly needed a shave. Personal hygiene was something of a challenge when he was stuck in a wheelchair. "God, Cara. Stop talking for two seconds and I'll answer your infernal questions. And give me back my note."

"Don't pay attention to the nasty-tempered man, Kitty. He's just cranky because he's hurting and won't take his pain pills."

Not much got by his sharp-eyed sister. "Yeah, well, I don't want to get through all this just to end up a junkie. Tylenol is fine. Now do you want to hear the story or are you going to keep harassing me?"

"I'm done harassing you. For the moment." She handed him back the sheet of paper.

He reluctantly chuckled and told his sister how the cat had shown up on his second morning home, slipping in the front door when he'd opened it for the mailman, who was kind enough to hand Finn his newspaper and mail when he delivered a package and realized his customer was in a wheelchair. He'd promised to keep it up until Finn could manage for himself. The cat had since discovered the dog door and now made daily use of it. "She showed up with the brand-new collar and tag yesterday. I sent a note back, attached to the collar, letting the owner know the cat's female and I call her CJ." He handed her the note he'd received in return.

Cara read it, smiling. "She sounds fun. Do you have any idea which neighbor it is?"

"Two doors down on the left." He winced as he realized he'd given too much information. Damn. He'd never been able to keep anything from Cara.

"How do you—oooh!" She'd spied the binoculars. "How Jimmy Stewart of you, Finn!" She leapt out of her chair, released the cat, and danced into the living room to grab them up. "So, has anyone murdered his wife and chopped her into tiny pieces?"

"Not as far as I can tell, but the old lady across the street has been digging in her flower beds, so maybe there's hope."

Cara laughed. "I thought you were crazy when you bought a house in this senior citizen neighborhood, but maybe it's more exciting than I expected." She peered out the window through the binoculars for a few moments. "I can't see any sign of Nice Lady."

Finn had bought the house six months ago when his former partner's wife, a real estate agent, had told him what a great deal it was. Small, neat, with a gorgeous yard and old, established trees, the one-story brick house was perfect for a single guy who was tired of throwing away money on rent. The older, quiet neighborhood appealed to him and he'd had visions of settling down and starting a family. He was twenty-nine and it was starting to feel like the right thing to do. He'd been on the verge of asking his girlfriend to move in, had actually been thinking about it during his run that morning nearly three months before. It was the last thing he'd thought about until he woke up ten days later in the hospital. "She doesn't poke her nose out very often. I've only seen her a couple times."

"Well, maybe Miss CJ will help you meet her and a few more of your neighbors. Who knows?"

"Yeah, who knows?" But he only said it to shut Cara up.

Chapter Two

Melanie

Dear Nice Lady,

Nice Man says you should never doubt him, at least when it comes to pets. He says he and his five siblings had every possible pet known to man when they were growing up, including a piglet. The sure-fire way to tell I am indeed a girl is to 1) lift my tail. Go ahead. I'll get over the indignity eventually. 2) The opening just under the tail is the anus. Below the anus is the genital opening, which is round in males, and is a vertical slit in females. See? Mine is quite vertical, isn't it? Therefore, I am a girl. The nice man wants me to assure you he is not really an insufferable know-it-all and is willing to call me Cooper if it's important to you.

On the off chance you're not terribly attached to the name Cooper, CJ stands for Calamity Jane. He won't tell me why he calls me that and I am quite irritated with him. I certainly hope you will have the courtesy to explain his rude laughter. I don't like when people have fun at my expense. I am twitching my tail at him as he writes. I may have to bite him. I'll let you know.

Sincerely,

CJ/Cooper Catson

P.S. Nice Man hopes you have a nice day too.

Melanie chuckled and kissed the cat's head. "Well, Cooper, it appears he has a sense of humor. I wonder what his name is?" She had no intention of actually finding out, of course. That wasn't an option. No, she'd stay in her aunt's house—hers now, she supposed, although it didn't seem real yet—and mind her own business. She wasn't a hermit by any stretch, but she worked from home and preferred to keep to herself in her leisure hours. There weren't many of those between her graphic design clients and her writing, but she had a very limited social circle and she liked it that way. She wasn't good with people she didn't know.

"Mrow."

"Would you mind if I took a quick peek under your tail? I know it's terribly intrusive, but he sounds like he knows what he's talking about." She turned the cat and lifted the tail. "He's right. You're a girl. CJ, huh? I guess I can go with it, but you don't need all the gritty details about your namesake." She smiled as she thought about the similarities between the street-wise, sometimes prostitute from the Old West and the feline sitting on her lap. She decided she'd make a quick trip to PetSmart after dinner for a new collar and tag.

Both CJ and Fluff perked up when they smelled the salmon Melanie was searing on the stovetop and she ended up splitting the fillet with them. CJ jumped on the table when she finished her portion and proceeded to wash, licking her paws and rubbing them across her furry face. Fluff retreated to his little blue bed and was soon snoring. "Don't get used to this kind of dinner every night. You caught me in a weak moment." She cleared the table and washed her dishes by hand, enjoying the warmth of the sudsy water. Aunt Karen had finally had a dishwasher installed last year, right before Melanie moved in. She had never bothered before, claiming a single woman had no need for one, but had wanted to make things as easy as possible for her great-niece. Melanie wouldn't have cared and often still washed up by hand. She changed out of her yoga pants, donning a pair of jeans in honor of actually leaving the house for the first time in several days, and checked her hair. She sighed at her reflection, wishing there was just a bit more...oomph. There was nothing hideous, of course, but everything about her was so average: average height, common brown hair, brown eyes, and an extremely average figure. Nothing like any of the women she'd seen coming and going from her neighbor's house. Ugh! Why did she have to think about that now? Her fragile self-esteem certainly didn't need any more blows. *Snap out of it, girl! Nobody likes a pity party.*

At the store, she chose a pink rhinestone collar for CJ and added a few toys and treats, including some for Fluff. For someone who never planned to own a pet, she was suddenly spending an inordinate amount of money and time on two of them. Oh, well. She could afford it, especially since Aunt Karen had left everything to Melanie, including the house. It wasn't riches, exactly, but it certainly eased the budget strain. Melanie would trade it all for five more minutes with her aunt, but knew it was a selfish wish since the elderly woman had been in such pain toward the end, the cancer eating away at her wasted body. She pushed the maudlin memories aside and focused her thoughts on the furry beasts waiting for her at home. The two animals were company and kept her from talking to herself. Besides, they were awfully cute.

"Miss CJ, you look glorious!" she said as she sat back to admire the new collar and tag she'd fastened around the cat's neck. CJ was practically prancing, showing off her new collar. "And you too, Fluff. You are so handsome." She'd picked out a blue plaid collar she thought would look nice against his white fur. Was it her imagination, or did the elderly dog seem younger since the cat showed up? "You two will have to amuse yourselves with your new toys because I still have several hours of work ahead." Nevertheless, she spent a few more minutes throwing the catnip mouse for CJ.

She stepped onto the front porch for a few minutes of fresh evening air and gazed down the street toward *his* house. The curtains were closed, but the lights were on and a car was in the driveway. Another girlfriend? Or the same one as before? She wondered where he'd been for the past few months and why he was suddenly back. She stared for a few more minutes then went back inside to write for several hours. Days were for graphic design, her paying job, but evenings were set aside for the romance novels she adored writing. She dreamed of one day writing full time, but her current royalty checks were somewhat underwhelming, to say the least. Nevertheless, it was pure joy to create characters and plot twists and to hear from readers who loved her book.

She fired up her laptop and lost herself for the

next three hours.

***

Finn

Dear Nice Man,

Well, it's official: I'm a girl. Nice Lady checked and realized you were correct. She's somewhat embarrassed, but she'll get over it, I'm sure. Best of all, she gave me a bit of salmon to make up for getting all up in my business. All she will tell me about my name is that it is in honor of a heroine of the Old West, but she was definitely smirking when she said it, so I'm not sure I trust her.

Nice Lady is still reeling about the fact that you have five siblings! She's an only child and says she can't imagine what growing up in such a large family was like. She wants to know if you're the oldest, youngest, etc.? She worries that she's being nosy, though, and, if so, apologizes and retracts the question.

Either way, she hopes you have a lovely day and enjoy reading your newspaper.
Sincerely,
CJ Catson

Finn grinned and stroked the cat purring on his lap. He'd noticed the glitzy pink collar right away and had eagerly checked for a note. He'd been worried his last note had offended her and the amusing exchange would be over, nixing the possibility of ever meeting her. *God, I need to get out of this chair! I'm desperate enough to look forward to passing notes with my mysterious neighbor via a damn cat. If she'd wanted to meet, she would have come by to introduce herself when I first moved in.* He refused to entertain the idea that he could have done the same thing. He'd been so busy with work, family, and his girlfriend he hadn't made time to meet neighbors. But two of those things were no longer an issue, so he found himself with enough time on his hands to be curious.

The pounding on the front door startled the cat and she leaped off his lap, using plenty of claw to gain traction on his leg, and hid under the sofa. "Finn? You in there? Open the goddamn door! My hands are full!"

He wheeled to the door and opened it to reveal his partner, Chris, holding two cups of coffee with a brown bag clutched precariously under one arm. "Where else would I be? Please say you brought bagels."

She stepped past him, dropping the bag in his lap. "Of course I brought bagels. You look like shit, by the way."

"Really?" he asked around a giant bite of green chile bagel with a plain shmear—Chris knew exactly what he liked—and wheeled after her to the kitchen table. "I guess I should go change into my tux, huh? You think it'll fit over this big-ass cast?"

"I'll help you rip the pants open. Okay, no tux, but when was the last time you shaved? This homeless look doesn't do much for you." She handed him the coffee she'd brought for him, strong and dark, as he preferred.

He scratched his scruffy beard at her words. "I agree, but I can't stand in front of the mirror yet, so homeless it is. Unless you want to lend a hand?"

"Ah, hell to the no, partner. That's definitely a job for your mom or Tat—" She stopped, horrified at her slip. "God, Finn! I'm sorry. I forgot."

"Don't worry about it. It's fine." It was anything but fine.

"That bitch! She didn't deserve you." Chris tossed her half-eaten bagel on the table and grabbed her coffee cup angrily.

"Yeah, well, it doesn't matter anymore. So, what's new at the precinct? Any interesting cases?" He was grateful she hadn't requested a new partner, apparently resigned to waiting for him to recuperate. They'd only been working together for a couple months when a hit-and-run driver had taken him out of commission. She was a great partner and they balanced each other well.

"Not really. We picked up that John Doe

19

discovered behind the dumpster. Other than that it's been pretty slow. People just aren't killing each other in this town lately."

"Selfish bastards! Are they trying to put us out of a job?"

She chuckled and he hoped they could move past her inadvertent mention of his ex. "Well, we may be light on new cases, but there are plenty of cold cases sitting around gathering dust. You game for glancing through a few files while you sit around here on your ass?"

He was barely able to tamp down his enthusiasm. He was dying of boredom and would kill for a chance to do some actual work. "I guess I could set aside my bonbons and turn off my soaps for a couple hours. Can you bring them by tomorrow?"

Chris grinned and took another bite of her bagel, chewing slowly. "They're in the car."

He crumpled his napkin and threw it at her. "Brat."

"You love me. You know you do."

"It's a good thing, huh?" She was his first partner since he'd made detective and they had hit it off immediately. She was a tall, intimidating woman a few years older than Finn who took nonsense from no one. Whenever they questioned a perp, she was definitely the bad cop, something that amused Finn no end.

"So, what's with the cat? I thought you were allergic." CJ had made her way from under the sofa, onto Finn's lap, across the kitchen table, and onto Chris's lap.

"No, that was Tatiana. She was allergic to everything, even cinnamon."

"What? No one's allergic to cinnamon. That's bullshit!"

"Well, that's what she told me." He really didn't want to talk about his ex-girlfriend. He'd woken from a 10-day coma to discover she couldn't handle the stress of a boyfriend seriously injured and had left him. His family had to tell him about the break-up. Christ, he'd been about to ask her to move in with him! He'd actually contemplated marrying her! His relationship radar was obviously broken.

"I think she had a pathological need for attention, that's what I think. You can do so much better, Finn."

"Can we talk about something else, please? Anything but my love life, or lack thereof. I'm begging you."

"Sorry." She cleared her throat in the awkward silence. "So, did you watch the game last night?"

Finn was grateful and they spent the next few minutes dissecting the baseball game from the night before. Before she left for work, she brought in the cold case files she'd promised.

"Maybe you can find something. It would sure be nice to make some headway with any of these."

"Yeah, well, I can give them my total attention since I've got literally nothing better to do."

"You won't forgo your PT, though, will you?" She looked worried.

"Nah. I need to get out of this chair, so I won't neglect physical therapy. I may be able to start using crutches soon."

21

"That's great, Finn! How soon before you can come back to work?"

He was saved from answering the question by the arrival of his older brother, Hugh, who let himself in and joined them in the kitchen. "Hey, Finn. I just stopped by to tell you I'm sending a crew over to build the ramp for your wheel chair. Oh, hey, Chrissy. Good to see you."

Chrissy? He'd never heard anyone refer to his partner as *Chrissy*. He valiantly attempted to hide a smirk as he prepared to hear her rip Hugh a new one. He glanced across the table and was shocked to see her glancing down at the tabletop and—was she blushing? What. The. Hell?

"Hi, Hugh. Nice to see you too." She fumbled with her coffee cup, knocking it over and spilling a bit. Her mumbled curse was perfectly audible.

Finn flipped his head back and forth between the two of them, confused. *What am I missing?* He wasn't even aware they'd met. It must have been at the hospital while he was unconscious. "Hugh, man, I appreciate it. You'll make sure it doesn't wreck my porch, won't you? I don't plan to need it very long."

"Sure, of course I will. You're gonna be up and out of that chair before we know it. Hey, I didn't know you have a cat." CJ had been winding herself around Hugh's ankles and he bent down to pet her.

"I have joint custody. She spends her mornings here."

"Huh. Okay. Well, I need to get going. The crew should be here in about an hour. You up for watching the game tonight? I'll bring the beer."

22

"Cool. I'll order the pizza."

"Great. I'll be here around seven. See you, Chrissy." He left after giving the cat one last pat.

Finn switched his gaze to his partner, who busied herself cleaning up the spilled coffee, bagel wrappers, and paper bag, not meeting Finn's eyes. "Chrissy?"

"Shut up."

Chapter Three

Melanie

Dear Nice Lady,

I love my new collar! You are the nicest of nice ladies! Nice Man says he would have gotten off his butt and bought me one himself, but his stupid broken leg is still keeping him housebound. He would like the first vet visit to be on him, but wonders if you are able to take me since he can't drive right now. I DO NOT like the sound of this and must insist that any plans to take me to the vet be run by me first! I've heard they stick things under your tail and poke you with sharp sticks. That is simply not acceptable. But I digress.

Nice Man wants me to assure you that asking about his family is not nosy in the least. They're a crazy, big bunch and he loves to talk about them. He is third in line and has an older brother and sister. He also has a younger sister and two younger brothers. It's a giant Irish/Italian circus when they all get together for Sunday dinner.

Sincerely,

CJ Catson

P.S. Nice Man hopes you have a great day and wonders if the two of you could meet sometime. To discuss the vet visit, of course. He'd also love to tell you more about his family.

Broken leg...housebound...can't drive right now. Melanie lowered the note, horrified. "Oh, my God! That's why I haven't seen him in so long." The natural caretaker side of her mentally warred with the chronic introvert as she sat on her sofa, the note clutched in her hand. It took only a few seconds for the caretaker to win the battle and she leaped up, startling the cat, as she strode purposefully to her kitchen. *Don't be such a chicken! The poor man can't even leave the house. You can check on him, at the very least. Just a quick visit to make sure he's all right and see if he needs anything.* She cast her gaze around the room, thinking it would be nice to take him something homemade. She spied the banana bread she'd baked earlier and grabbed the foil-wrapped loaf before she could talk herself out of it. "Fluff, CJ, I'll be back in a few minutes. I just need to check on him." It was a mark of her distraction she didn't stop to check her appearance before leaving the house. Concern for her injured neighbor carried her the short distance between their houses; any greater distance and she would have had more time to re-think her impulsive decision. As it was, she found herself walking up a handicap ramp and knocking on his red front door before she was quite ready.

"Just a sec," a deep, muffled voice sounded from inside the house. "Who is it?" The voice now sounded much nearer, just on the other side of the door.

"It's uh, me. Nice Lady. You know, the cat?" Melanie winced as she realized how ridiculous she sounded. She heard the deadbolt release and then the door opened. She looked down as she realized he was in a wheelchair. Any thoughts of pity flew completely out of her mind as she saw him up close for the first time. He was gorgeous—there was simply no other word for it. Black wavy hair, deep blue eyes, and a strong jaw covered with a few

26

days' worth of scruffy black whiskers all added up to the most handsome man Melanie had seen in a long time. Or ever.

"Hi!" His grin was cheerful, but she detected weariness, possibly pain, around the edges, reflected in the purplish smudges beneath his eyes. "I'm so glad you came over. I'm Finn, by the way."

"Oh. I'm M—Mel." Her throat completely closed up before she could even finish her name. *God, what a spaz!*

"It's great to meet you, Mel. Come on in." He wheeled backward and gestured for her to enter. His arms, visible below the sleeves of the band t-shirt he wore, were magnificent—golden brown, muscular, and corded, but not bulging like a body builder. Masculine arms had always fascinated Melanie and Finn's were some of the best she'd ever seen.

She watched him struggle to close the front door and turn his wheelchair. She bit her lip and forced herself to let him do it himself.

"Have a seat." He gestured toward the living room, where an inviting overstuffed sofa and loveseat combo sat in front of a large flat screen television.

She perched on the edge of the loveseat while he wheeled his chair to a spot that looked like an armchair might usually occupy the space. "I'm so sorry."

"About what?"

"I didn't know about…" She gestured vaguely to his right leg, the entire length encased in a white cast and propped straight on the wheelchair extension. "I would have…I don't know." She shrugged with a nervous laugh. "Oh!" She stood abruptly. "I brought banana bread." She held the foil packet out toward him stupidly, then pulled it back when he simply raised his eyebrows. "Um, I'll just put it in your kitchen, if that's okay?" She found the kitchen through the dining room and set the bread on the counter, despising herself for her lack of anything resembling a social grace. She shrieked when he cleared his throat close behind her. How had she not heard him?

"Sorry. I didn't mean to startle you. Why don't we have some of that right now? Do you mind getting the plates down, though? The cabinet above the dishwasher." He pointed in the general direction.

"Of course." She turned to retrieve the plates, happy to have a task. She located a serrated knife in the block on the counter and found a cutting board with his direction. In short order, she set a platter of banana bread, a tub of margarine, and a small plate each on the kitchen table. At his suggestion, she then busied herself making them each a cup of coffee in the Keurig machine, brushing away his apologies for not doing anything himself.

"This is delicious, Mel. Did you make it?" he asked around a bite.

She smiled and nodded as she sipped the coffee. "This morning. I like to bake." She helped herself to a small piece, mostly to be sociable. "When did this happen?" She gestured to his leg again. "How?"

"Hit and run while I was jogging. It was almost three months ago." He shrugged as if it wasn't a big deal. "I've been in the hospital and then rehab ever since. Well, I was staying with my parents most recently, but I needed to get back to my own place. I'll be out of this chair soon. Hopefully. I had another surgery last week that should enable me to begin using crutches in a week or so."

"That will be nice for you. You must be going nuts being stuck in that chair, huh? You're a police officer, aren't you?" She was using all her latent social skills, trying to maintain something of a conversation. He was so good-looking it was hard to believe she was sitting here talking to him. *Can you say way out of my league?*

"Yeah, I'm a cop. I actually just made detective, literally two months before I got hit. Rotten luck, huh? What do you do, Mel?" He reached for another piece of banana bread, slathering it with butter. "This is really great. Thanks." He grinned, causing her insides to actually flutter. She didn't get out much; being in such close proximity to an incredibly handsome man was messing with her equilibrium. She needed to get out of here before she said something stupid. He was staring at her, eyebrows raised, and she realized she'd been so busy thinking she'd missed what he'd said.

"Sorry. What was the question?"

"What do you do? For a living, I mean."

"Oh. I'm a graphic designer. I work from home. Contract stuff, mostly. I also write." She bit her lip and started clearing their plates.

"That's cool. What do you write? Here, let me get that." He took the plates from her, set them on his lap, and wheeled to the sink.

"Um, I write contemporary romance." Why was

29

she always embarrassed to talk about her writing? She certainly wasn't ashamed of it—in fact, she was proud of what she'd achieved—finding an agent and landing a publishing deal—yet she always found herself downplaying it.

"Really? Can I read one of your books?"

"Oh, I'm sure you wouldn't like what I write. Guys don't like to read romance."

"How do you know? I've never read a book written by someone I know. It would be cool." He smiled at her in a way that probably got him whatever he wanted on a regular basis.

"Oh." Wow, she must sound brilliant, indeed. "Sure, yeah. I'll bring you a copy…sometime." Of course she wouldn't. She followed him back to the living room. "Well, I better—" She was interrupted by the doorbell.

"That'll be the pizza. You haven't had dinner yet, have you?" He wheeled toward the front door, not really waiting for an answer. "You want to grab a couple beers from the fridge? I hope you like Italian sausage."

And that's how she ended up sharing pizza and beer with her gorgeous neighbor, whom she'd just met.

***

Finn

Finn sent the text while he wheeled, one-handed, to the front door to pay for the pizza.

Finn: Gotta cancel. Sorry.

Hugh: Seriously? I'm at the store buying beer.

Finn: Go home.

Hugh: Girl?

Finn: Maybe.

Hugh: You little shit! Pretty?

Finn: Duh.

Hugh: You owe me.

Finn: Whatever.

Finn grinned as he shoved his phone between his good leg and the side of the wheelchair. He wasn't worried about Hugh. He'd be pissed for a while, but he'd get over it soon enough. Finn had been ditched for a pretty girl more than once, so he knew his brother's anger wouldn't last long. He'd seen Mel was preparing to bolt and he figured he'd have a hard time getting her back. And he definitely wasn't ready to let her go yet. He'd known she was cute from spying on her with the binoculars, but he hadn't been prepared for how pretty she was up close. Her long brown hair, looped messily on top of her head, was shiny and soft-looking, while her creamy skin was the most tempting thing he'd seen in quite a while. It didn't appear as if she had a speck of makeup on, either. Tatiana had worn way too much and he'd always hated how he had to wipe her lipstick off his mouth when they kissed. The attraction he felt when he'd opened the door and seen his reclusive neighbor standing there was instant and undeniable. And she'd brought him home-baked banana bread. God, how sweet was that? So, although he had no intention or desire to start another relationship so soon after his last disastrous one, he'd invited her in and set about getting to know her. She wasn't going to be easy to get to know, however. She seemed a bit on the shy side and Finn figured he'd better break out the charm he hadn't had to use in a while. The doorbell signaling the arrival of the pizzas had been fortuitous, allowing him to wrangle her into staying for dinner. He paid the delivery guy and set the boxes on his lap to return to his guest.

"Are you sure you want me to stay? I don't want to intrude," she said as she set a cold beer on the side table near his chair. "Were you expecting someone else?" She gestured to the amount of pizza, clearly too much for one person.

"My brother had to cancel at the last minute, so it's perfect." He felt the tiniest bit guilty about taking liberties with the truth, but didn't stop to closely examine his desire to keep her near. He set the pizzas on the coffee table and opened the boxes. "We've got pepperoni with green chile and sausage with mushrooms. You're not a vegetarian, are you?" Tatiana had been and it made eating with her no damn fun.

She smiled and shook her head as she reached

for a slice of the sausage. "Mmm. This is wonderful! Where's it from?"

Finn forgot to breathe, his slice frozen halfway to his mouth, as he watched her tongue slide over her lower lip to catch a stray bit of sauce.

"Finn? What's wrong?"

"Huh? Sorry. Nothing's wrong." He cleared his throat and took a bite. She was right: it was wonderful, as always. "It's from Mario's. Best pizza in town, in my opinion. I'm probably biased, though, since my cousin owns the place. You ever eaten there?"

She shook her head. "My aunt was bedridden when I moved here to take care of her, so we didn't go out to eat. I haven't ventured out much since her death."

"I'm sorry to hear she died. When?"

"Almost two weeks ago now."

"I never got a chance to meet her." They were both silent for a few moments and he took the time to study her face as she glanced away, obviously attempting to maintain her composure as she recalled the recent death. She wasn't drop-dead gorgeous like most of the women he dated, but there was a wholesome beauty to her he found incredibly alluring. She was pretty, although that particular word seemed too tame for her. He sternly told himself he was only interested in casual friendship as he tried to quash the attraction building stronger with every second he spent in her company. "Where did you move from?"

"Chicago. I moved there for college and was working in an advertising firm when Aunt Karen got sick. She didn't have anyone else, so I moved here to help out."

"What about your parents? You said you didn't have any brothers or sisters, right?" He found he was curious about every aspect of her life.

She shook her head. "My dad died a long time ago and my mother and I don't get along. No siblings. A couple of half-brothers, but I don't know them well. Not like you. Tell me about your family. Explain the whole Irish/Italian thing, please."

He was happy to comply, hoping to reverse the suddenly shuttered expression that had fallen across her features when he asked about her family. "Well, my dad is Italian, one generation removed from Italy. His parents emigrated and somehow wound up here in Albuquerque. My grandad started a construction company and my dad took it over when he retired. My mom is from Ireland. She came over here on a study abroad program, met my dad, and never went back. Long story short, they multiplied like rabbits and that's why I have five brothers and sisters." He checked to see if she was glazed over or drooling with boredom, but she seemed interested, so he continued. "My parents took turns naming us; my mom picked Irish names and my dad picked Italian names. My mom went first, so my oldest brother is Hugh. He's thirty-four and works with my dad. Then there's Isabella, who's thirty-two and has a four-year old daughter, my niece, Janey. Then there's yours truly. Next is my sister Cara, who's twenty-seven and is a high school English teacher. Seamus is twenty-five and a firefighter. Last but not least, there's little Tony.

He's twenty-two and supposedly graduating from college this year if he can stop partying long enough to pass his last few classes."

"Wow," she said with a soft chuckle. "Your house must have been loud and crazy when you were growing up. So you're what? Thirty?"

"Twenty-nine. I'll be thirty in October. What about you?" He absolutely loved the way she laughed. It was light and lilting, falling softly around them, causing him to grin, absurdly proud he was responsible for the sound.

"I'm twenty-four. So, I've never had green chile before, but I think I'll give it a try." She reached hesitantly for a slice of the other pizza.

"Never had green chile? What? That's almost a crime! You've lived here for how long?"

"Almost a year now. Aunt Karen couldn't go out, so I've never had it." She nibbled at the slice.

"So? What's the verdict? You need to like it or we can't be friends, but no pressure." He smiled to let her know he was kidding—mostly.

"Hmm." She continued to chew and then took another larger bite. She swallowed and said, "Well, I like it on pizza, at least. I'd like to go to a real New Mexican restaurant, though, and try more."

"The second I get out of this chair, I would love to take you out for Mexican food. How about it, Mel?" Holy crap! Had he just asked her out on a date? The words had slipped out before he even had a chance to consider them. He'd had every intention of cooling it on the whole dating scene for a while after the fiasco with Tatiana, but this little slip of a girl had waltzed into his house and next thing you knew, he was asking her out on a date.

"Oh." She looked surprised and a bit flushed. "I, uh, okay. Yeah. That would be great." She was silent for a moment, staring down at the slice of pizza in her hand. "My name's really Melanie. I just choked up when you answered the door." She didn't meet his eyes.

He could tell he needed to tread lightly, but he couldn't hold back the grin at her shy admission. "Mel suits you. Do you mind if I call you that?"

She bit her lip and shook her head, which he found utterly charming.

"Cool. Mel it is. You can call me Finn."

"Isn't that your name?" She glanced up at him, a small frown wrinkling between her eyes.

"Yeah." He grinned again, enjoying teasing her.

She smiled and rolled her eyes.

Chapter Four

Melanie

Three hours had never flown by so fast. Melanie wrenched her eyes away from Finn's handsome face long enough to take in the nearly empty pizza boxes and the array of empty beer bottles on his coffee table and realized she had certainly overstayed her welcome. She quickly gathered the trash, brushing away his protests that she didn't have to clean up, and bid her new friend good night. They'd exchanged cell numbers before she left and she made him promise to call or text if he needed anything. She didn't know how he was managing on his own and decided she would check in on him frequently, at least while he was still in the wheelchair. It had nothing to do with how gorgeous he was. That was simply a fortuitous benefit. She giggled a bit, and turned back to see him sitting on his porch, watching her walk home. She waved, hoping he hadn't heard her. What was she— thirteen? Giggling over the cute boy in her class?

Get it together, Melanie! This isn't like you! She hadn't been silly over a guy since college. The thought of her college years wiped any trace of a smile from her face. She didn't like to think about that time in her life.

She was nearly past grouchy old Mr. Taylor's house, situated between hers and Finn's, when she first felt it: the prickling on the back of her neck that made her feel like she was being watched. She whisked her head back around to Finn's porch, but he was gone and his front door closed. She rubbed her hand up and down her arm, suddenly chilled, as she picked up the pace, glancing around when she could swear she heard a branch cracking underfoot somewhere to her right. She stopped and peered into the dark space between the two yards across the street. "Hello? Is anyone there?" No answer, of course. She shook her head at her foolishness and hurried home, grateful she'd had the foresight to leave her own front porch light on.

CJ and Fluff were both waiting for her inside the front door. While the cat wound itself around Melanie's ankles, doing her best to trip her, the dog pranced and yipped impatiently.

"I know, I'm sorry! You both must be starving! Come on, I'll get your dinner." She rushed straight to the kitchen and fixed them each an extra-special dish of kibble, stirring in some leftover broiled chicken to help make up for her tardiness. CJ finished and stalked to the chair opposite the sofa where she licked her whiskers and stared moodily at Melanie. "I said I'm sorry." No response from the taciturn feline. "What can I say? You *have* noticed how cute he is, haven't you? I lost track of time staring into those dreamy blue eyes." But CJ didn't seem in the mood to forgive easily. She finished her post-dinner bath and curled up in a tight ball for her evening nap while Melanie fired up her laptop, ready for a few hours of uninterrupted writing time.

She found her thoughts wandering, however, back to the unexpected evening spent with her neighbor. *He called me Mel.* No one had ever called her that. *So what? It doesn't mean anything! He's the kind of guy who oozes charm without even trying. He's not your type!* The truth was she hadn't had any type of guy in years. Since college. Since Evan. She grimaced as she thought about the college boyfriend who had broken her heart—and for a while, her spirit. *Ugh! Stop it! Do not let that jerk have any more power over you!* It was a wonderful sentiment, but a whole lot easier said than done. She shook her head and forced her attention back to her latest novel. Her agent was expecting a first draft in less than a month, so Melanie couldn't afford to procrastinate. She managed to put all thoughts of her gorgeous neighbor aside and added nearly four thousand words to her manuscript before closing her laptop with a huge yawn.

"That's it for me, guys. Let's head to bed." CJ and Fluff both rose and stretched before following Melanie to her bedroom. She stopped to check the front and back doors, reminded of the creepy feeling she'd had walking home from Finn's house earlier. The neighborhood was in a decent area, but you never knew in Albuquerque. Just the week before, there had been a pair of escaped convicts in the area and they'd only captured one of them. The police helicopters flying overhead had kept her awake for hours.

CJ left, as usual, bright and early the next morning, and Melanie figured she was heading straight for Finn's. She briefly considered following the cat, but firmly told herself 'no' and set to work on the logo she was designing for a startup company in California. She had several designs to present, but wanted to have a few more to offer before sending it to her boss. She was completely caught up in her work when her cell phone buzzed with a text message.

Finn: Good morning Mel. This is CJ. Come over.

She smiled as she texted back.

Melanie: I'm working.

Finn: So is the man. Bring your laptop and work here. We can all have lunch together. You'll have to make it, but the man has groceries. Bring Fluffy.

She smiled at his attempt at her dog's name. She must have mentioned him last night and was touched he'd remembered.

"Well, Fluff? What do you think? You want to go down to Finn's?" Fluff lifted his head from the sofa at the mention of his name. "We can work there as easily as we can here. Besides, I can make lunch for him. He might not eat much if I don't. It's the neighborly thing to do." She stuffed her laptop and Wacom drawing tablet in a tote bag then scooped up the small dog before she could think too deeply about her rationalization.

"So, this is Fluffy, huh?" Finn was waiting for her at the front door. He had shaved and his hair was still damp and curling around the collar of his t-shirt—AC/DC today. He was apparently a classic rock fan.

"It's just Fluff. His full name is Sir Fluffers McNutt. Don't look at me like that! My aunt named him and he was the light of her life. It was basically a deathbed promise I made to take care of him."

"Sorry! I shouldn't laugh, but I've never heard a name quite like that. He's cute."

She set the elderly dog on the ground and watched, amused, as he walked straight to Finn and asked to be picked up by putting his front paws on Finn's good leg. Finn met Melanie's gaze, surprised, but reached to lift the small dog onto his lap.

They spent several hours working in companionable silence. Finn had wheeled his chair to the dining room table, where he had at least a dozen manila folders spread across the rectangular oak table. She curled up on his couch to continue her design work. Her growling stomach finally caused her to close her laptop and stand, stretching to get the kinks out. She wandered over to see what had engrossed him so completely—she hadn't heard a peep from him since he'd made sure she had everything she needed to work. She stepped behind him quietly and peered over his shoulder. He had spread the contents of one of the file folders across the table and was scratching notes on a yellow legal pad. There were various typed reports and at least a dozen gruesome photos of a nude female body that looked like it had been dumped in a ditch of some sort.

"God, that poor girl!"

"Oh, hey Mel." He quickly set his notepad over the worst of the photos. "You don't need to see this. Sorry about that. I guess I lost track of time. You must be starving." He backed his chair away from the table and led the way to the kitchen.

"I could definitely eat."

He produced an array of cold cuts and sliced cheeses for sandwiches and showed her where to find everything. He actually handled most of the lunch prep, making her doubt his need for her help, and only allowed her to set the table and reach for the items he couldn't from his chair. In short order they were seated opposite each other at his kitchen table, ham and cheese sandwiches, apple slices, potato chips, and iced tea.

"So, those pictures…a case you're working on?" She nibbled the edge of potato chip, something she rarely allowed herself; she was way too prone to eat the entire bag.

"Yeah. My partner dropped off a few cold cases to keep me busy. It might just keep me from going completely insane." He chuckled and took another bite of his sandwich.

"So, how's that working for you?"

He choked as he laughed and took a few gulps of his iced tea. She froze with a chip halfway to her mouth, intrigued by the way the muscles in his throat worked as he swallowed. She was entranced by the corded strength and noticed a small patch of black whiskers he must have missed this morning when he shaved. She was just starting to imagine what it would feel like to run her lips across the expanse of tan throat when he caught her staring. *Crap. I'm in so much trouble.*

***

Finn

Quiet, but sassy. That's how he decided to categorize his neighbor as he watched her take a bite of the sandwich he'd made for her. He made an effort to hide his grin as he realized he'd caught her staring. Fair enough. He'd done his fair share of staring at her pretty face. Yeah, he hadn't really needed her help fixing lunch, but he wanted her company. He'd really enjoyed talking to her the night before and hadn't been able to stop thinking about her since, including a fairly sexy dream that ended far too soon. He had made it through a tough physical therapy session earlier that morning by thinking about her, planning to call as soon as he was done. He'd chickened out at the last minute and sent a text—from the damn cat, of all things. How lame could he get? He was nervous. Him. Finn DeLuca, who had dated some of the most beautiful women in Albuquerque. His last girlfriend was the ten o' clock anchor for one of the local news stations and was stunning. And he was nervous about calling his neighbor? Go figure. But she'd said yes and came over, curling up in the corner of his couch and working on her computer for several hours. Her ridiculous little dog was still asleep in his lap. Didn't it ever have to pee? He'd been able to concentrate—truly focus for the first time since the accident—and dug into the files Chris had dropped off the day before. Something about knowing she was there, being able to look over and see her on his couch, had quieted his mind and he'd been able to get some good work done. He'd started to worry he'd lost his touch and would have to find a new job when he could finally walk again. God, please let him be able to walk again and be strong enough to return to his job! Today, both the grueling physical workout and the headway he'd made with a decades-old murder case, gave him a brand-new hope for his immediate future.

"So, my physical therapist told me I could start using crutches next week." He broke the somewhat awkward silence.

"That's great, Finn! You must be pretty sick of that chair, huh?"

"You have no idea. Yeah, I get this big cast off on Monday and, if all looks good, I'll have a boot for my ankle and be able to use crutches."

"How much of your leg did you break?"

"I'd like to point out that I didn't break it. The person who ran me over broke it. I was minding my own business, jogging, trying to be healthy." He grinned when she rolled her eyes. "Anyway, my femur was broken, but it was a clean break and has healed pretty well. My ankle is what's really giving me fits. It was crushed and isn't healing as well as the doctors had hoped." He shrugged and took another bite of his own sandwich to hide his fear. He didn't want her to know how worried he was about his ankle.

"Did they find the person who hit you? You said it was a hit-and-run, right?"

"It was, yeah. Nope. We have no idea who or what hit me. I had my headphones in and was hit from behind. The next thing I remember was waking up in the hospital ten days later."

"Oh my God. You were in a coma?"

He nodded and shrugged again. He wasn't trying to impress her and didn't care to dwell on how close he'd come to death. Existential crises simply weren't his forte. "So, I read your book last night." He figured that would change the subject.

"Excuse me?"

"Your book, *Taking Chances*. I read it last night after you left."

"How did you—you don't even know my last name!" She looked appalled and embarrassed, making him feel like a putz.

"I'm a cop, Mel. One phone call got me the name Melanie Blythe. I found your book on Amazon and downloaded it to my Kindle. I really liked it, by the way. You have a gift for creating memorable characters."

"You really read my book?"

"Yep. Kept me awake 'til nearly three a.m. I had to find out if Danae and Chance finally got together.

I'm glad you went for the happily-ever-after. I'd have been pissed if they stayed broken up."

She bit her lip and appeared to be trying to decide whether or not to smile. "You really liked it? I wouldn't have pegged you for a romance reader."

"It was my first, but I might be hooked. You write a pretty hot sex scene, Ms. Blythe. I had no idea there was such fun stuff in romance novels." He absolutely loved the blush creeping across her cheeks. He'd always been attracted to bold, flashy women who'd forgotten how to blush long before. The girl sitting across the table from him was a breath of fresh air.

"Oh, well...you know." She shrugged and busied herself with eating another potato chip.

He was enchanted. "No, I don't know. But I'm sure I'd like to find out." He raised his eyebrows up and down in a suggestive manner. When she snorted in laughter, he knew he was in trouble. *She is entirely too adorable for my peace of mind.* Yet he liked being with her. He liked her company. "So, when does the sequel come out?"

"I'm working on it. It's not exactly a sequel, though. It's the next story, about Danae's sister. You didn't have to buy it, you know. I would have given you a copy." She still didn't seem able to meet his eyes.

"No way! It's too good to give away. I wrote a great review. Did you see it?"

She shook her head. "I never read them. The good ones make me feel good, but the bad ones really mess with me."

Finn experienced a rather primal shot of

protectiveness that shocked him. He was distracted from his fantasy of punching a bad reviewer in the face by the sound of the front door being unlocked and opened.

"Finn? You here?"

He rolled his eyes at his sister's question. "Where else would I be?"

"I thought you might have escaped by now." She appeared around the corner of the kitchen, a laundry basket propped against one hip. "I brought back the wash Mom did for you. All your tidy-whities are bright and—ooh, you have company!" She set the basket on the floor and crossed to seat herself at the table, intrusive as always. "Hi, I'm Cara." She snagged a chip from Finn's plate as she sat.

Finn sensed Mel withdrawing in the face of Cara's ebullient greeting and silently cursed his sister's intrusion. "Mel, this is my sister, Cara."

"Nice to meet you, Mel. So, how do you know Finn?" She was smiling, and he could see the gleeful light in her eyes.

"Oh, I…uh…I live down the street and—"

"Mel is CJ's other owner," Finn broke in to explain. "You know, the cat and the notes?"

"You finally met her! So, how did you lure her down here?"

"Oh, he didn't! I just didn't know about his broken leg—" Mel looked horrified by Cara's assumption.

"Ah! He used sympathy. I get it." She laughed again, waking Fluff, who sat up and peered over the edge of the table, managing to grab the discarded crust of Finn's sandwich. "What is that?"

"This is Fluff, Mel's dog."

"Oh, he's so cute! Can I hold him?" Cara stood and leaned over her brother, holding out her arms for the small dog. *"She's adorable!"* She mouthed the words at him and he was positive she didn't mean the dog.

Finn flashed her an admonishing look. He didn't need his well-meaning, but nosy sister butting in to his fledgling friendship with Mel. He backed his chair away from the table and wheeled into the kitchen. "You want a sandwich, Sis?"

"Sure, thanks. Oh, Mel, he's so cute and cuddly! It must be so fun to have such a little-ittie-bittie doggie. Yes, it must!" The last part of her statement was directed to Fluff as she held him in front of her face and rubbed her nose against his.

Mel vainly tried to hold back an amused smile. "Well, he spends most of the day sleeping, but, yeah. He's pretty cute, I guess. He's my first dog, so I'm not a really good judge."

Finn listened, amused, as his sister prodded and fished for information from Mel. He set the plate he'd prepared in front of Cara and offered Mel another sandwich from the plate of extras he'd also prepared. She politely refused and he returned to his place, busying himself eating another sandwich while his sister worked her magic. By the time she finished with Mel, they had plans for a girls' night out later that evening and he'd promised to dogsit Fluff. His sister was a force to be reckoned with.

Chapter Five

Mel

What just happened? How did I end up with plans for a girls' night out with someone I just met? Mel shook her head and chuckled. "At least I won't have to leave you and CJ all alone. It was nice of Finn to offer to watch you, huh?" She addressed the dog tucked under her arm. "He's a nice guy. And very nice-looking. Don't look at me like that! I noticed, that's all. I'm not dead, you know."

"Who's not dead?" A gruff voice nearby startled her, nearly causing her to drop Fluff.

"Oh, hi, Mr. Taylor." Mel juggled the dog to her other arm and waved to the man who lived in the house between hers and Finn's, a crotchety senior citizen who spent hours every day sitting on his front porch. She felt bad for him since he was confined to a wheelchair, but he wasn't very friendly.

"Hi yourself. Who's not dead?"

"Oh. Me, I guess. I was just talking to my dog.

It's nonsense."

"Sounds like it. That cop next door doing okay?"

"His name's Finn, and yeah, he's doing okay. Not great, but he's getting better."

"They brung him home in a wheelchair. What happened?"

Mel sighed and walked across the lawn toward the man. "He was hit by a car while he was running. He broke his leg and his ankle."

"That's too bad. Hope he gets better. It's good to have a cop living next door, I suppose. Keeps the riff-raff away."

"Yeah, it is. Well, have a good day, Mr. Taylor."

"Hmmph."

She half-smiled as she turned to leave. What a grump! Oh, well. The poor man didn't have a lot to be happy about. Aunt Karen had told her Mrs. Taylor died the year before. They'd been married nearly sixty years. Mel couldn't find it in her heart to be too irritated with him for his grumpiness. She let herself into her house through the side kitchen door, making sure Fluff went outside to do his business before he returned to his little bed for the afternoon. CJ had left Finn's house at the same time she had, disappearing to wherever she spent her afternoons. Mel set her tote bag on the counter and set about making a cup of tea to get her through a few more hours of work before she had to get ready for the evening.

It was when she opened the cabinet to retrieve the honey bear that she first noticed it. She froze, her hand halfway to the bottle, and frowned at the sink to her left. Hadn't she left her breakfast dishes in the sink? Yes, she had received the text from Finn before she had the chance to put them in the dishwasher and had rushed off without giving a second thought to mundane household chores. But there were no dishes in the sink now. She opened the dishwasher and saw her cereal bowl and coffee mug. *What the hell?* She shut the dishwasher as a cold shiver slithered down her spine. Unless she'd suddenly acquired a house elf, someone had entered her home and filled her dishwasher. Had she forgotten to lock up when she went to Finn's? No, she'd used her key in the kitchen door and hadn't unlocked the front door that morning. She turned, gazing around her kitchen. Nothing else seemed out of place. *Get a grip, Melanie! Stop being ridiculous! No one came into your house and washed your dishes! You obviously forgot you put them in the dishwasher. Having lunch with a handsome man has apparently addled your brain!* She purposefully shook off the creepy feeling that lingered and finished preparing her tea.

At ten minutes before six, she was staring at her reflection in her closet mirror, trying to decide if the black leggings and silky peach sleeveless tunic she'd donned were appropriate. Cara had said they were going to a fun bar and to dress casual, but Melanie didn't really know what that meant. She added a long necklace and turned from the mirror. She'd left her hair long and straight, hanging nearly to her waist. It absolutely wouldn't hold a curl and she normally pulled it back or clipped it on top of her head to get it out of the way, but tonight she wanted to look special. "I know it's silly, but he's only ever seen me in my sweats and looking like a rat. I have to take Fluff over, and Cara's going to pick me up there." She addressed CJ, who was sitting on the bed, licking her paw, looking unimpressed. "I just want him to realize I can, you know, step it up a bit." She added a touch of blush, mascara, and lip gloss, hoping she didn't look ridiculous. She'd never been good with all the girly stuff. She gave herself a final glance, refusing to dwell on how she compared to the girls she'd seen going in and out of Finn's house. *It doesn't matter. He's a friend, that's all.*

Cara answered the door and scooped Fluff out of Melanie's arms as she ushered her new friend inside. "You look great, Mel! Wow, your hair is so long and gorgeous! We'll have to beat the guys away at the bar tonight."

Melanie walked into the living room and stopped short at the sight of yet another gorgeous woman in Finn's house. The man was apparently a magnet for them. She instantly felt frumpy and dowdy as she took in the woman's gleaming black hair, cut in a stylish bob, and willow-thin figure encased in a short black dress and some killer heels. Cara looked amazing as well, in tight, shiny black pants and a glittering blue tank top, her dark brown curly hair loose about her shoulders. She also wore a pair of spike heels Melanie envied. She looked down at her own flats and oh-so-normal outfit and sighed inwardly.

"Mel, this is my sister, Izzy. I convinced her to come with us. She desperately needs a night out. Finn!" She turned and hollered down the hall. "Get in here! We gotta go!"

"Do you have any idea how hard it is to take a pi—Mel!" He gave his sister an evil look as he wheeled in from the hallway. "I didn't know you were here yet. Wow! You look beautiful. Wow."

Mel stood awkwardly while Finn stared at her and his sisters stared at him, amused expressions on their faces.

"Super smooth, big brother." Cara snickered as she handed him the small dog. "You ordered a pizza?"

"Yeah. Hugh's coming over in a bit."

"Good." She kissed the top of his head. "Don't let him drive home if he drinks more than a couple beers, okay? I'll take him when we get back."

"Yes, Mother," Finn sighed. "Why don't you three get going? And try not to completely corrupt Mel. Okay?"

"Aw, where's the fun in that?" She rubbed Fluff's ears and turned to gather her purse. "Let's get out of here, ladies."

The bar Cara had chosen was called Nexus and was full of loud music and louder conversation. Melanie checked slightly at the door, suddenly unsure this was such a good idea. She felt her heartbeat kick up several notches as her stomach clenched in dread. Why had she agreed to this? She hated crowds. Izzy bumped into her from behind with a soft 'oof' and Cara turned back to grab her hand and pull her into the bar.

"You are not chickening out, Mel! No way! The three of us look amazing and we are going in there to knock 'em dead!" She dragged Melanie to a table right in the middle of the bar and caught a waiter's attention. "First round's on me. What do you want, Mel?"

"Oh, um..." She grabbed a drink menu to stall for time. To say she wasn't much of a drinker was to put it lightly. The beer she'd shared with Finn the night before had been the first alcohol she'd had since college, other than a very occasional glass of wine. She swiftly scanned the list of drinks on the menu and spotted one she recognized. "I guess I'll have a Long Island Iced Tea?" She glanced up to see the waiter smirking and Cara and Izzy both with raised eyebrows. "Is that bad?"

"I'll give you all a few minutes," the waiter said with a chuckle.

"Mel, I know we just met, but I'm guessing you don't drink a lot." Izzy's eyes were kind, causing Mel to not take offense.

"And I'm guessing I ordered the wrong drink, but I have no idea why. I remember people drinking it in college."

"Yeah, it's a college drink. It pretty much means 'I want to get laid tonight and I'm not really picky about by who.' Do you agree, Cara?"

"With everything except 'by who.' It's 'by whom.'" Cara grinned at her sister.

"Wow, I didn't know we brought the grammar Nazi with us tonight," Izzy muttered as she perused the drink menu.

"Occupational hazard." She turned to Melanie. "I'm an English teacher. Anyway, how about a coconut margarita, Mel?"

"As long as it doesn't say I'm a slutty whore, it

54

sounds great."

Cara and Izzy looked at her in shock then broke into laughter. "Oh, God, Mel! I'm so glad Finn found you!" Izzy said when she'd finally stopped laughing.

"Yeah, so much better than Tittyana," Cara muttered. "Ow." She flashed a dirty look at her sister, who must have kicked her under the table.

"Who?" Mel hadn't missed the whispered words.

"She's talking about Tatiana, Finn's ex-girlfriend," Izzy explained.

"Oh." Mel had known there was someone, and had wondered what happened to her. It was probably the blonde beauty she'd seen going in and out of his house when he'd first moved in. "Ex?" The word slipped out completely against her will.

Cara and Izzy exchanged knowing glances. "Definitely ex," Cara said and then paused to give their order to the waiter, who had returned. "She apparently couldn't handle the stress of Finn being in the hospital and took off. She didn't even wait until he woke up."

"That's terrible! Were they together long?" Mel hated herself for asking.

"More than a year." Izzy paused to take a sip of water, which the waiter had brought. "They were practically living together. I think he was planning to ask her to marry him. God, talk about dodging a bullet! I'm sorry he got hurt so bad, but it did mean the end of her. If we had ended up with her as a sister-in-law, I don't know what I would have done."

"We would have had to poison her," Cara said

nonchalantly as she sipped her water.

"Probably," agreed Izzy. "We could have done it slowly over several months while we built our own immunity to the poison. They never would have caught us."

"I'm pretty sure that's a better movie plot than a real-life option." Mel paused as the waiter delivered their drinks. They all spent a few moments tasting each other's and getting to know one another better, chatting about what each did for a living. Mel knew Cara was a high school English teacher, but she hadn't known Izzy, short for Isabelle, helped their oldest brother, Hugh, run the family construction company.

Mel finished her margarita, realizing it had slid down way too easily. Her lips were feeling pleasantly numb and she wished she had eaten before she came. "Do they have food here? I'm going to be drunk if I don't eat something."

"Me too, and I want another margarita. You're the designated driver tonight, Cara, by the way." Izzy caught the waiter's attention and ordered another margarita apiece for her and Mel and a club soda for her sister.

Melanie decided to throw caution to the wind and enjoy the evening with these two women who seemed to want to be friends. It had been an awfully long time since she'd had anyone close to her own age to simply hang out with.

***

Finn

He heard the key in the lock and turned the TV volume down. He would usually take issue with his brother entering his house without permission, but he knew Hugh was simply trying to save him the trouble of answering the door from his wheelchair. All his siblings had been making liberal use lately of the keys he'd given them. God, he was ready to ditch this thing. "Hey, Hugh. Pizza's not here yet. You better have brought the beer, cuz I'm out."

But it wasn't Hugh who appeared around the corner. It was Seamus, his next youngest brother. "I not only brought beer, I brought wings." He grinned as he held up the bulging bag and the twelve pack. "And none of that fancy imported shit Hugh likes, either. How you doin' Finn? Sorry I haven't stopped by for a few days."

"No problem. It's not exactly a barrel of laughs around here, so I don't blame you."

"I heard it's a lot more fun since he got a new girlfriend." Tony, the youngest member of the DeLuca clan entered on Seamus' heels, holding a grocery bag and a six-pack of PBR.

"I don't know where you're getting your information, brat. I don't have a new girlfriend." The doorbell rang at that moment, waking Fluff, who had been snoozing in his lap.

"What the hell is that?" Tony stared at the yapping dog in disgust.

"This is Fluff, Mel's dog. I'm dogsitting while she's out painting the town with Cara and Izzy. Here. Go pay for the pies." He handed his little brother several twenties.

Hugh came in holding the pizzas. "I got it." He set them on the coffee table along with the beer he'd brought. "I got something decent since I knew these two hipsters would bring that PBR swill."

Seamus and Tony laughed delightedly. "God, you're old, Hugh!" Tony added.

"Shut up," Hugh said softly as he opened a bottle of the Belgian lager he'd brought. "Not too old to kick your scrawny ass." Since Tony was six foot two and anything but scrawny, he took no offense.

They settled in to watch the baseball game and devour the pizza, wings, and chips, along with a fair amount of beer. It was the first time since the accident the four of them had gotten together for a game night and Finn had missed it—had missed spending time with his brothers. He'd almost lost it all thanks to some damn driver not paying attention. He was determined to never take his family for granted again. He reached up to quickly wipe the start of an angry tear away, hoping to God none of his brothers had noticed. No such luck, of course.

"You okay?" Hugh was always hyper-aware of what went on with his family members.

"I'm fine. It's time for more painkillers, that's all. Be right back." He wheeled into the kitchen and grabbed a glass of water and a couple ibuprofen. It was important to stay ahead of the throbbing pain in his ankle. If he let it get ahead of him, he'd be in for a bitch of a night. The alcohol would help, but it was times like these he almost wished he wasn't a cop because a little pot would certainly do the trick and take the edge off the pain. It wasn't worth it, though. If he wasn't willing to take the narcotics legally prescribed to him, he wasn't about to risk his career to smoke a joint.

"So, you ever gonna tell us about this new girl who is definitely not your girlfriend?" Seamus lobbed a decorative pillow at him as he returned to the living room. Finn caught it before it could hit Fluff. "Cara and Izzy took her out for a girls' night? You sure you want them getting their hooks into her before you've sealed the deal?"

"Can you 'seal the deal' with that big ass cast on your leg?" Tony said with a laugh. "This new girl may have to do most of the work."

"Shut the fuck up! Don't *ever* talk about Mel like that!" His sudden hot anger even surprised him. The mere thought that they might be thinking about Mel in a sexual way infuriated him. His brothers were staring at him, shocked. Except Hugh. He had a small, somewhat wistful smile on his face. "Sorry, guys. Just don't—I don't know." He ran his hands through his hair, unsure of what he wanted to say. "Mel's off limits, that's all. And we're just friends."

"Uh huh." Tony and Seamus exchanged amused glances, which made Finn grind his teeth. "So, tell us about her. Cara was stingy with the details. She's pretty, I assume? You never go for anyone less than stunning." Seamus passed him another beer as a peace offering.

"She's beautiful, of course. And smart. She's really shy, so you guys take it easy, okay?" He realized they would almost certainly still be here when the girls got back and didn't want them scaring her away.

"Smart, huh? Well, that's new and different for you." This from Seamus.

"No, Tatiana was wicked smart." Hugh leaned forward for another slice of pizza. "She was just a shallow, cold bitch. Good riddance."

"Don't hold back on account of my tender feelings." Finn took a swig of his beer, irritated, but silently in agreement with his older brother. He had definitely misjudged his former girlfriend and realized he was probably a bit gun-shy. "Can we please watch the game and stop talking about my love life?"

"Sure. Doesn't sound like there's all that much to talk about, anyway." Tony laughed, but thankfully stopped talking.

The game was in extra innings when the girls came back. Finn, using his finely honed cop skills from years of DWI checkpoints, could tell Mel and Izzy were definitely buzzed, but Cara seemed fine and he assumed she'd been the designated driver. He was suddenly eager to see what a buzzed Mel was like, so he made every effort to get rid of his unwanted siblings as soon as possible. His efforts were for naught, however, and it looked like his brothers were settled in for a while. It was probably best she met the whole fam damily while she was drunk; they were a lot to handle at one time, even for the strongest of constitutions. His brothers, unexpectedly, took his warning to heart and asked her only the simplest of questions and let Cara and Izzy carry most of the conversation. They finally began cleaning up and left, Cara promising to make sure Izzy got home safely. The guys had all been careful not to go over their limit, so Finn felt fine about them driving. Mel was dozing on the couch, so he went to the kitchen to get her a bottle of water from the fridge. She was still asleep, her head propped in her hand.

"Mel? Hey, wake up and drink some water. You'll have a hell of a headache in the morning if you don't hydrate."

"Huh? Oh, sorry. I didn't mean to fall asleep. Did everyone leave?" She pushed her hair behind her ear and twisted the top off the water bottle. Finn wondered if that gorgeous hair was as soft and silky as it looked. He entertained a very masculine fantasy of seeing her hair spread out across his pillow for about ten seconds while she drank half her water. *Okay, enough of that! Down, boy!* He was grateful he still held the dog on his lap.

"Yeah. How was your evening with my sisters? They can be a handful."

"It was really nice. It's been...awhile since I went out for an evening like that. It was fun." She smiled sleepily and Finn was launched straight back into his fantasy.

He cleared his throat and shifted uncomfortably. "How long?"

"What?" She looked adorably confused.

"How long since you went out for a girls' night?"

"Um, since college, I guess." She shrugged as if it didn't matter. Finn had a feeling it mattered quite a bit.

"Why? I know you've been busy taking care of your aunt for the last year or so, but what about before that?"

She shrugged again. "I don't have a lot of friends. I just…I don't make friends easily. Pathetic, huh?" She laughed lightly and drank more water.

"Mel." He didn't know what to say. She was so amazing. Why couldn't everyone see that? She should have people beating down the door to be her friend. He hated to see the sad smile on her face so he changed the subject. "How are you feeling? Why don't you stay here tonight?"

"Oh, no! That's not necessary, Finn. Thanks, but I need to get home. CJ will be waiting."

"The cat will be fine. Mel, I think you should stay. I've got a bed made up in the guest room. You won't be any trouble."

"Thanks, but I am perfectly fine to walk the thirty or so yards to my house." She stood, a bit wobbly, and gathered her bag. She held out her arms for Fluff.

"He can ride in my lap." Finn rolled toward the door.

"What? You're walking me home? That's not necessary."

"Technically, I'm rolling you home. Let's go." He ushered her toward the front door.

"Oh, Finn," she sighed. "You don't need to—"

"No arguments. I can be as stubborn as you. I'm perfectly capable of escorting you home. It's late and you're tipsy."

"I'll text you when I get home." She shrugged when he refused to agree. "Fine. Be stubborn." She marched out his front door, ruining all her righteous indignation by stumbling on the wheelchair ramp, barely catching herself before she fell.

He wisely said nothing and simply followed her down the walkway to the sidewalk. It was an older neighborhood and the sidewalks were raised at the seams in several places, making it difficult for a wheelchair. Finn had plenty of upper body strength to compensate, but he realized an elderly person, such as the neighbor between his and Mel's house, would find it impossible. He decided to make a call to the city in the morning.

"Looks like we're getting a new neighbor." Mel's soft voice broke into his thoughts.

"Huh?"

"Across the street." She pointed to the house directly across the street between theirs. "The **'For Rent'** sign is gone. Either they took it off the market or rented it out."

He hadn't been outside since he got home for more than quick trips to and from the doctor and certainly hadn't paid any attention to what was going on in the neighborhood. "Great. All we need is a rental property on our street. Our property values just plummeted."

"Okay, Mr. Glass-Half-Full. Maybe we'll get a responsible renter who will take care of the house and yard." She smiled at his disbelieving look. "It could happen." They reached the bottom of her porch steps and she turned to him, her hand reaching to steady herself against the railing. "Thanks for rolling me home, Finn. You are a true gentleman."

"And you're a bit of a smart ass." He held his breath as she leaned down to scoop Fluff off his lap.

Her loose hair fell into his face and he inhaled the delicious fragrance of her shampoo—peaches, if he wasn't mistaken. He couldn't stop himself from tucking the right side behind her ear. He was right—it was every bit as silky as he'd dreamed. She froze as his hand caressed her cheek, her eyes darting to his, panicked. He reluctantly let his hand fall away, realizing he would have to take anything with her more slowly than he was used to. Wait, what was he even thinking? He wasn't ready for another relationship. *Whoa, slow down, buddy!* "Goodnight, Mel. I'll wait 'til you get inside. Don't forget to lock up, okay?"

Chapter Six

Mel

Her cell phone vibrating on the nightstand woke her. She was shocked to see it was nearly eleven o'clock. She usually rose by nine at the latest. The nasty taste in her mouth was something she hoped never to experience again and she made a vow on the spot to severely limit her tequila intake in the future. The margaritas were fine, but why on earth had she allowed Cara to talk her into the shots? She grabbed the cell phone and saw that Finn had messaged her.

Finn: Morning, Sunshine! How's your head?

Mel: Not sure yet.

Finn: Did I wake you up? Sorry.

Mel: No, of course not. I've been up for hours.

Finn: Liar. How about I make it up to you by fixing you a gourmet lunch? And by gourmet I mean sandwiches.

Melanie laughed and pushed the hair out of her face. She knew spending more time with him was probably a bad idea, but she couldn't help herself. She liked him. She also liked his sisters, and it had been so long since she'd had any friends her own age. So, although it was likely to do nothing but strengthen the silly crush she'd already developed, she agreed.

Mel: What about if I come over later this afternoon and make you dinner? I'm a little worried all you ever have is pizza and beer.

Finn: Vicious rumors! I'm not a bad cook when I'm not in this %$@# wheelchair. How about both? Unless you have a hot date for lunch? Bring Fluff. CJ's already here.

"Oh, Fluff! Why does he have to be so nice? How am I supposed to not fall in love with him?" Fluff refused to answer, so Melanie dragged herself out of bed and into the shower. She refused to consider why she chose to dress in a casual sundress rather than her usual yoga pants/t-shirt combo. She gathered the ingredients for chicken spaghetti into a wicker basket and scooped Fluff under her other arm, along with her tote bag full of her work paraphernalia. As she locked the kitchen door behind her, she paused. The door hadn't been locked. She could have sworn she locked it the night before when she went to bed. Hadn't she? Finn had reminded her before she went inside and she'd locked the front door behind her, then immediately gone through to lock the kitchen door. Was she going insane? Her heart began to pound as she considered the alternative: someone had somehow unlocked it and come into her house. No. That was crazy. Wasn't it? She shook off the disturbing thoughts and walked to Finn's house, waving to Mr. Taylor as she passed.

A strange woman answered the door, causing Melanie to do a double take. "Hi. I'm Anna. I'm Finn's physical therapist. He said to come on in. We're just about done." She left Melanie to follow and shut the door.

"Hey, Mel. You can go on into the kitchen and make yourself at home. I'm just about done with the daily torture. I'll join you in a few minutes," Finn's voice called to her from the living room to her left.

"Good God, Finn! It's not like I'm water boarding you, you big baby! If you want to get out of that chair, you better stop whining and finish this set!"

"*Jawohl herr kommandant*," Finn muttered. Mel caught a glimpse of him lying on a mat, pushing with his good leg against the physical therapist.

She decided to take him at his word and made herself at home in his kitchen, preparing lunch for both of them so it would be waiting when he finished with his session. He would surely be exhausted, and fixing lunch was probably something he didn't want to even think about. She found cold cuts and sliced cheese readily enough, along with the bread and some baby carrots. She put some potato chips on his plate, but left them off her own. They represented a slippery slope she was all too wont to slide down, crunching all the way.

She heard the front door open and shut, then Finn rolled into the kitchen. He immediately reached for the bottle of Tylenol on the table and swallowed three capsules, dry. She bit her lip, worried at the way the lines around his mouth and between his eyes were deeper than she'd ever seen.

"Here." She handed him a bottle of water from the fridge. "I can clear out, Finn. I don't mind."

He smiled tiredly. "Nah, I'm good. PT's a bitch, that's all. Thanks for fixing lunch. That was really nice."

"No problem. I didn't know physical therapists made house calls."

He chuckled as he recapped the water bottle. "I'm sure they normally don't, but the police department arranged it since it's so hard for me to get around with this cast. Shit pay, but they take care of their own. Once this cast is off she'll stop coming to me. That'll be fun since I can't drive yet. Good thing I have so many siblings."

"I can help too. I'm home all day and totally available."

"Thanks, Mel. That's really sweet. I will probably take you up on it." He took a bite of his sandwich and chewed unenthusiastically, still looking exhausted.

"I don't suppose there's any way I could convince you to lie down for a while this afternoon?

Maybe while I'm making dinner?" She wasn't sure how he'd take her suggestion.

She was relieved when he laughed softly. "Yeah. That might be a good idea. Anna pushed me harder than usual today. I'm scheduled to get this cast off Friday, so she wants me to be ready, which translates to 'let's torture Finn especially hard.' I'm sorry to be so lame. We can reschedule if you want."

"I don't mind at all. I don't need to be entertained, Finn. So, this Friday, huh? No more wheelchair?"

"God, yes! Finally! I need to see if Cara can take me. At least this all happened in the summer when she's on break from teaching."

"Why don't I take you?" She nibbled a carrot nonchalantly while she waited for him to answer. She didn't know why she was so eager to torture herself by spending more time with him, but helping people came second nature to her. She could rationalize away her infatuation when it coincided with a chance to help.

He met her gaze with a half-smile. "You sure you want to volunteer? It will probably be a fairly long visit."

She shrugged. "I don't mind. I can take my laptop and get some work done. I really want to help, Finn."

"Okay. Thanks. I really appreciate it. I can't believe we just met for the first time a few days ago. I feel like I've known you a lot longer."

"Maybe it's because you read my book. It's kind of like seeing deep into my soul, in a way."

He smiled at her fully now. "That could be it. There's nothing like reading a sexy scene written by someone you know. Makes a guy wonder."

She could feel the heat rising in her face. "That's not what I meant."

He laughed. "I know. You're fun to tease." He finished his sandwich and carried both their plates to the sink. "I'm going to try to put in at least an hour of work before my nap. God, I sound like a four-year-old."

"Well, if you're good, I might fix some graham crackers and milk for you."

"I was right. You're definitely a smart ass."

They worked in companionable silence for a couple hours before he yawned and excused himself to go to his bedroom for a short nap. Melanie knew how much the admission of weakness must cost him; it was obvious he was used to being strong and healthy. This recuperation had to be getting on his nerves. She silently promised herself she'd do whatever she could to keep his spirits up.

With that in mind, she put the chicken on to boil and rifled through his cabinets to see what she could come up with for a special dessert. She found nearly all the ingredients for chocolate chip cookies and a quick trip to her house for real butter and pecans— she much preferred them to walnuts—made it possible. She found his kitchen reasonably well stocked and organized, although much of the equipment seemed to be hand-me-downs, probably from his mother. She managed quite well and soon had a cookie sheet loaded in the oven while the chicken cooled on the counter. She fetched her laptop and opened Pandora so she could have some soft music while she worked.

An hour later, with the last of the cookies cooling on newspaper and the casserole tucked in the oven to bake, she peeked in on Finn. He'd been asleep longer than she expected and she had to check. He was on his back—the huge cast probably made any other position impossible—and Fluff was curled beside him on the bed. They made an adorable picture that completely melted her heart. *I could so easily fall in love with him.* But love was something she'd managed to avoid for years and she had good reason to still keep her guard up. Didn't she? The reasons, once so clear, seemed to be fading swiftly from her grasp.

***

Finn

He dreamed he was eating chocolate chip cookies. He slowly came fully awake, the delicious aroma still with him, taking him straight back to his childhood. The small dog stretched and yawned beside him.

"Make yourself at home," he muttered as he hopped into the bathroom and then flopped into the hateful wheelchair, out of breath. He scooped the little dog into his lap and followed his nose to the kitchen, where a glorious sight met his eyes: Mel bending over to pull a large casserole dish from the oven. He fully enjoyed the curve of her backside and the glimpse of her creamy thighs where her

71

dress rode up. He'd be willing to bet they were as silky smooth as he'd dreamed—dreams which were occurring with uncomfortable regularity. Seeing this domestic side of her unleashed a sudden lust in him and he realized it was a good thing he was confined to his chair, otherwise he knew he wouldn't have been able to resist stepping behind her and pulling her into his arms. Dinner would most likely be stone cold by the time he was through. *What am I thinking? What happened to holding off on starting any new relationships until you're at least fully mobile? Tatiana shredded your heart, you dumbass!* But he knew exactly what happened—Mel. She was so different from any of the women he'd dated before; she'd sneaked in under his radar and now he didn't want to hold off. And when he really thought about it, he realized the only thing Tatiana had truly shredded was his pride. *How in the world did I ever convince myself I was in love with her?* Maybe he did need to slow down. But she straightened at that moment and caught sight of him. Her smile chased any silly thoughts of slowing down clear out of his mind.

"Evening, Sleepyhead. You must have been really exhausted." She set the dish on the stove. "Are you feeling better?"

"You know, I'm not sure. One of those cookies would probably make me feel pretty good, though." He raised his eyebrows and gestured toward where they were cooling.

"Oh, really? One of these?" She plucked one off the counter and held it out to him, just out of his reach. "What do you say?"

He loved when she was in a teasing mood. "I say you are a goddess divine and I am your most humble slave."

She laughed delightedly and gave him the cookie. "I was just looking for 'please,' but I'll take goddess divine, since I don't get it every day."

He groaned in appreciation as he bit into the crispy, buttery confection. It was chock full of silky dark chocolate and toasted pecans. "This is amazing, Mel. I'm in heaven. You *are* a goddess divine. Marry me. Right now." He wasn't quite sure how that last bit had slipped out and quickly shoved the rest of the cookie in his mouth to forestall any more verbal stupidity.

Luckily, she took it as the joke he'd originally intended and simply laughed. "We should probably get to know each other a bit more first. You'll be a lot less enthralled when I get so wrapped up in my writing I forget to eat and don't sleep for two days. It's not a pretty sight." She handed him another cookie. "That's all until after dinner."

"Yes, ma'am." She was so cute when she was sassy. "Will that dinner be soon by any chance? I'm starving."

"It's nearly ready. I just need to toss the salad."

She refused to let him help set the table, but handed him two cold beers to open for them. He loved the creamy, cheesy chicken spaghetti—he ate three helpings to prove it—as well as the salad and garlic bread. She insisted on stacking their dishes in the dishwasher and he swore to himself he would have her over as soon as he was mobile and she would do nothing but sit and eat. He felt like such a bum, sitting around while everyone waited on him. He insisted on escorting her home again, feeling like it was the absolute least he could do. She tried to talk him out of it, but he refused to be dissuaded.

He waited beside her, in front of her porch, while she fished deep in her tote bag for her house keys.

"If I even locked it this time," she muttered.

"Huh? What are you talking about?"

"Oh, I'm just being ridiculous. It's nothing." She shrugged and laughed lightly.

But he detected a strain to the laugh he didn't care for. He reached out and clasped her hand before she could gain the steps. "Mel. Tell me."

She stared at their joined hands for a moment. "It's just that I thought I locked my kitchen door last night and it was unlocked this morning." She shivered noticeably.

All his cop instincts suddenly went on full alert. "What else? Tell me everything." He listened, growing progressively grim, as she detailed the feeling of being watched as she walked home from his house, the dishes that had mysteriously migrated into the dishwasher, and the unlocked door. "Shit," he muttered under his breath. "Okay, here's what we're going to do." He was already reaching for his phone. "Chris? You busy? Yeah, I need you to swing by real quick. Thanks."

"Finn? What are you doing?"

"We'll wait at my house." He tugged lightly on her hand. "My partner is on her way. She'll do a check of your house—"

"No! That's ridiculous, Finn!" She tried to tug her hand free. "I can't believe you called someone!

How embarrassing!"

He held firmly and forced her to look at him. "It's not, Mel. Trust me. Let's go back to my house and wait for Chris. I just need to know you're safe."

She bit her lip and shrugged. "I'm sure I'm imagining everything. I shouldn't have told you."

"Yes, you absolutely should have. I don't like the sound of this. It won't take Chris long to check your house. I wish I could do it myself, but I can't right now. Now stop whining and let's go." He tried a stern look.

She looked at him for a long moment before rolling her eyes. "Fine. You're kinda bossy, you know that?"

He chuckled and ushered her to walk in front of his chair. "When it comes to the safety of—" He'd been about to say 'those I love,' but caught himself and finished with, "my friends and family, I can indeed be super-bossy. Get used to it."

Once back inside his house, she busied herself making tea while he waited for his partner to arrive. When her car pulled up outside, he met her on the front sidewalk and handed her the keys he'd gotten from Mel. "Thanks for coming over, Chris." He ran his hand through his hair in frustration. "It's probably a waste of time, but I didn't like the sound of what she was telling me. She's not the kind to create unnecessary drama."

"No problem. I'll take a look around and be back." She grabbed the keys and headed to Mel's house. Finn waited for her on his porch.

She was back within five minutes. "Looks okay, but her locks are a joke. On the off chance there is someone messing with her, you should get her to install something more secure. A child with a bobby pin wouldn't be challenged by hers."

"Yeah, I'll make sure she gets some better ones, even if I have to do it myself. You want to come in for a beer?"

"Sure. I'm dying to meet this girl who has you so wrapped around the axle."

"I am literally begging you to not say anything, Chris. She's...I don't know—skittish is the best word for it."

She smirked as she reached out to mess his hair up. "Don't worry. I won't scare her away. After all, she managed to get you to shave for the first time in weeks."

"Shut up." He could hear her laughing as she entered the house ahead of him. He followed her into the kitchen, where Mel was sitting at the table with a mug of tea. She appeared surprised as she gazed at Chris. "Mel, this is my partner, Chris."

"Hi, Mel. It's nice to meet you." Chris shook her hand and took a seat. "Your house is secure and both doors were locked when I got there. I would get better locks installed, however. Yours are way too flimsy."

"Oh. Okay. I had no idea." Mel frowned into her tea. "I'm sure I'm imagining everything. I hate that you had to come over and check."

"It was no problem. Thanks, Finn." She took a long pull of the beer he handed her.

He offered one to Mel, but she shook her head and took another sip of her tea. He grabbed one for himself and joined the two women at the table.

Chris was on her best behavior—thank God—and was engaging Mel in a bit of chitchat, obviously attempting to draw her out. He let them talk for the most part and simply enjoyed watching Mel's face. She was so beautiful and he was kicking himself for living so close to her for nearly six months and not even meeting her. He knew he should slow down— he was on the rebound, after all—but fate, or whatever controlled his destiny—seemed to have other ideas. She had appeared in his life and he wanted her to stay there. He wasn't going to rush anything, but he had every intention of getting to know his adorable, shy neighbor much better in the coming weeks.

Chapter Seven

Melanie

On Friday morning Melanie sat at her dining room table, struggling to finish a brochure design for a finicky client before she was scheduled to drive Finn to his appointment to have his cast removed. She wanted to be free for the rest of the afternoon so she could be totally focused on him. Not that she wasn't totally focused on him every other moment of the day since they'd met. *Can you blame me? Guys like him don't drop into my lap every day! And he seems to like me for some reason.* It had been so long since she'd enjoyed being with a guy and Finn was surely only interested in friendship, so all she had to do was keep her silly crush to herself. Her mother had drilled into her head from early on that an infatuation with a boy was strictly Melanie's problem. It wasn't the boy's fault that she liked him and she should never make him uncomfortable by revealing her silly crush. Things like that stuck with a person even into adulthood.

The knock on the door made her jump; she was that deep in her work and daydreaming about Finn. She sighed and went to answer, hoping it would be quick.

"Hi! I'm Lena. I just moved in across the street." The young woman on the porch was smiling widely, flashing white teeth in an extremely tan face. Her hair was bright blonde and surely not the color she was born with.

"Oh." Melanie knew she sounded stupid, but she'd never been good with this sort of thing. "Um, hi. Welcome to the neighborhood." She mentally chastised herself for her uncharitable thoughts and forced a friendly smile. "I'm Melanie."

"Thanks. Listen, do you mind if I come in for just a minute? I'd love some coffee, if you have it. I can't remember what box I packed my coffeemaker in." Lena was already moving forward, not giving Melanie much chance to refuse.

"Uh, sure. Come on in." Melanie stepped back to let the pushy woman in, although it was definitely not what she wanted to do.

"Thanks! So tell me all about yourself." The woman followed her to the kitchen and took a seat at the table.

Make yourself at home. And I have no intention of telling you all about myself! "Well, I've lived here for about a year." She reached for a mug and poured her new neighbor a cup. She didn't know if it was still hot and didn't really care. She reluctantly fetched the bottle of creamer from the fridge and set it, along with the sugar bowl, in front of Lena,

79

somehow unable to completely forget about hospitality.

"Oh, thanks, sweetie! This may just save my life! I hate moving, don't you? So what do you do? Are you married?"

Ugh! I do not want to chitchat with this woman! But Melanie knew what it was like to move somewhere new and not know anyone, so she swallowed her irritation, realizing it was mostly due to the interruption, not the woman herself. "I'm a graphic designer and I work from home. I'm not married. I lived here with my great aunt, but she died a few weeks ago."

"Oh, that's terrible! Well, you must have a boyfriend, as pretty as you are." Lena took a sip of coffee, staring across the table at Melanie.

This is why I usually avoid conversations with people I don't know. So intrusive! She chose to simply shrug—why was her love life any of this woman's business, anyway?—and changed the subject. "So, what brings you to Albuquerque?"

"Oh, a messy divorce. You know how it is." She took another sip of coffee and then stood. "Well, those boxes are not going to unpack themselves. It's so nice to meet you, Melanie. I just know we're going to be great friends." She left as abruptly as she had come, leaving Melanie rather dumbfounded.

"What the heck was that, Fluff?" The little dog sat up when he heard his name, but dropped his head back on his bed when it became obvious no treat was forthcoming. "You're no help. Okay, I need to get this brochure done before noon. Now stop demanding my attention and let me work!" She smiled at the small dog curled up in his little bed. Fluff was probably the lowest maintenance dog in the history of dogdom and was pretty good company when she thought about it. At least he kept her from talking to herself. CJ had, as usual, left right after breakfast and was probably curled up on Finn's couch.

She finished the brochure and sent it to the client, glad to have it done. She headed to her bedroom to change into something better looking than her yoga pants and t-shirt, but not as obvious as the dress she wore the other day. She chose a pair of black capris with a newish soft pink top that she felt good wearing. She couldn't help wanting to look nice for Finn. She backed her aunt's Lincoln Continental out of the garage and drove it the short distance to his house.

He was waiting for her on the front porch. "That is one heck of a luxury automobile," he said with a chuckle. "I had no idea I would be going to the doctor in such style."

"Well, it is a bit much, I guess. I'll need to think about trading it in and getting something smaller. But for now it's a lucky thing I still have it because I'm guessing your giant cast wouldn't fit in a cute little car like the Mini Cooper I've got my eye on."

"Well, we could have taken my Jeep. That's what Cara's been driving me around in. I sure hope I still remember how to drive when I finally get done with all these casts. It had to be my right leg." He shook his head ruefully.

"I'm sure you will, Finn." She got a rare glimpse

of the frustration he kept hidden most of the time and her heart went out to him. "Hey, if you're up to it after your appointment, would you want to stop and eat somewhere?" She tried for a casual tone, hoping he wouldn't think she was trying to pressure him into taking her on a date.

"Absolutely! Great idea, Mel. I believe I promised to take you out for your first New Mexican food, and I know the perfect place."

She couldn't stop her smile. "Sure, but if you're too tired from the doctor we can do it another time."

"I'll be fine. I just have to sit there while they cut off the cast." He wheeled himself to the large car and Melanie was impressed by how efficiently he maneuvered himself out of his chair and into the backseat. She'd be lying if she didn't admit to enjoying the play of muscles in his strong arms.

She followed his instructions for folding his wheelchair and hefted it into the trunk. Once at the clinic he'd directed her to, they reversed the process and she followed him inside, noting the lines of pain around his mouth and eyes. She would be glad, for his sake, when he was fully recovered. Once he'd checked in and they were sitting beside each other in the waiting room, he reached over and laid his hand gently on hers. It was incredibly warm and she was barely able to stop herself from turning her hand over and entwining their fingers.

"Thanks for doing this, Mel. I feel like such a burden on my family right now. It's nice to give them a break."

"I'm sure they don't mind. I don't either, you know. I'm happy to help, so feel free to call on me whenever." She smiled at him, captivated by how he smiled at her in return, looking deeply into her eyes. When was the last time someone had taken the time to look at her like that? It felt incredibly good.

"I'm glad we finally met, Mel. I feel like I've known you for a lot longer than a week. I owe that silly cat big time for bringing us together."

She had no idea how to reply and was relieved when the nurse stepped into the waiting room to call him back. Since she'd finished her work earlier, she'd left her laptop at home and brought her Kindle. Reading for pleasure was a luxury these days, so she used the time waiting for Finn to start a new book. She'd picked a good one, and was soon caught up in the adventure and romance. Patients came and went, but Finn had yet to reappear nearly two hours later. She was checking her watch every few minutes now, and had decided to ask the receptionist when the door to the waiting room opened and he finally appeared. He was walking— albeit with crutches—but the cast was gone, replaced by a boot apparatus encasing his broken ankle. He grinned at her across the waiting room and she shoved her Kindle in her bag and leaped up to meet him.

"What do you think?"

"I think you're a lot taller than I expected." She had to look up to meet his gaze. She'd known he would be tall based on the size of his brothers, but it was still a bit of a shock. He had to be at least six foot two. "How does it feel?"

"Amazing. You tend to take walking for granted until you can't do it. They gave me a pain shot while they sawed off the cast, so I'm feeling pretty good right now. I hope you're still up for a late lunch, because I'm starving."

"Of course. You said you had a place in mind?" She held the door for him and adjusted her pace to his slower one. When they arrived at her car, she reached to open the passenger side door for him.

"I got it, Mel. I don't need you to open doors for me anymore, okay? You're messing with my masculinity." He smiled, taking away any sting in his words.

"Sorry. Habit."

"God, it's good to ride in the front seat again. Makes me feel like a big boy."

She laughed and started the car. He gave her the directions to the restaurant he'd chosen and sat back to apparently enjoy the drive. She cranked the air conditioner up, grateful it worked so well. The summer heat was intense, in the upper nineties today, with little to no humidity. It was so different from the climate she'd grown up with, as was the landscape. Everything here was brown, with only the occasional tree or scrub bush to break the monotony. She'd hated it at first, but found the desert southwest growing on her now.

"There's certainly no shortage of Mexican restaurants in Albuquerque, but if you've really never been to one, El Patron is a good one for kitsch. If we're lucky they'll have the mariachis there this afternoon."

"The what?"

"Mariachis. You know, musicians. Guitar, violins, trumpet, guitarrón? They sing too."

"Sounds fun. Do you play an instrument?"

"Me? Nah. I never had time for band in school. Sports took all my spare time. You?"

She laughed self-consciously. "I played the flute. I even played in college for a while."

"Really? That is a fascinating aspect of your life, Mel. Will you play for me sometime?"

"I'm trying to imagine anything more boring for you than sitting and listening to me squawk on my old flute." She was actually quite good and still practiced occasionally, but couldn't imagine playing for him.

"Oh, you're quite wrong, Ms. Blythe. I think I'd find anything you do absolutely fascinating." He reached for her hand as he said this, holding it lightly for the rest of the drive.

If he had any idea how it messed with her ability to even breathe normally, he would surely stop, fearing for his safety. *I could get used to holding hands with him. I like it way too much.*

***

Finn

He refused when she offered to drop him off at the door before parking her giant boat of a car. God, this woman needed to stop babying him! He wasn't really annoyed; she was too cute and sweet for that. "Mel, just park the car." When they got to the front door of the restaurant, he made sure to reach for it before her. "And I will open the damn door for my date. My mother raised me to be gentleman." There.

Let her deal with that. This was a date and she could damn well get used to it.

"And she did a wonderful job." She walked past him. "For the most part."

He chuckled at her sauciness and followed her. He gave his name to the hostess and took the small black pager she handed him, dropping it into his shirt pocket. "It's about a twenty minute wait. This place is always busy. Let's get a beer in the bar." He suggested she find a table while he ordered them each a Dos Equis. "To walking, even with crutches." He offered the toast as soon as the waitress dropped off the bottles.

She smiled at him and took a sip. "Congratulations, Finn. I know you worked hard to get out of that wheelchair."

He tipped his beer toward her and then drank deeply. It was either that or lean across the small table and kiss her, which he knew would be rushing his fences. She was the best thing that had happened to him in a long time and he wasn't about to let her get away. But how to do that without spooking her? She was skittish as a colt and he knew he needed to take it slowly. But why? What was behind it? Something in her past? Or simply her shy personality? The pager went off a few minutes later and he allowed her to carry his beer to their table; a major drawback of crutches was no free hands.

Chips and salsa appeared nearly as soon as they were seated. "You want a margarita?" Finn offered as the waitress took their drink orders.

"Oh, no thanks. I'm driving, so one beer is all I get. You just got out of a wheelchair, so let's not court a car wreck on the way home. But you go ahead and order one for yourself."

"Why, you wouldn't be trying to get me drunk so you can take advantage of me, would you, Ms. Blythe?" He loved the blush that crept across her cheeks at his teasing.

"That certainly doesn't sound like me," she muttered as she glanced at the menu.

He let it go, although he wanted to tell her she could take advantage of him any time she wanted. "So, what looks good?"

"I have no idea. My experience with Mexican food up until now has been limited to Taco Bell and Chipotle. Maybe you should order for me."

He laughed. "Okay. You want the chile on the side or can you handle a little heat?"

"I can handle a little heat." She fairly bristled as she spoke.

"Good to know." He attempted a smoldering look, but ruined it by laughing when she raised her eyebrows in surprise. She laughed with him, burying her face in her napkin when she snorted. Oh, God, he was falling for her. *Too fast! Slow down, idiot!* The waitress came back for their orders and he chose a combination plate for her and enchiladas for himself.

"What's *Christmas*?" she asked as the waitress left.

"It means both red and green chile." He had ordered it for her combo platter. "You should try them both to see which you like better."

"But you just ordered red?"

"Yeah. It's my favorite." He shrugged and took

another pull at his beer. He watched as she tried the salsa, impressed when she went back for more; it packed a spicy punch today.

"So, you've met most of my family, except my parents. What about your family? Do they still live in Chicago?"

She shook her head as she took a sip of her water. "No. I'm from a very small town south of Chicago called Mendota. My mom still lives there. My dad was military; he died in the Gulf War. I never knew him. My mom got pregnant on his last leave and I was born eight months after he died. He never even knew she was pregnant."

"God, Mel. I'm so sorry. I shouldn't have asked."

"No, it's okay. It was a long time ago. When I was fifteen, Mom remarried a guy with four younger kids. She's happy." She shrugged.

Finn recognized a world of unspoken hurt in her simple statement: a lonely teenager whose mother remarried and acquired a new family and had little time for her older daughter. He reached across the table for her hand, picking it up and kissing the backs of her fingers. "Well, I'm really, really glad you found your way to Albuquerque." He was grateful when she didn't pull her hand away immediately. *Progress.*

Their dinners were delivered and he allowed her to reclaim her hand so she could eat. She seemed to enjoy hers, eating almost half of the food on the huge platter. He asked the waitress to bring her a box.

"I hope you saved room for a sopaipilla."

"A what?"

"You really have been living under a rock since you moved here, huh? Sopaipillas are delicious little pillows of deep fried dough. You tear the corner off and pour honey inside."

"They sound really healthy."

He laughed. "Oh, there's not much about Mexican food that's healthy. Sometimes you just gotta go with it." The box and a basket of piping hot sopaipillas were delivered. She enjoyed hers, licking a drop of honey from her lip, making him nearly swallow his tongue. *If I don't kiss her soon, I'm going to go crazy.* Instead, he reached for a sopaipilla and busied himself adding honey and eating it.

They finally wrapped up their meal and Finn paid the check. He was glad she didn't try to pay for half; this was a date and he wanted her to know it. It was late afternoon when they left the restaurant as he checked the time on his phone, noting a series of texts from his mother. *Crap. I got so distracted by Mel I forgot about my mom.* "I need to make a phone call real quick, Mel. Do you mind?"

"Of course not. I'll go get the car."

He caught her hand as she started toward the parking lot. "I didn't mean for you to leave. I need to call my mom. She's sent me a bunch of texts, probably freaking out because I forgot to let her know how the doctor's appointment went. Let's go sit on that bench." He led her to the bench by the fountain and pressed the button to call his mom.

She answered on the first ring. "Finn? What happened? Did you get your cast off? Are you all right?"

Guilt swamped him at the worry in her voice. "I'm fine. The cast is off and I'm hobbling tolerably well on crutches. I'm really sorry I forgot to call. I got, uh, distracted." He flashed a guilty smile at Mel.

"Oh, Finn! I was worried sick! Are you with your brothers? If you all are sitting around watching sports and drinking—"

"No, Mom. I'm actually on a date, so I need to go." He knew that would shut her up.

"Oh. Well, that's all right then. Who is the lucky girl?"

He smiled; his mother was obsessed with seeing her children, the older ones at least, married off. "Her name is Melanie." He took her hand as he said her name.

"Is she your neighbor? The one with the cat?"

"That's the one."

"Oh, wonderful! Cara and Izzy told me all about her. I'll let you go, but you're coming Sunday for dinner, aren't you? Bring Melanie."

"I'll ask her. Maybe she can give me a ride. I still won't be able to drive for a few more months. Gotta go, Mom. Love you and Dad. Bye." He slipped the phone in his pocket and turned to Mel. "So, how about it? Will you go with me Sunday for dinner at my parents'?"

"Of course. I'm happy to give you a ride." She stared down at her lap.

What had happened to make her doubt herself? With any other woman, he might assume she wasn't interested, but she was sending unmistakable signals of interest. He reminded himself he needed to tread carefully, but he had a strong feeling she would be worth it. "Mel." He intertwined his fingers with hers. "I can get a ride with any of my brothers or sisters. I want you to go with me. I want to introduce you to my parents." He picked her hand up and kissed the backs of her fingers. "This is a date, Mel. I want you to know that, and I want there to be others, better ones that don't start with a doctor's visit." He smiled as he let go of her hand and reached for her face, brushing her silky brown hair behind her ear, caressing her cheek along the way. "I need to know if you want that too."

She looked up at him with those big brown eyes, uncertainty shining through. "You do?"

He smiled gently, but wondered if he'd ever understand her. She didn't seem to have a coquettish bone in her body. He rubbed his thumb across her lips lightly, then, because he simply couldn't help himself, he leaned forward and pressed his lips against hers. He pulled back almost immediately; their first real kiss wouldn't be in such a public place. "I absolutely do. You haven't answered my question. Will you go out with me again, Mel?"

She placed her hand over his against her cheek and nodded. "I want to, Finn. But I'm scared."

"Of me?"

She shook her head. "Of me."

"Mel." His heart squeezed at the pain evident on her face. He wanted to ask questions, but this wasn't the place. "Give me a chance. Give us a chance."

She stared at him for an eternal moment. "Yes."

He grinned; he couldn't help it. Then he leaned in for another soft kiss; her lips were the best thing he'd ever tasted and he was determined to have more. "We're going to be good together, Mel."

"How can you be sure? I've never been good with anyone."

"Trust me."

Chapter Eight

Melanie

Finn was silent on the drive home, but he held her hand on the seat between them, rubbing his thumb along her fingers. She stole frequent glances at him while trying to force herself to keep her eyes on the road. *He wants to date me. How did this happen? It's like I'm living in a dream.* She knew it probably wouldn't last long; he'd soon discover she wasn't exciting enough or beautiful enough and move on. But that tiny seed of hope still lived inside her—deep inside—and she wanted to believe it could work out.

"Do you want me to drop you off at your house? You must be exhausted."

He laughed softly and squeezed her hand. "I am, but I'm not ready to end our day. I was kind of hoping to relax on the couch with you. We could watch a movie or something."

"That sounds nice. But you have to promise to kick me out when you're tired, okay?"

"I promise, Mel. But don't go if I fall asleep

93

during the movie, okay? It doesn't mean I want you to leave. I may not be a very exciting date for a while, but I'll make it up to you if you stick around."

She decided not to tell him simply looking at him excited her. She parked in his driveway and walked with him to the door. "I'm going to run down and get Fluff. I hate to leave him alone all afternoon." She fetched the dog and grabbed a bottle of wine as an afterthought. She checked suddenly as she chose the merlot from her pantry, her stomach clenching as she tripped over a potato rolling loose on the floor. She looked down and saw the five pounds of potatoes had been spilled out of the plastic bin she kept them in. *Calm down! It could easily have been CJ nosing around in the pantry.* She swallowed the bile in her throat and convinced herself that's what had happened. She wouldn't mention it to Finn; he'd probably insist on coming down and checking her house. It was almost certainly the cat that had spilled them.

She let herself into Finn's house through the kitchen door and set Fluff down so she could rummage through the cabinets for wine glasses. She came up empty and had to settle for mismatched tumblers, but she did find a corkscrew. Fluff had made himself comfortable on Finn's lap, and Finn had removed his boot and had his ace bandage-wrapped ankle propped on the table, resting on a pillow.

"I couldn't find your stemware." She handed him a glass of the merlot.

"If that means wine glasses, it's because I don't

have any. I'm usually a beer drinker." He took a sip. "But I could be persuaded to drink more wine. This is good."

She smiled over the top of her glass. "So what are we watching?"

"Whatever you want." He handed her the remote. "Choose something."

She took it, looked at it, then handed it back, laughing. "Too many buttons for me. You pick. Nothing too scary. I want to be able to sleep tonight."

He chuckled and navigated to Netflix. "So no slasher flick. How do you feel about sci-fi?" He clicked on a fairly recent blockbuster space drama. "Have you seen it?"

"Nope. Looks great."

"How would you feel about scooting over here and letting me put my arm around you while we watch?"

She wanted to, of course, but it scared her at the same time. *Stop being such a fraidy-cat! He's not Evan!* She moved closer, letting him drape his arm over her shoulders. She held herself a few inches away, however, not quite ready for so much physical contact. She was grateful he didn't say anything and let her get used to him, slowly relaxing until she was leaning against him. He was so warm and he smelled incredible, a blend of subtle aftershave, detergent, and clean male skin. They stayed that way for the entire movie, except when Mel leaned forward to refill their glasses. He fell asleep halfway through the movie, helped, no doubt, by the two glasses of wine. She gently removed the glass from his hand before he spilled the dregs in his lap. She leaned against him quietly and let him sleep. *Please let this work out. I like him so much! Probably too much.*

He woke as the credits rolled. "Well, I guess I still haven't seen it, huh?" He chuckled and rubbed the back of his neck.

"I better go. You need to get to bed." She took the empty glasses to the kitchen and loaded them in the dishwasher. When she returned to the living room, he was fastening the walking boot back on his right ankle.

"I'll walk you home."

"You don't need to do that."

"Yes, I do. Get used to it." The stubborn set of his chin told her arguing would be futile.

She sighed and bent to scoop Fluff into her arms. "Thank you."

When they arrived at her front door, he held his hand out for her keys. "I'd like to go in first and check, okay? It would be great if you'd let me do it without a huge argument."

"Fine. Go be a cop. My lips are sealed." She placed her key ring in his outstretched hand.

He winked at her and went inside, leaving her on the porch to cool her heels. He returned a few moments later. "All clear. Come on in."

"Thanks, Finn. I don't mean to be such a brat. I will actually sleep better tonight knowing you checked." She stepped inside and turned to glance back at him. "You want to come in for a while?"

He smiled at her crookedly. "I better not."

"Oh. Okay." She tried not to feel hurt.

He sighed and stepped toward her. "Hey. That's not it. Come here." He pulled her into his arms, rather awkwardly because of his crutches. "I want to stay. Believe me. But I don't want to rush anything."

"Oh. Well, that's different. Thanks." She looked up into his handsome face, grateful he was trying to be sensitive to her fear, but at the same time wanting more.

He framed her face with his hand. "Would it be all right if I kissed you before I leave?"

She swallowed hard and nodded.

"Good." The words were whispered against her lips.

His lips were firm and warm, sweeping her into a maelstrom of sensation as she clung to him. He moved his mouth against hers, gently nibbling her lower lip. It was the most romantic kiss she'd ever received. She sank against him, her hands creeping up to his shoulders. He pulled back after a moment, resting his forehead against hers. "I don't know about you, Mel, but that pretty much rocked my world."

She had rocked his world? This gorgeous man, who could have any woman he desired, was rocked by kissing her? Wow.

"Mel?" He looked adorably unsure.

She realized he was waiting for her answer, but she didn't think she was capable of speech just yet, so she lifted her face to his and kissed him again.

He groaned and pulled her closer, his hands slipping around her waist. Long moments later he finally lifted his head. "I could kiss you all night, but I better get home." He brushed his fingers across her soft cheek before securing his crutches and stepping away. "Any chance you'd be available for a date tomorrow night?"

"A pretty good chance, actually. I had a last-minute cancellation."

He chuckled and leaned down to kiss her again quickly. "Well, pencil me in, please. I've been cooped up for months. Maybe we could see a movie and then go to dinner. Dancing will have to wait, I'm afraid. Oh, and you'll have to drive. But we can take my car."

"Consider yourself penciled in, Mr. DeLuca. Call me tomorrow with a time?"

"Yeah. Lock up as soon as I leave, okay? I need to have Hugh stop by and look at your locks." He managed to get himself down the front steps and turned to wave before he made his way down the walkway.

She stood in the open doorway and watched until he reached his house, making sure he made it without incident. Once he had closed his door behind him, Melanie shut her own—making sure to lock it—and crossed the room to her couch, sinking down in a daze. *He kissed me! He took me on a date and he wants to take me out again tomorrow. He kissed me!* She hugged herself, hardly able to believe what had transpired through the afternoon and evening. Yes, she'd developed a crush on him—what red-blooded American female wouldn't? But she hadn't dreamed he would be interested in return. Her history in the romance department hadn't been anything that would lead her to believe a guy like Finn would want her. She had no idea how long she'd be able to keep his interest, but she made up her mind to enjoy it while she could.

***

Finn

He locked up and headed to the bathroom to take his first shower in three months. He'd made himself pull away from Mel's intoxicating mouth before he would need a cold shower, so he cranked the handle to hot and sat on the commode to remove his boot and the bandage beneath. His right ankle was now crisscrossed with scars, both from the accident and the surgeries he'd had since. He took off his clothes and stepped/hopped into the stall, sighing with pleasure as the scalding water ran over his shoulders. He'd never realized how wonderful a shower felt until it was taken away. He'd had to make do with sponge baths and washing his hair in the sink since the accident and hadn't felt really clean. He washed his overly long hair—he needed a haircut in the worst way—and scrubbed himself all over, letting the water wash over him until it cooled, a sure sign he'd emptied his hot water heater. He deserved the small luxury.

He dried himself and hobbled back into his bedroom to find a clean pair of boxers, and then re-wrap his ankle. The pain shot the doctor had given him earlier was beginning to wear off, so he needed some ibuprofen before he went to bed. He turned off the lights and crawled into bed, finally allowing himself to review the events of the afternoon and evening. *Mel. Ah, God. She was...amazing.* He'd certainly kissed his fair share of women—maybe more than his share—but none like her. He'd wanted to deepen the kiss, but had felt her stiffen when he wrapped his arms around her waist. *Skittish.* He would have to be patient and earn her trust before their relationship became physical. And he certainly wanted it to be physical. She was obviously gun-shy, though, so he'd have to be careful and try not to rush her. He could do that. He'd never been one to try to rush a woman into bed, and Mel was special. Every atom in his body and soul was screaming at him to pay attention because this girl was important. Well, he was awake. He was paying attention.

He slept late the next morning, finally waking when he heard the key in his front door. He threw on a pair of sweats and grabbed his crutches to hobble out to the kitchen. Cara was fiddling with his coffeemaker, pressing random buttons and swearing under her breath.

"Did you run out of coffee at your place?"

She swore louder, startled. "God, Finn! You scared the shit out of me! You're walking!" She skipped across the kitchen to hug him.

"Yeah, sort of. What are you doing here?" He took over the coffee-making before she ruined his machine.

"I stopped by to see if you needed anything from Costco. Why didn't you set your coffeemaker last night? You always set it before you go to bed. I'm in desperate need of caffeine."

"You could always make your own. Or stop by Starbucks. There's one like, a block away."

"I like yours better. Plus, it's free." She flashed him the smile that nearly always got the spoiled brat what she wanted. "You didn't answer my question."

He rolled his eyes and finished setting the coffeemaker. "I had a late night and forgot to make coffee."

"A late night? What, did you get your cast off and then party all night? Why didn't you call me?"

"Because I don't usually care to take my sister on dates." He leaned against the counter and waited.

"A date? The day you get your cast off you already had a date? I'm impressed. Was it Mel?"

He nodded, unable to keep the grin from his face. "And?"

"And we're going out again tonight. And I'm taking her to dinner Sunday at Mom and Dad's."

"Yay!" She hugged him again. "I like her a lot, Finn, so don't screw this up, okay?"

"I'll give it my best, Cara. I'd hate to let you down."

"Shut up. When is that coffee going to be ready?"

He scrambled them some eggs while she drank a cup of coffee. She'd offered to fix breakfast, but he was sick to death of everyone waiting on him hand and foot. He did allow her to fetch the salsa and butter from the refrigerator—carrying things was a challenge with crutches.

"You need to teach me how you get your eggs so good someday." She forked another fluffy mound in her mouth.

He smirked; she was a terrible cook and unlikely to have the patience to wait for scrambled eggs to cook on the lower heat that ensured a creamy finished product.

"So, where are you taking Mel tonight?"

"She's technically taking me, since she'll have to drive, but we're going to see a movie and then grab some dinner. I am beyond ready to get out of this house for a while."

"I'm sure you are. Hey, you want me to pick you up any, you know, *supplies* while I'm at Costco?"

"If 'supplies' is a thinly veiled euphemism for prophylactics, then no, thanks. You must have an inflated opinion of my stamina if you think I need a seventy-five-pack of condoms on my second date. I still have a broken ankle, you know."

She laughed and carried her plate to the sink. "I was thinking of a nice bottle of wine, actually."

"Of course you were. Yeah, pick up something red. I think she likes red wine. And see if they have any wine glasses."

***

Mel arrived promptly for their date, looking fresh and tempting in a pair of tight jeans with a flowing top that skimmed her shoulders and had him itching to touch and taste. She'd braided her hair, leaving her long neck exposed; Finn was distracted all evening by various fantasies, all involving his lips on her creamy skin.

Tonight he insisted she drive his Jeep, saying she

would love how easy it was to park compared to the boat she drove. They decided to see a movie first and she suggested the new theater with reclining seats so he could prop his leg up. He'd been meaning to check it out, but hadn't had a chance, so was amenable to her suggestion. They saw a fairly forgettable earthquake saga, but reclining next to her with a bucket of popcorn and a shared soft drink was something he didn't think he'd forget any time soon. Once the popcorn was finished, he set the empty bucket on the ground and held her hand, linking their fingers. She turned her head and smiled at him, making his heart ache with her beauty and grace. He knew he was falling fast, but he couldn't seem to care.

For dinner, he suggested a favorite pub that featured some good local craft beer. Over the last few years, Albuquerque had become a contender in the craft brew scene, with lots of new micro-breweries appearing. The one he chose had adopted an Irish theme and served some of the best fish and chips in the city. His mother, a native of Belfast, even approved, although she claimed it wasn't quite as good as it would be in Ireland. Mel seemed to enjoy it and the Irish Red brew quite a lot. After dinner, they went back to his house and sat on the back patio, talking and sipping wine from his new glasses, for hours. The warm summer evening was perfect as they watched the sun sink behind the West Mesa, silhouetting the inactive volcanoes known as the Three Sisters.

"I've never seen such gorgeous sunsets before," she mused. "The colors are stunning."

The vivid orange and pink watercolors painted the western horizon as they gazed. Finn thought it was one of the most perfect moments of his life. "They say it's all the dust in our atmosphere that makes New Mexico sunsets so pretty."

She turned and smiled at him; the glorious sunset was immediately forgotten. He wanted to know everything about her: what she was like as a little girl, who she dated in high school, what she studied in college, etcetera. As she spoke about her past, he noticed she glossed over her college years and he tucked that information away for later. There was something she wasn't comfortable sharing with him yet. He would have to be patient and give her time. He had a feeling it might be related to why she was so skittish.

He walked her home when they finished the bottle, grateful she didn't try to talk him out of it. He did a quick check of the house, but everything seemed to be in place. Finally, when nothing else was standing in his way, he pulled her into his arms and lowered his mouth to hers, quickly losing himself in the wonder of kissing her again. Tonight, he couldn't stop himself from going a bit further, letting his tongue taste her lower lip before seeking entrance to her warm mouth. She complied and he swept inside, groaning, as he truly tasted her for the first time. She met him, tasting him stroke for stroke as he tightened his hold on her waist. He got a bit carried away and let his hand steal down to caress her shapely bottom and pull her closer, clueing her into how much he desired her. He realized his mistake when she stiffened and pulled away.

"Mel, hey." He cupped her cheek and forced her to look at him. "I'm sorry. I got carried away. I won't push."

"It's okay, Finn. It's my fault. I'm just—"

"What? What in the hell are you talking about?"

"Nothing. I don't, I mean I'm not...I don't know." She stepped away from him, her arms wrapped around her middle as if protecting herself.

His heart melted at her obvious pain. What had happened to make her like this? Or rather, who? He'd like to bash the bastard's face who had done this to her. He stepped close to her again, brushing a stray wisp of her silky hair behind her ear. "Mel, sweetheart. I don't know what happened to you in the past, but I need you to know something. I like you. A lot. And I want to explore this relationship. I want to get to know you better, and I hope you want to get to know me better. And yes, that includes a physical relationship." He stopped as she looked away. "But I would never push you into something you're not ready for. I can be a very patient man when necessary. You're worth waiting for, Mel."

She finally looked at him again and he was appalled to see tears shining in her eyes, threatening to spill over. "Finn. I like you too. A lot. I'm scared. I haven't been in a relationship for a long time, and I'm not sure I'm any good at it."

He smiled and leaned in to kiss her quickly. "Why don't you let me worry about that? So far, you've impressed me with your abilities."

She laughed slightly, as he'd intended. Now wasn't the time to get heavy and serious. He'd prefer to wait a few dates and maybe not be on her front porch. He pulled her close again and kissed her thoroughly, leaving his hands firmly on her waist.

"Good night, sweet Mel. Sleep tight. We have dinner with my family tomorrow, so get plenty of rest. They're a handful."

Chapter Nine

Mel

She changed three times. The dress had been too…dressy. The jeans were too casual. She finally decided on a skirt and matching top in a light coral shade her aunt had always told her complemented her coloring. She wanted to look good this evening when she met his parents. *I'm not ready for this. I can't do this. His family is huge! There will be too many people. I need to cancel.* But then she thought about Finn. He'd been so sweet and patient with her. They'd gone out for brunch earlier and he'd talked about his family, about how they drove him crazy, but he was still good friends with all his siblings, especially Cara, Hugh, and Izzy, who were closest to him in age. When he told her about his niece, Janey, his eyes had lit up and Melanie had thought about what a great father he would be someday. He'd told her about how Izzy had sat them all down one day, nearly six years ago, and dropped a huge bomb: she was pregnant. They'd been shocked, he said, since she wasn't even dating, having broken up with her long-time fiancé months before. She'd refused to talk about the father and they'd swallowed their surprise and supported her. He was so proud of his parents for not reacting badly and letting any of the disappointment they must have felt show to their daughter, who exhibited steely determination to have the baby and raise it herself. Love for his family had practically oozed from every pore.

You can't let him down. Stop being such a baby and get yourself over to his house. Now! She turned from the mirror and grabbed her purse before she could second-guess herself again. She knocked lightly before letting herself in with the key Finn had presented her with at brunch. He'd told her it was simply to make it easier for her since he was so slow on his crutches. He wasn't trying to pressure her in any way. She knew that. She believed him and trusted him. It was herself she didn't trust.

"Finn? You here?" The house was awfully quiet and she wondered if maybe he'd fallen asleep.

"Back here," he called.

She followed the sound of his voice, stopping short at his open bedroom door. He exited his bathroom, shirtless, wearing a pair of low-slung jeans. Holy. God. Wow. His torso was magnificent: sculpted, tan, with defined abs below a mat of black chest hair. She'd never cared for the waxed look on men. She couldn't quite make herself look away from him and struggled to swallow with a throat that had suddenly gone bone-dry.

"Hey, Mel. Sorry I'm running late. Ironing my

shirt took longer than I thought it would. Crutches make ordinary chores awkward." He hobbled over to the closet door, where an Oxford-type blue shirt was hanging from the knob. "You look great." He buttoned his shirt, apparently unaware she had frozen at the sight of him.

"Thanks." She cleared her throat and looked away from the tempting sight of him dressing. "I brought a bottle of wine for your parents. Do they like Chardonnay? I thought it would be good for a summer evening. I figured a red would be too heavy, but I don't know what's on the menu. I can run home real quick and get the red if you think they'd like that better."

He finished buttoning his shirt and crossed the room to her. He leaned down to kiss her softly. "Shh, sweetheart. They'll love it. You're nervous, huh?"

"I almost called to cancel. I'm not good with big groups."

He chuckled and put his arms around her, tucking her head under his chin. "Don't worry about my family. You've already met all my brothers and sisters and survived the trauma. My parents will love you, trust me."

"Okay. I'll try." She inhaled his scent: soap, aftershave, and laundry detergent, and was comforted.

"That's all anyone can ask. Come on. Time to go."

She followed his directions and drove them to the Albuquerque Acres area of town, parking in front of a sprawling adobe multi-level home.

"Wow." She stared at the beautiful house.

"Yeah. My dad built it."

"By himself?"

He chuckled. "No. He owns a construction company. He's semi-retired now. Hugh and Izzy run the company for the most part, these days. Dad still shows up at the office or on a job site a few times a week, mostly to drive everyone crazy." He ushered her up the front walkway and held the door for her, daring her with a look to try and hold it for him.

"Oh, Finn! Look at you!"

Melanie saw a flash of black hair rush by her and into Finn's arms. "Yeah, I'm walking and everything. Almost." He hugged the woman and then turned her around. "Mom, this is Mel."

"Hello, Mel. I've heard so much about you. Welcome. Call me Moira, please. I'm so glad to meet you." Her voice was lovely with a slight Irish lilt Melanie found charming. "Let's go out back. Everyone's here, except Seamus, of course. That boy…" She walked quickly, too quickly for Finn.

He smiled at Melanie, rolling his eyes. "After you."

The rest of Finn's family, minus one of his younger brothers, was in the vast backyard. "Mel!" Cara squealed and ran over to her, carrying what looked like a croquet mallet. "I'm so glad Finn brought you! Come play croquet with us. You can be on my team. Tony cheats, so watch out."

"I heard that, Cara. Don't be a brat. Hey, Mel. Wuz up?" Finn's youngest brother jogged up and slung his arm around Mel's neck.

110

"Hi, Tony. It's nice to see you again." She smiled at the young man, so like Finn, yet without the fine lines and care-worn appearance his age and recent accident had caused.

"You hear that? Mel likes me." He stuck his tongue out at his sister and led Mel away to the croquet game.

They played one game before Finn claimed her back, leading her toward the cooler for a couple beers and then ushering her toward the large barbecue grill. "Dad, I want you to meet my girlfriend, Mel."

She nearly choked on her beer; *I'm his girlfriend? Yeah. I'm his girlfriend. Take that, world!*

Finn's father flipped a piece of meat and turned to greet her. "Well, she's even prettier than you said, Finn. Hi, Mel. Nice to meet you." He pulled her into a bear hug, causing her to slosh the beer slightly.

"Sorry about that, Mr. DeLuca."

"Call me Big Tony. Everyone else does. Finn, get me one of those, why don't you?" He gestured toward the beer.

"I can't carry anything with these damn crutches, but I'm sure I can get someone to bring you one." Finn saluted jauntily and hobbled away toward the cooler.

Big Tony watched his son, concern evident on his face. "How's he doing, Mel? He seems much better, but his mother and I have been so worried."

She looked up at the older man, her heart aching at the concern on his face. "He's doing better.

111

Getting out of the wheelchair was really important to him."

"Yes, I can see that. We almost lost him." His voice faltered on the last words. He sniffed and looked down at her. "I'm glad he's found you, young lady. I haven't seen him this happy in months."

She didn't know what to say.

Finn returned with a young child in tow. "Hand Poppa his beer, Janey." The adorable girl with golden brown pigtails handed her grandfather a bottle.

"Here, Poppa." She smiled delightedly and turned to Finn, holding her arms up. "Will you pick me up, Uncle Finn!"

"Sorry, Janey-bear. I can't. Come over here and maybe I can put you on my lap." He led the child to a seating area and scooped her into his lap, tickling her until she was screeching with giggles. Mel noticed he made sure to keep her on his good leg.

"Janey! I told you we have to be gentle with Uncle Finn, remember?" Izzy quickly approached, reaching for her daughter.

"It's fine, Iz. Let her be." Finn flashed his sister an impatient look, then turned back to play with his niece.

"He's impossible," Izzy muttered. "Hi, Mel. So, you and Finn, huh?"

Melanie looked quickly at Finn's older sister, trying to gauge whether or not she was expressing disapproval. She was relieved to see only slight amusement in Izzy's gaze as she watched her brother entertain her small daughter. "Yeah.

He's…well, he's special."

Izzy turned and smiled at her. "Funny. That's what he said about you." She stared at her for a long moment. "Mom made some white sangria. What do you say we ditch the beer and try some?"

Mel smiled and followed her inside to sample the fruity wine concoction, which was delicious. She made a mental note to ask Moira for the recipe. As she sipped, she thought about how worried she'd been about this gathering: meeting his parents and seeing his siblings again, but it was working out fine. She could do this. She felt her confidence building with every minute she spent with this family. They were simply people; people she happened to like very much.

Big Tony announced the steaks were ready and the family gathered around the large outdoor table to eat. Seamus arrived a few minutes after they started eating, with his girlfriend in tow. Her name was Sloane, and it took Mel approximately thirty seconds to sense the family didn't love her. Mel watched closely throughout dinner, trying to figure out why. It didn't take long; Sloane was a full-on diva, demanding Seamus' attention exclusively and attempting to control his every action. She seemed completely oblivious to the tension she'd created and Melanie wondered what the story was. She'd be sure to ask Finn later.

It was several hours later when Finn collected her from where she was talking with Cara and Izzy, planning a shopping afternoon as soon as Izzy could get her mom to babysit Janey. She hugged her two new friends, promising to join them for the outing, then left with Finn.

Once they got in his car, he reached for her hand. "That wasn't so bad, was it?"

"No. I worried for no reason, which is what I always do. I almost canceled this afternoon because I was so freaked out."

"I'm really glad you didn't, Mel. Thanks for coming. It meant a lot to me."

"Well, it was my first, so I hope I did okay." She laughed lightly, hoping he saw the humor in it.

"Your first what?" He turned to her, frowning.

"My first time to meet the parents." Now she was worried; he seemed so concerned.

"Wait. You've never been introduced to your boyfriend's parents before? How is that possible? I'm not your first boyfriend, am I? That's impossible."

"No, of course not." She stared out the windshield, refusing to meet his eyes. "You're my second."

***

Finn

He was flabbergasted. How in the world had this beautiful, smart, funny, sexy woman sitting in the car next to him only had one boyfriend before him? "Mel, sweetheart, how is that possible?"

She shrugged and continued to stare out the windshield. "I was really shy in high school. No one ever asked me out. It got better in college and I dated a guy for about a year."

She still wouldn't look at him and his gut clenched at the unspoken pain he could detect in her voice. He remembered how hard it was in high school to figure out which girls might possibly say yes if you asked them out; the silent ones who gave no signals or encouragement were stricken from the list, no matter how pretty they were. Fragile male teenage egos simply couldn't handle that kind of pressure. "What happened to college boy?"

She shrugged, but he noticed the set of her mouth grow hard. "It didn't work out. We both moved on."

There was more to the story, but it didn't appear she wanted to tell it at the moment. He understood. There had been a girl in college, Sarah, who had pretty much crushed him when she broke it off. "And since college?"

She shrugged again. "A lot of first dates."

He didn't know what to say or even think. Why? Did the guys never call again? He had a hard time believing that. She was fun, a great conversationalist, and one heck of a kisser. It must be Mel, then, who refused any follow-up dates. So how did that explain the fact that he was sitting here with her on what amounted to their third date—fourth if you counted brunch earlier in the day? How did he get so lucky?

She pulled into his driveway, clicked the garage-door opener, and pulled into the garage. He met her around the back at the bumper.

"Thank you." He brushed her hair behind her ear.

She stared up at him, eyebrows raised. "For

what? Driving you home?"

He chuckled. "No, but thanks for that. I meant for giving me a chance and a second date."

She stepped closer to him, a bit unsure, but reached her arms around his neck. "You're welcome." Then she kissed him.

Knowing she instigated it made the kiss all the more amazing and Finn gladly sunk into the wonder of her mouth. He pulled her tightly against his body and spent the next few minutes—hours?—kissing his girlfriend, deepening it when she made no move to pull away. Finally, realizing they were giving any neighbors who happened to be walking by or looking out their windows quite a show, he softened the kiss and pulled away slightly. "I better walk you home. We could continue this fascinating conversation on your couch, if you like." He wiggled his eyebrows up and down in a hopefully salacious manner.

She laughed and nodded. They exited the garage and made the short walk to her house. As they turned up her walkway, a small white ball of fur charged at them, tail wagging madly.

"Fluff? What on earth are you doing outside?" Melanie bent to scoop the small dog into her arms.

Finn's senses were suddenly on high alert and he began searching the surrounding area with his gaze, attempting to penetrate the dusk. Melanie started toward her front door, which he could now see was standing partly open. "Mel! Stop!"

She halted, looking back at him. "What?"

"Don't go inside." He held his hand out, beckoning her to return to his side. "Did you lock up when you left? Are you sure?" he prodded at her nod.

"Positive." Her voice sounded hollow, afraid.

"Take Fluff and go back to my place."

"Finn? What's going on? Come with me."

He turned and put an arm around her, balancing somewhat precariously on his crutches while still peering through the near-darkness. "Mel, I need you to let me do my job. It looks like someone may have broken into your house. I'm going to call it in and go check it out, but I need you to wait for me at my house, okay?"

"But what about you?"

"I'll be fine. This is what I do and I'm really good at it. Now take Fluff and go." He softened his order with a kiss on her forehead. He watched as she walked quickly to his house and let herself in; then he pulled his phone out and called it in. He waited in the yard for the unit to arrive; he knew better than to investigate on his own. Even if he had his gun—safely stashed in the gun safe in his bedroom—he had no free hands to hold it. This friggin' broken ankle was really starting to piss him off!

A marked police car arrived within ten minutes and the two officers checked the house. Nothing appeared disturbed and the officers suggested Mel must have not closed the door properly, allowing the wind to open it. Finn knew the officers well and realized they had certainly checked thoroughly. Finn thanked them and headed back to his house, not looking forward to facing Mel.

"Do you think that's what happened, Finn? Do

you think it was just the wind?"

He sighed and pulled her closer. They were sitting on his couch, drinking out of his new wine glasses. "I don't know, sweetheart. If it were just this, yeah, I'd probably think you didn't shut the door all the way. But with the other stuff—the unlocked doors and feeling like someone's watching you—I'm not convinced. Why don't you stay here tonight? In the guest room, I mean." He knew they weren't ready for more yet.

She smiled, but shook her head. "No. I'm a big girl and I refuse to be spooked. I probably didn't close it all the way. I was pretty nervous about meeting your parents, you know."

"What? You, nervous? Nah." He watched as she sipped her wine. "Are you sure, Mel?"

"No, but I need to do this. I need to not be a wimp."

"Nobody with any sense would ever think you're a wimp." He poured her another glass of wine, then sat back to put his arm back around her. She'd freaked out about meeting his parents, but was determined to stay at her house after a possible B&E. What was he going to do with her?

He walked her home and insisted on going in to look around. Everything looked clear, but he didn't like the nervous way Mel's gaze was darting around. "Why don't I stay here tonight? I can crash on the couch."

She put her arms around his neck and pulled his head down for a kiss. "You are super-sweet, Finn, but no. I will be fine and you need to sleep in your bed. You probably need some Tylenol too, and I don't think I have any, so go home."

He sighed and held her. "Why do you have to be so damn brave? Okay, but you have to swear to keep your phone with you at all times. I mean it, Mel. Promise."

She smiled up at him. "I promise."

Chapter Ten

Mel

Her phone buzzed on the nightstand at eight. She opened a bleary eye and grabbed it, sending Finn a short text to assure him she was fine. He'd called last night as soon as he got back to his house, repeating his offer to sleep on her couch if she was feeling the slightest bit nervous. She'd again told him she was fine. She had lain awake for several hours, however, hearing every noise and creak the house made. CJ had kept watch with her, purring contentedly while Mel stroked her fur. She'd finally fallen asleep around three, and as a consequence had slept later than she intended. She rolled over, intending to catch another hour or so of sleep, but the phone buzzed again, this time with an invitation to breakfast. *Extra sleep or breakfast with my gorgeous boyfriend? Not even close.* She threw the covers off and headed to the shower.

He prepared pancakes and bacon, the aroma greeting her as she opened his front door. She offered to take over for him at the stove, but he shooed her away with a kiss, telling her to enjoy her coffee while he finished. It was painful to watch him struggle to balance with his crutches while moving around the kitchen, but she knew he needed to be independent. He did allow her to carry the platters of steaming pancakes and crispy bacon to the table.

"Cara called to see if I wanted to meet her for lunch."

"That sounds fun. I'm glad you two are getting along. She and I are pretty close, so it will be very convenient if you two are friends." He grinned and reached for another pancake.

She shook her head when offered her another. "I'm stuffed; pancakes fill me up fast. You're a pretty good cook, at least for breakfast. I feel like I've gotten quite a bargain bagging you for a boyfriend."

He laughed, nearly choking at her teasing. "This is just the tip of the iceberg, sweetheart. You wait 'til I get off these crutches. I've got way more in my bag of tricks than pancakes and bacon."

"Ooh, I can hardly wait."

"You're a saucy little minx, you know that? You come off as shy, but you're not, really." He reached for her hand, linking their fingers atop the kitchen table.

She loved how he seemed to want to touch her all the time. She'd been raised by a woman who didn't give a lot of hugs and her college boyfriend had only been interested in touching her when he wanted to sleep with her. Aunt Karen had been affectionate, but bedridden for the last few months. Mel hadn't realized how hungry for simple human touch she'd been. "I don't feel like I have to be shy with you. I can be myself."

He leaned over to kiss her. "Did you get any sleep last night?" He brushed his thumb gently over the slight smudge under her eye.

She shrugged and looked down. "It took me a while to fall asleep, that's all."

They were interrupted by a rapping on the kitchen door. "Yoo hoo! Hi Melanie! Can I come in?" Lena, the new neighbor from across the street was waving madly through the window.

"Who the hell is that?" Finn muttered, sounding cranky.

"She just moved in across the street. You know, the rental?" Mel stood to open the door for the woman. "Hi, Lena."

Lena nearly shoved her aside as she entered— technically uninvited—Finn's home. "Hello again! And who is this?"

"This is Finn." Mel performed the introduction, noting Finn seemed somewhat ambivalent about meeting their new neighbor.

"Nice to meet you, Finn! I'm trying to meet all the neighbors. I just talked to that adorable Mr. Taylor next door and thought I'd try this house next."

Melanie didn't think adorable was anywhere near the right word for the neighbor between her and Finn; why was it okay to refer to the elderly as 'adorable' or 'sweet'? They were simply people who had lived a long time and deserved to be treated as such, not as cute little pets to be admired and then ignored. Besides, Mr. Taylor was habitually cranky, which she found neither cute nor endearing. Melanie felt her teeth begin to grind.

Finn also seemed less than thrilled by the woman, judging by his expression, which was somewhere between horror and disgust. "You, uh, want some coffee, Laina?"

"It's Lena." The woman spoke in a clipped manner that bespoke her irritation, then seemed to relent. "Thanks. That would be great."

Melanie poured a cup for her as Lena launched her interrogation on Finn. "So what do you do, Finn? And how did you do that?" She gestured to his injured leg.

"I'm a cop. I got hit by a car." He pushed himself up and grabbed his crutches. "If you'll excuse me, ladies?" He hobbled out of the kitchen.

Mel watched him go, slightly bemused, before turning back to their guest, determined to be polite. Her mother had always drilled into her the importance of good manners, even when you didn't feel like it. "So, are you getting settled? Did all your furniture arrive?"

"Oh, sure. Everything's great. I'll have you all over for a barbecue real soon." She took another sip of her coffee. "I was surprised to see you over here, Melanie. Are you and Finn together?"

Melanie smiled tightly; why did the woman sound surprised? Was it so difficult to believe? "Yes, we are. It's pretty recent, but, yeah."

"Well, that's just great." She stood. "Say goodbye to Finn for me. I've got so much to do, so I

Amy Reece

better not stay."

Had Melanie given the impression she was looking to extend this visit? "Thanks for stopping by. Let me know if you need anything." She saw her to the door, then went looking for Finn. She found him skulking in the living room.

"Is she gone?" he asked with a guilty look.

"Yeah. What happened to you?" She'd never seen him so...rude before. He was usually so charming and affable.

He chuckled ruefully. "I don't know. I'm sorry. Something about her just set me off. I figured I would be better off ducking out than saying something unpleasant. She's...interesting, huh?"

Melanie laughed. "You could say that. Yeah, she's not my cup of tea, either. The first time we met, she was all nosy and up in my business. I didn't care for it."

He lowered himself into the easy chair—newly restored to its original spot since he got out of his wheelchair—and beckoned to her. "Let's not waste time talking about the new neighbor. I haven't had a proper kiss yet this morning, Ms. Blythe. Come here." He held his hand out to her.

She grinned and took his hand. "Are you sure? I don't want to hurt your leg."

"My left leg is fine." He pulled her down to his lap and draped her legs across the arm of the chair. "Now this is what I'm talking about."

They were silent for several minutes as their mouths met. He nibbled at the corner of her mouth, then let his lips wander along her jawline and up to her earlobe, taking it gently between his teeth. He

124

hadn't shaved that morning and his black whiskers were scratchy against her face in a way that she loved. This man's kisses did things to her she didn't even begin to understand. A low clenching in her belly—and somewhat lower, if she were perfectly honest—had her moaning his name softly. She felt him grin and then his intoxicating lips were back on hers, his warm tongue seeking entrance to her mouth. The taste of him was a heady mix of coffee, sweet maple syrup, and his own special flavor. She speared her hands through his hair and hung on as he swept them into a maelstrom of passion. She'd never felt this level of desire and hunger before. *More.* The word, the feeling repeated in her brain as she melted into him, her lips leaving his to begin their own exploration of his whisker-covered jaw and neck. She smiled as he groaned and let his hand wander up her leg to her hip and around to her bottom. The heady sense of power filled her as she realized he wanted her—plain, boring Melanie whose college boyfriend dumped her because she wasn't exciting enough in or out of bed.

A sudden movement at the window startled her and she jerked in Finn's arms.

"What's wrong?" He sat up and looked across the room where she was staring.

"Nothing. It's just...I thought I saw something at the window."

"Some*thing* or some*one?*" He pushed her off his lap with a quick kiss. "Let me take a look." He quickly grabbed his crutches and crossed to look out the window. "I don't see anything. It could have been a bird flying by."

It could have, but Melanie had thought she'd seen the outline of a person. It had been nothing more than an impression really, but it stuck in her mind. "That's probably what it was. Sorry. I guess I'm a bit jumpy after last night. I'm not usually such a nervous Nelly." Her first thought had been that Lena was peeping in at them, but why in the world would she want to do that? Finn was probably right and a dove had flown too close to the house. They were known to fly into windows, often killing themselves in the process.

He walked back to her and reached his hand to cup her cheek. "I know you're not, Mel. Hey, while you were talking to Laina—"

"Lena."

"Whatever. I called Hugh and he's going to drop by to install some new locks on your front and kitchen doors. Could you leave me a set of keys so we can get in while you're at lunch with Cara?"

"Oh, I hate to bother him with that. I'll call a locksmith tomorrow and get it done."

"Mel." He forced her to look into his eyes. "It's not a problem. Let me do this, okay? It's a cop thing. And a boyfriend thing. Your locks are shit and I won't sleep until I know you're safe. Please don't make a fuss." He followed with a searing kiss.

"Mmmm. What?"

He chuckled and kissed her again. "Good. I'm glad to have found a secret weapon. Any time I need you to cooperate I'll simply kiss you into submission. It's a tough job, but I think I'm up to the challenge."

"Fine, but be sure he leaves me a bill. I'm not

taking freebies from your brother."

"I can see I need to kiss you some more." He grinned and set about his task.

***

Finn

"So, do you think it was a bird?" Hugh looked up from his position on the floor where he was installing a new state-of-the-art security lock and deadbolt on Mel's kitchen door.

"Probably not." Finn ran his hands distractedly through his hair. "Shit, Hugh. I think someone may be stalking her."

"Which would explain why I'm sitting on her kitchen floor first thing on a Monday morning instead of making sure Izzy and Dad aren't reorganizing the company in my absence." He returned his focus to the task for a few moments. "Any idea who it could be?"

"Not a clue."

"You really like this girl."

"Is that a question?" He was starting to get irritated with his older brother.

"Nope. An observation. Mom and Dad really seemed to like her. She's…different than your usual type."

"I don't have a type."

"Yeah, you do. All your other girlfriends over the past few years—and there have been a lot— were gorgeous, smart, and shallow."

"You don't think Mel is pretty?" He forced

himself to stay seated. It was either that or hobble across the kitchen to punch his brother in the face, which would most likely leave him to finish installing the locks, something he would have difficulty managing with his crutches.

"Calm down," Hugh muttered without even looking up. He was always the calm one, rarely getting involved in the many fights of his younger siblings. "Mel is beautiful. Everyone can see that, Finn. And I'm sure she's smart. But she's obviously not shallow or mean or self-obsessed like Tatiana or Celia or Kabira or any of the others. Are you ready for what this means?"

"What do you *think* this means?" Sometimes Hugh's big brother unsought wisdom was downright annoying. Who the hell did he think he was?

"I *think* this means you may just find yourself with a girlfriend you won't want to get rid of once the initial glow of romance and sex wears off."

"May I remind you Tatiana left me?" he asked through gritted teeth.

"It was only a matter of time."

"I was thinking about asking her to move in when I got hit."

"I never thought I'd be glad for that accident."

"Shut up."

Hugh laughed. "Sorry. I'm kidding. Mostly. Finn, if you have to spend a bunch of time thinking about whether or not to ask a woman to move in, then you're with the wrong woman."

"What in the hell makes you such a goddamn expert? Last time I checked, you live by yourself and I haven't noticed a steady girlfriend in over a year."

"I'm waiting for the right woman. I'll know her when I meet her and I sure as hell won't bother thinking about asking her to move in. I'll put a ring on her finger and we'll start a life together." Hugh finished with the kitchen door and stood to begin the cleanup.

"You make it sound so simple."

"It is simple. I just need to find the woman."

This time Finn laughed. "Yeah, well, good luck with that." He was silent for a moment. "I really like her, Hugh."

"Yeah, I can tell."

***

The next two weeks flew by. He and Mel spent every minute they possibly could together. She drove him to his physical therapy and doctor appointments, they watched movies and went out to dinner. They didn't sleep together, unless you counted the times they fell asleep on the couch. He wanted to, of course, but he knew he couldn't rush her. He had a feeling if he was patient it would happen in its own time when Mel was ready. There was obviously a bad relationship in her past, but he refused to push her to share the details until she was ready. There was also the small matter of his broken ankle. He was still in a lot of pain and wasn't altogether too sure how well everything would go their first time, so he was stalling.

They had made plans to spend Saturday together

at a craft beer festival and maybe a movie later. Her text thirty minutes before the time they'd agreed to leave was unexpected and unlike her.

Mel: I have to cancel today. I'm really sorry.

Finn: What's up? Everything ok?

Mel: Fine. I just can't go. Sorry.

Weird. He thought about calling but decided to walk down and look in her eyes. If she needed to be alone, fine. They'd been spending a lot of time together lately and he realized an introvert like Mel probably just needed a day to herself. He would assure her he understood and let her be.

She answered the door and he could tell she'd been crying, her eyes red and her face a bit blotchy. She was not a pretty crier, but his heart ached for her.

"Mel, what's wrong?" He opened the screen door and stepped inside.

"I'm fine. I didn't want to bother you. I'm not very good company today, that's all. Can we reschedule?"

"Of course, but I need to know what's wrong. Why are you crying, sweetheart? Come here." He pulled her into his arms.

She held herself stiffly for a moment as he rubbed his hands on her back. Finally she melted into his embrace and wrapped her arms around his waist. "It's stupid. You don't need to deal with my ridiculous emotions."

"Hey." He pulled back and tipped her chin up. "Tell me."

"It's Aunt Karen's birthday. I thought it wouldn't bother me, but I've been weepy all morning. I can't seem to shake it, so I don't want to inflict myself on you today."

Who had made her feel like this, like she couldn't share the way she felt or what made her sad? Finn burned with anger at the person in her past. "Mel, honey. That's not the way this works. I absolutely want to know when you're feeling weepy or whatever. I want to be here for you. Let's go sit on the couch and you can tell me about it, okay?" He pulled her against him, stroking his hand over her silky hair, breathing in the scent of her peach shampoo. "Tell me about her."

"About Aunt Karen?" At his nod, she began to talk. "She was my great-aunt actually, my mother's aunt. She never married, never had any kids of her own, but whenever she visited us she was so much fun. She played 'cats' with me when I was little." She chuckled through her tears.

"Cats?"

"Yeah. We just crawled around on the floor for hours, meowing and purring. Silly, but I loved it."

"That sounds really sweet." He kissed the top of her head.

"She was really special." Her voice was still wavering. "She sent me money every month while I was in college. She moved out here to New Mexico a few years ago when she finally retired, saying she was sick of the harsh Illinois winters. When she was diagnosed with cancer, I moved here to help her.

She went so fast, Finn. It was barely a year, and the last few months were so hard on her. She was in so much pain."

"I'm so sorry, Mel." He let her cry softly for a while. "Hey, why don't we go put some flowers on her grave? Have you done that, yet?"

She shook her head. "Not since the funeral. Are you sure you don't mind? I don't want to spoil your day."

"The only thing that would spoil my day would be to spend it without you."

She drove them to a floral shop and bought two bunches of cheerful mixed flowers. He didn't question her, but was curious what the other bouquet was for. Once at the cemetery, he followed her through the grass surrounding the headstones until she stopped at the one belonging to her aunt. He stood back and let her take as much time as she needed. When she finally rose, she still held the second bouquet and he wondered what she planned. He watched as she walked around to a nearby headstone; it looked much older than those nearby. Mel cleared a few weeds away before arranging the flowers in the container near the grave. She finished and joined Finn.

"Whose grave is that?"

"His name was George Hanover. He died way back in the sixties. He was only three years old."

"Was he a relative?" He was trying to figure out the connection.

"No. I have no idea who he was. I just noticed his grave here during Aunt Karen's funeral and figured no one probably ever put flowers on it anymore. I just thought it would be nice." She shrugged, as if it were nothing.

He stared at her, unable to fathom the depth of her beauty—body and soul—in that moment. *God, what an amazing woman.* He pulled her close, tucking her head under his chin. *I love her.* He recognized the feeling—but so much more than a simple feeling—mostly because he realized he'd never truly experienced it before. What he'd thought was love for Tatiana was so pale and anemic compared with what he felt for Mel. *I'm completely in love with this woman. I've only known her for a few weeks, but it doesn't seem to matter. I love her.* He smiled hugely and wanted to tell her, wanted to shout it to the world at large, but figured a cemetery wasn't the most romantic place. *Soon.*

"Are you ready to go?"

"I am." She hugged him again. "Thanks for this, Finn. Thanks for understanding."

"Always."

Chapter Eleven

Mel

I will get this chapter finished tonight! Finn was spending the evening with his brothers—they had swooped in and kidnapped him earlier in the evening, laughingly claiming Mel was hogging him. There was apparently a pub-crawl downtown they tried to attend every year. Finn had complained it would truly be a crawl this year, courtesy of his crutches, but he'd gone along willingly enough. Hugh had assured her they were taking an Uber, so she had kissed Finn and sent him on his way.

She'd fallen behind on her writing in the weeks since they'd started dating and had received a few increasingly irritated emails from her editor. It was difficult to concentrate on the fictional romance she was creating when she had a real one to participate in, especially with Finn sitting next to her on the sofa nearly every evening. Cuddling and kissing him was a whole lot more fun than living vicariously through her protagonists. And it could be considered research. Of course it could. She grinned and fired up her laptop, wondering if she could adequately describe the way Finn's kisses made her feel. It would add something to her romantic scenes that had been sadly missing for a long, *long* time. She frowned as she thought about how reticent Finn seemed to be to take their relationship to the next level beyond merely kissing. Didn't he want to? She was starting to wonder and to worry a bit. Of course, she was relieved he wasn't pressuring her, but while his kisses blew her mind, that was pretty much all he ever tried to do. His hands would wander some, but he always stopped short of anything more than PG-13. She was ready for more. Maybe. Ugh! It was so frustrating, but what could she do? Ask him? Yeah, that would go over well. *"Hey, Finn. So tell me why exactly you seem to not want to sleep with me, hmm?"* That would be an uncomfortable conversation, to say the least. She knew he'd practically lived with his last girlfriend, so why was he holding back with her? Several answers came to mind; none of them made her feel any better about herself.

She shook off the gloomy thoughts and managed to immerse herself in her manuscript for several hours, gaining back some of the ground she'd lost in the last few weeks. Her editor would at least speak to her again. She reached the end of the chapter and stood to stretch, arching her back, amused when CJ did the same.

"I don't know about you, CJ, but I deserve a glass of wine." She scratched the cat right above her tail, then headed to the kitchen to pour herself a glass of the red blend she'd bought earlier in the week. She'd discovered the wonderful world of wine blends through some research for her newest book and was in love. The one she'd just opened was tart and fruity—absolutely delicious! She took her glass back to the living room and turned on the TV, hoping to catch the late news. She chose the first channel with local news and settled on the sofa to watch. The female anchor was gorgeous—so beautiful it was hard to concentrate on what she was reporting. *Why are some people so blessed with good looks? Not fair.* When the anchor's name flashed across the screen, Melanie frowned and sat up. Tatiana Barrett. Why did that name seem so familiar? Melanie was sure she'd seen her somewhere before, but couldn't think where.

It took her until nearly the weather segment to figure it out: Tatiana was the name of Finn's ex-girlfriend. The one who had left him while he was in a coma in the hospital. Cara had said she was an anchor for a local news station, so this had to be her. How many Tatianas could there be? Melanie's heart sank as she was confronted with how beautiful the woman was. *That's what he's used to. That's the kind of woman he can get. Why is he settling for someone like me? He is so far out of my league it's ridiculous.* The voices—the same ones that had been destroying her self-esteem for years—clamored in her head. She told herself she was being silly, that Finn had chosen her, Melanie, and they were happy. *But maybe he misses her. Maybe he wishes it were different.*

Stop! She left and he chose you! Stop doing this to yourself! She knew she was worrying needlessly, but it was hard to shake it off completely. She clicked off the TV and slugged back the last of her wine, determined not to think about it anymore tonight. She would see Finn tomorrow and he would put her mind at ease. And maybe she would see about testing the waters in regards to taking their relationship to the next level. She was enormously nervous about the thought of sleeping with him—she had extremely limited experience, after all. He obviously knew what he was doing and had a lot of experience, the thought of which made her slightly sick to her stomach. She'd only ever slept with one guy in her life and the experience had been less than stellar. Evan had pressured her into a sexual relationship before she was ready—she'd always planned to wait until she was in love to take such a big step. She'd allowed Evan to convince her they were in love and had a future together, but she realized what she had felt for him was nowhere close to what she already felt for Finn. Was she in love with him? She wasn't sure, and didn't trust herself to recognize what it even looked like.

She checked to make sure she'd locked up—the new locks Hugh had installed made her feel like she was living in Fort Knox—and went to bed. Her phone buzzed with a text as she tucked herself in.

Finn: Goodnight, sweetheart. See you tomorrow. Lock up, please.

Melanie smiled and texted back a smiley face

emoji.

***

She woke early, determined to get through her design work before lunch so she could spend the afternoon with Finn. CJ left right after breakfast, as usual, and Melanie sat at the dining room table to work. She worked steadily for a couple hours before standing to stretch and take a short break. *I love working from home, but I miss having a workstation with everything at hand. Maybe I should turn one of the bedrooms into a home office.* She took a short trip down the hall and peered into the spare bedrooms. The most likely candidate was the corner room, which had a nice window with a view of the pretty backyard. *I should probably move into the master bedroom, as well.* It was time to begin sorting through Aunt Karen's belongings. Most would go to charity; Melanie would only keep a few mementos. She'd never been overly interested in material possessions—a good thing, given her relatively low-paying career choices—and she had a lot of good memories of her aunt. She'd been dragging her feet about the sad chore, but it was time.

Another hour and a half was enough to finish the most pressing of her work. She changed into capris and a tank top before scooping up Fluff and locking the front door. She crossed her lawn and was nearly to the edge of her property when she stopped short. There was a strange car in Finn's driveway. Maybe she should wait until whoever it was left—she didn't want to interrupt, especially if it was someone from work. He was hoping to start back to work—half days and chained to a desk—the next week. While she was trying to decide, his front door opened and a woman exited. Even from this distance Melanie recognized her. *Tatiana.* That gleaming golden hair was burned into Mel's brain, courtesy of the ten o'clock news the night before. Mel froze, unsure what to do. *Why is she there? She dumped him!* Mel watched, willing the woman to leave. She did, but not before looping her arms around Finn's neck and kissing him. It didn't look like a quick peck, either. And Finn didn't push her away and wipe his mouth—far from it. He smiled at her. Smiled! Melanie's heart squeezed painfully as her eyes filled. Another woman might have charged across his yard and demanded answers. But Melanie had years of crushed confidence behind her. She hugged Fluff to her chest and turned back to her own house.

***

Finn

Well, that was uncomfortable. Finn leaned against his front door after closing it behind Tatiana. She'd shown up out of the blue, insisting they talk. He'd been worried at first that she wanted to get back together, but it turned out she simply wanted to clear the air. And she wanted to return his house key. He was relieved and wondered why he felt so little anger toward her. He'd been absolutely

139

livid for weeks after he awoke from the coma; in fact that anger had helped him focus on recovering. She had torn him apart and he'd feared seeing her again would rip open the wound. But he'd felt nothing except impatience to get rid of her. Mel was due soon and he certainly didn't want them meeting quite yet—that would be awkward. Even when she'd pressed the quick kiss on him at the door he'd been completely unaffected. He'd simply smiled and bid her goodbye.

He chuckled ruefully and made his way to the kitchen to prepare lunch for the woman who did affect him, who was currently driving him to the brink of insanity with wanting her. He'd been taking it so slowly over the past few weeks, determined to make sure she was completely comfortable with him before suggesting they take the next step in their relationship. Now that he realized he loved her it was especially important; she was the most precious thing in the world and he'd never do anything to make her feel pressured or uncomfortable.

He finished tossing the salad, wondering where she was. She was late and he wondered if she'd forgotten. It wasn't like her. She was one of the most punctual people he'd ever met, and she always called or texted if she was running late. His stomach clenched as he thought about the recent weird stuff happening to her. He grabbed his phone.

Finn: Hey, you ok? Lunch is ready.

She didn't reply. His heart began hammering as

140

he punched the speed dial button for her. No answer. *Shit.* He hobbled as quickly as he could to his bedroom and fumbled with the combination to his gun safe. He shoved his Glock 9mm in his back waistband and maneuvered out the door and down the street to her house. He took up a position to the side of her front door—clumsy and feeling off-balance on his crutches—and knocked.

"Mel? Are you home?"

It took several agonizing minutes before he heard the locks clicking and her door opened. A wedge of her face appeared, but she kept the screen door shut between them.

"Mel? What's wrong? Are you okay?" He tried to peer into the house to see if she was alone.

"I'm fine."

"O-kay." She didn't sound fine. She sounded like she'd been crying. "Can I come in?"

"Um, not right now."

"Mel." He reached for the screen door handle and jiggled, but found it locked. "What's going on? Is someone in there with you?"

"No. I'm fine. I just…I want you to leave."

"What? Why?" He was at a complete loss. What the hell?

"Please, Finn. Go. I need to be alone." She shut the door and he heard her lock it.

"Mel! Talk to me, dammit! Don't do this!" Silence from the other side of the door. He pounded on the frame, but she didn't respond. He waited several minutes, but the door remained firmly shut. He finally hobbled home, dejected but not wanting the entire neighborhood to hear them. As soon as he got home he tried calling and texting her repeatedly, but she must have turned her phone off. What in the world had happened? Everything had been fine yesterday. What could have happened between then and...*oh, shit*. Tatiana. Mel must have seen her. He tried to imagine what their encounter on the porch must have looked like to an outsider and realized she certainly might have construed it as a romantic interlude. Well, crap. This was just perfect. She wouldn't answer her phone or her door so he couldn't explain. He thought about sending a note with CJ, but the damn cat had disappeared, as usual, shortly before noon. "Fine! If she wants to be mad, that's her choice. I didn't do anything wrong!" His righteous indignation lasted all of five minutes. He soon realized if he'd seen her kiss another man, he'd probably flip his lid. He returned his Glock to the safe and threw himself down on his bed. *What am I gonna do?*

It took him nearly an hour to realize he didn't have a prayer by himself. He called Cara. She promised to come over as soon as she got home from a professional development workshop. He tried to spend the time until she arrived working on the cold cases Chris had brought, but he couldn't concentrate. She would get over it, wouldn't she? She had to. He couldn't fathom the alternative and found himself near panicked when he thought about it too long. He shut the manila folder disgustedly and scrubbed his hands over his face. *Oh, God! Three hours without her and I'm a basket case! Pull your shit together, DeLuca!*

By the time Cara showed up a few hours later, he

had managed to calm himself somewhat, but he was near desperate to talk to Mel. She still wasn't answering her phone.

"Okay, big brother, what is going on? What did you do?" Cara had let herself in, going straight to the fridge for a diet soda, which he kept stocked for her. She had obviously come directly from her workshop, judging by her work clothes and the computer bag she dropped on the couch.

"I didn't do anything!"

Cara simply raised her eyebrows over the rim of her soda can.

He sighed. "Tatiana stopped by earlier. I think Mel saw her leave. And she probably saw her kiss me."

"You kissed Tatiana?"

"No! She kissed me, I swear!" He ran his hands through his hair.

"Oh, and I'm sure you shoved her away indignantly, huh?"

"Yeah, well, I didn't think my girlfriend was watching!"

"I hate it when that happens." She didn't even try to hide her smirk.

"Shut up. I thought you came over to help me." He slumped back on the couch. "Please, Cara. I'm going nuts. I need Mel. What did I ever see in Tatiana?"

"It probably had something to do with her giant tits."

"Are you gonna help me or insult me?"

"I can't do both? I'm a pretty good multi-tasker." She had the good sense to take his dangerous look seriously. "Fine, calm down. Yes, I'm going to help you. Now, have you tried talking to her?"

"Seriously? Of course I've tried talking to her! She shut the door in my face and she's not answering my calls or texts. I think she turned her phone off."

"I think you're right. I tried calling and it went straight to voice mail. I thought she might be ignoring only your calls." Cara was silent for a few minutes as she sipped her drink. "Okay. I think this calls for a direct assault. Do you still have any of that wine I bought for you?"

"Yeah, why?"

She disappeared into the kitchen, returning with two bottles. "Because I have a feeling I'm going to need it to even get in the door." She pocketed her keys and opened the front door. "Don't wait up, but do turn the covers down in the guest room. I'm pretty sure I won't be able to drive home."

***

Mel

She heard him leave, clump-clumping down the steps, and let herself slide down the door. Arms wrapped around her knees, she finally gave in to the tears that had been so near the surface since she'd watched him kiss his ex-girlfriend. Were they already back together? It was surely just a matter of time. She couldn't begin to compare with the curvy blonde goddess who obviously wanted him back. Who could blame her? Finn was amazing, the best thing that had ever happened to Mel, but she wasn't the kind of woman he'd want to be with when he had someone like Tatiana. *All right, stop feeling sorry for yourself! You'll be fine. You always have been.* She wiped her eyes impatiently and stood, determined to stop sulking. *You don't need him. You don't need anyone.* Maybe not, but she wanted him and she didn't think she could be entirely happy without him.

"Melanie?" The knock on the door startled her. "It's me, Lena. Are you home?"

Crap. She's the last person I want to deal with right now. She wondered if she could remain perfectly still long enough for her to leave. Finally deciding it was best to get it over with, she turned and unlocked the door. "Hey, Lena. What's up?"

"Is everything okay? I saw Finn leaving and he looked upset."

Intrusive much? "Oh, no. Everything's fine."

"Well, good. Do you mind if I come in for a minute? I have something I need to ask you."

Ugh. Mel was not in the mood. "Sure." Why could she only be rude in her mind? She unlocked the screen and opened it for her neighbor. "Come in."

Lena followed her to the kitchen and sat at the table expectantly, so Mel continued in the neighborly vein and poured them each a glass of iced tea. "So, what did you need?"

"I'm going out of town next weekend and wondered if you'd mind picking up my mail and newspaper while I'm gone." Lena ran a hot pink-tipped fingernail around the rim of her glass.

145

"Um, sure. No problem."

"Wonderful! Oh, I'm so glad I found such a nice neighborhood. Everyone has been so great here. Thanks so much." She paused to take a few more sips of her tea. "Are you sure you're okay, Melanie? It kind of looks like you've been crying."

"I'm fine. I was crying earlier; my eyes stay red for a while, that's all. I did have a fight with Finn, but everything is fine." It was nowhere near fine, but Mel didn't want to talk about it with this woman she barely knew. She needed a friend in the worst way, but Lena wasn't even on the list. The problem was her friend list was extremely short.

"Oh, you poor thing! Well, I'm glad you worked it all out. Can I ask one more favor? It's kind of embarrassing."

"Sure, no problem." Mel would do pretty much anything to get rid of her.

"Well, I wonder if I can borrow a roll of toilet paper? I ran out this morning and won't have a chance to run to the store until later. Isn't that silly?"

Mel chuckled. "Not at all. When you gotta go...I'll be right back." She left Lena in the kitchen while she fetched the toilet paper. She brought two rolls and found her standing by the refrigerator. "Here you go. Did you need anything else?"

"Oh, no, thanks. You're a doll." She took the toilet paper from Melanie and carried her glass to the sink. "Thanks so much. See you later!" And she was gone.

Lena's visit, while annoying, had served to distract her from her troubles with Finn, at least momentarily. She found herself not wanting to work or write, but with an excess of nervous energy, so she decided to clean her house. Top to bottom. Maybe she could exhaust herself enough so she would be able to sleep tonight. Fat chance, but it was worth a try.

Four hours later, she was hot and dusty, but her house gleamed. She'd even begun to tackle packing up Aunt Karen's belongings. She'd make a call to a local charity later in the week to arrange for a pick up. It was nearing dinnertime and she had skipped lunch, but she couldn't work up any interest in food. The best she could manage was a cool shower and a handful of crackers. She was trying to decide between hard liquor and wine—tough because the only liquor in the pantry was cream sherry—when she heard yet another knock on her door. This time she ignored it. She wasn't ready to talk to Finn yet and she couldn't stand the thought of another round with Lena.

"Mel? Open up! It's Cara and my hands are full."

Yes! It's what she'd wished for earlier—a friend to talk to. Maybe it was a bit awkward because she was his sister, but Mel couldn't afford to be picky. She yanked open the door and reached to pull Cara inside. "You are a sight for sore eyes! Oh, my God, Cara!" She felt the wretched tears building again.

"Trouble in paradise, sweetie?" Cara set both bottles on a side table and pulled Melanie into her arms.

Mel hung on and let the tears flow.

Cara steered her over to the couch and let her cry

for a few minutes. "Okay. Tell Auntie Cara all about it. What did my idiotic brother do?"

"He didn't do anything! It's me. But I saw her last night and then she was there this morning and they were kissing and—"

"Mel, sweetie. Shh. Calm down and take a few deep breaths. You aren't making much sense." Cara reached for a tissue and shoved it in Melanie's hand. "Now wipe your eyes and let's talk about this. You saw Tittyana kiss Finn, right?"

Laughter bubbled up at Cara's interesting and accurate nomenclature for Mel's nemesis. It quickly turned a bit hysterical and they both laughed uncontrollably. Finally, Cara grabbed a tissue to wipe her own eyes and walked into the kitchen, returning a few moments later with a corkscrew and two wine glasses. She opened a bottle, poured them both a generous glass, and handed one to Mel. "You did see the kiss, right?"

"Yes." Melanie took a large sip. "I saw her last night on the news. I never realized how gorgeous she was. Then when I saw her leaving his house earlier and that kiss—I assume she wants him back, right?"

"Even if she does, why on earth would that matter? Finn is with you now."

"Yeah, but if she wants him—you have seen her, haven't you? I can't begin to compare." She felt tears again and took another sip of wine to keep them at bay.

"You don't compare, Mel, and thank God! She was so totally wrong for Finn. He hasn't always had the best taste in women, sad to say, which is why everyone is so thrilled about you."

"But—"

"But nothing! You do know Finn called me, right? He's freaking out, worried that you're trying to break up with him or something. Tatiana stopped by to clear the air and return his house key. She doesn't want to get back together and neither does Finn. He wants you, Mel. Why are you having such a hard time believing that?" Cara reached to squeeze her hand.

Mel shrugged and drank more wine. "He's way out of my league, Cara."

Cara snorted while she sipped. "Oh, God! Please don't ever let him hear that! His head is big enough, thanks. Plus, it's complete and total bullshit. You seriously underestimate yourself." She paused to top their glasses off. "I'm starving and I'm gonna be full-on drunk if I don't get some food in me. Let's order a pizza."

"How about Chinese? I'm not really feeling pizza tonight." Mel wasn't really feeling anything, but the thought of greasy pizza made her stomach churn.

"You're adorable, Mel. I keep forgetting you're from Chicago. I don't think Albuquerque even does Chinese delivery, unless maybe down by the university. Sorry, sweetie."

"Sure it does." She stood, a bit wobbly, and walked to the kitchen to retrieve the Chinese take-out menus she kept in a drawer. She returned to the living room and tossed them on Cara's lap. "Here. I have it delivered all the time. Dragon Wok is my favorite."

"Huh. Well, you learn something new every day." She perused the colorful brochure. "I could definitely go for some Szechuan chicken."

They finished the first bottle of wine by the time the food arrived and neither was feeling any pain. Mel reached for an eggroll, completely forgetting she wasn't hungry. "If he's not out of my league, why doesn't he want to sleep with me?" The wine had done its job and lowered her inhibitions; she found herself confessing her deepest fears.

Cara stopped chewing and stared at her blankly. She swallowed carefully and said, "You guys haven't slept together yet?"

Mel took a bite of the eggroll and shook her head.

"Okay. Wow. Well, I can assure it's not for lack of interest on his part. This is interesting. Have you asked him?"

"No, of course not. I wouldn't know how to bring up something like that."

Cara took a sip of wine, then set her glass carefully on the coffee table, looking hesitantly at her friend. "Mel, are you a virgin?"

"No, of course not. But..."

"But?" Cara raised her eyebrows.

Courtesy of the wine, Mel found herself spilling the whole sordid story of her college romance with Evan. "He was a senior and I was a freshman. He was so handsome and popular and I couldn't believe it when he asked me out. I was really shy back then; I had never even been on a date. He completely swept me off my feet, taking me to frat parties, things like that. He started pressuring me to have sex with him a few weeks after we started dating and made it clear it was a condition of our continuing relationship. So I did. I convinced myself I was in love with him and that he loved me." She shrugged and set her half-eaten eggroll aside and took up her wine glass again.

Cara opened the second bottle and filled Mel's glass. "What happened to this Evan? How long did it last?"

"About a year. I showed up at a party one night—unexpected. He thought I had gone home for the weekend, but I came back early to surprise him. The surprise was on me when I found him screwing another girl in an upstairs bedroom at the party. Turns out he'd never been faithful to me. I was just one more hookup in a long line."

"Oh, Mel. I'm so sorry. That's a horrible first experience."

"Yeah, well, it pretty much put me off relationships for a long time. Finn is the first guy I've really dated since then."

"Are you in love with him? I mean, you implied that you wanted to be in love with Evan before you slept with him. Does that still hold? Are in love with Finn?"

Mel bit her lip and frowned. "I don't know. I'm not sure I trust myself to know what it really feels like. How do you *know*? Have you ever been in love?"

Cara smiled crookedly. "Yeah, I have, but I'm not sure I'm the one to tell you how to know for sure. My story didn't work out very well."

"What happened? If you don't mind telling me, I

mean."

She shrugged. "I don't mind. I'm actually kind of surprised Finn didn't tell you." She sipped her wine and stared blankly past Mel. "Aidan and I were high school sweethearts and we were crazy in love. I never questioned it. He loved me and I loved him. Period. We knew we were meant for each other. Soulmates."

"What happened?" Mel asked again.

"We got married. I was eighteen and he was nineteen."

"Oh my God! You were married?"

"Yup. For four years." Cara reached for the carton of fried rice. "I've been divorced for nearly five."

"Did he cheat on you?"

Cara smiled ruefully. "No. Aidan would never do that. Neither would I. No, that wasn't our problem. Aidan started acting strange shortly after we got married. He changed—so quickly. I couldn't keep up. First, he decided he was a vegetarian. Then, within weeks, he was a vegan. Not that there's anything wrong with either of those things, but that wasn't all. He started talking about Eastern mysticism and then he became possessive and jealous. I couldn't spend time with any of my friends; he called me twenty or thirty times a day to see where I was. I wasn't allowed to handle any of the money or the shopping. He wanted to drive me everywhere. There was also a lot of verbal abuse. I kept as much of it as I could from my family, but then he started trying to keep me from spending time with them. I finally left him before it had a chance to become physically abusive."

"God, Cara! I'm so sorry."

"Thanks. Like I said, I'm really surprised Finn didn't mention it. He took it pretty hard. I guess he thought he should have known or something. But I didn't talk about it. I was embarrassed."

"Where's Aidan now? Do you ever see him?"

"Never. He moved away right after he signed the divorce papers. He literally took a suitcase and left everything else." She paused to take another drink, as if fortifying herself. "I think he was mentally ill, schizophrenia or bipolar disorder, maybe. I wish I could have helped him, but at the time I was too close to it and scared. I had to get out. My parents were so supportive. They helped me financially—I had to pay a huge amount to break my lease as well as for the divorce. I moved back in with them for a few months until I could get on my feet and finish getting my teaching license."

"Wow. I had no idea." Mel took a bite of her now-cold eggroll and grimaced. "Your story makes my issues with Finn seem ridiculous."

"It's not a contest, Mel, and your feelings aren't ridiculous. I hope you'll give him another chance, though. You and Finn are so great together. I haven't seen him this happy in, well, ever. This could be the real thing for you two."

They foraged for ice cream in Mel's freezer and finished the second bottle of wine, their conversation getting much less serious the closer to the bottom of the bottle they got. Cara left a few hours later, wobbling more than a little as she walked back to Finn's house.

Mel watched her leave, then locked her house securely before returning to the kitchen. She spied the left over bottle of wine on the counter she'd opened the other night. It looked like there was about a half glassful left and Mel decided it was just what she needed to insure a sound sleep; she feared she was still a bit too sober and inclined to obsess about Finn and Tatiana rather than dropping into a sound sleep. She would rather think about the whole situation tomorrow; maybe the light of a new day would clear her mind. She poured the wine and took it back to her bedroom. Once she'd brushed her teeth and donned her sleep tee, she crawled under the covers and reached for the novel on her nightstand and the wine. *Ugh*. She didn't remember it tasting so bitter. *I guess that's what I get for drinking wine after I brush my teeth.* She slugged back the remainder quickly and opened her book. She didn't get more than two pages read before her head nodded and the book dropped from her hands.

Chapter Twelve

Finn

Hugh showed up soon after Cara left. "Let's go grab a few beers. I'm buying. You don't need to hang out here, pacing and waiting for Cara to get back."

"Pacing's tough on crutches. She called you, huh?" He wasn't surprised; all his siblings, especially Hugh, Izzy, and Cara, had been extra-watchful of him since the accident. He tried not to be annoyed since he knew he would act the same way if it were one of them.

"Yep. So, Tatiana came slinking back, huh? What did she want?" Hugh's expression revealed his dislike of Finn's former girlfriend; none of his family had been too thrilled with her.

"Mostly to return my house key, which I appreciated. I still think I'll have the locks re-keyed, however."

"Good call."

"She didn't want to get back together. I know

you and Cara were worried about that, but she pretty much wanted to clear the air. She apologized for leaving me that way." Finn smiled crookedly.

"Oh, really? That's big of her," Hugh said with a sneer.

"Cut her some slack. She was never as serious as I was. I realize now I was totally jumping the gun even thinking about asking her to move in. She's more interested in her career than anything else right now and wants to be free to move whenever she gets an opportunity in a bigger market."

"Yeah, well, did she make that crystal clear from the start of your relationship? I'm pretty sure you would never have contemplated such a serious step if she had. What she did to you was shitty, Finn, and you can't excuse it."

Finn chuckled ruefully. "Yeah, it was. God, I hope I don't lose Mel over this. Tatiana kissed me goodbye on the porch and I'm pretty sure Mel saw it. She won't talk to me."

"Well, hell. Women. I can't figure them out. Come on. Let's get out of here." Hugh ushered Finn out to his truck. As he backed out of the driveway, he asked, "You okay with The Dirty Bourbon?" He referred to a bar Finn frequently visited after work with his cop friends.

"Nah. Too many badge bunnies. I don't want to deal with that tonight. Let's do The Red Door. I like their double IPA."

"What's a badge bunny?" Hugh laughed as he turned the corner.

Finn sighed and ran his hand through his hair, realizing he badly needed a haircut and hadn't made time over the past few weeks to get one. "Girls who get off on dating cops. They're not too picky and they can always spot a cop out of uniform."

"Huh. I had no idea." Hugh drove in silence for a few moments. "You ever date one of them?"

"Nah. I like to think I have higher standards, usually."

"Usually?"

Finn laughed, a bit shamefaced. "Well, yeah. The night after I got my promotion to detective I may not have shown the highest level of discretion."

"You got shit-faced, huh?" Hugh laughed.

"And then some. I was making out with one of them—I think her name was RayAnna or something—when Brett pulled me away and reminded me I had a girlfriend waiting at home. Maybe it was RayLynn. I can't remember."

"Brett's a good guy. You still see him?" Hugh referred to Finn's former partner.

"Occasionally. He and his wife had a baby a few months ago, so he's got his hands pretty full." Finn missed him, but was learning to appreciate his new partner and looked forward to getting back to work with her next week, depending on how things went in physical therapy.

They were silent the rest of the short drive to the brewery Finn had suggested. Once they found a table in the crowded establishment and had ordered beers and sandwiches, Hugh reached for a pretzel from the basket in the middle of the table, saying, "Do you ever think about having kids? Do you want them?"

Finn bit into a pretzel before answering. "Yeah, I

do. I never really thought about it before Janey was born, but lately…yeah, I want kids someday. I mean, I'd like to have a wife first. I admire Izzy and all, but I don't want to do it by myself."

"God, she's a piece of work, huh? She just drops that giant bomb one day and boom! We're uncles. She's a great mom, though. Did she ever tell you who the dad was?"

"No. I figured she would have told you if she told anyone. No idea?" He'd been curious, of course, but hadn't felt comfortable asking her. She'd made it clear the subject was off limits.

"None. I'd sure like to find out who the bastard is. He should be here, helping her raise that little girl." Hugh sat back as the waiter delivered their beers. "So, a wife first, huh? Mel?"

Finn took a gulp of his beer, enjoying the smooth, hoppy taste. "Maybe. It's early days yet, but she's pretty special. Of course, she would have to be willing to talk to me again."

Hugh chuckled and sampled his own beer, the house lager. Finn knew he didn't enjoy the IPAs his brother was so fond of, finding them too bitter. "Don't worry. Cara will talk to her and get her to calm down. I've seen the way you two look at each other. I'm happy for you, Finn."

Finn grinned and took another gulp. "If she'll give me another chance, I'm not gonna waste it."

"She will. Just give her some time."

Their sandwiches were delivered, so they devoted their attention to dinner for several minutes; two hungry men presented with fries and grilled Reubens with green chile had better things to do than chitchat. Once each had finished half his sandwich and a good portion of fries—along with another beer apiece—Finn shoved his plate away. His appetite since the accident was a fraction of what it used to be. He'd lost a good ten pounds in the months since he was hit by the car and had only gained a few back.

"What about you, Hugh? Do you want kids?" He wondered why they'd never talked about this before. It seemed like their conversations since his accident had been more serious. Perhaps that's what a near-death experience did for you. He knew it had affected his entire family. His parents seemed to need to touch him, hug him more often these days and his brothers and sisters were dropping by a whole lot more often than they used to. What would he do if he lost one of them? He swallowed hard as he realized how precious his family was to him. He stared across the table at his oldest brother, this man who had taught him how to ride a two-wheeler, who had held his head as he puked in the gutter during his first high school party, and who had supplied him with his first box of condoms—with dubious instructions—and realized how utterly devastated he would be if he were to lose him. He reached for his napkin and tried to cover his sudden emotion with a cough. Hugh would give him such shit if he said anything about this.

"Kids? Well, yeah. I guess." He was silent for a moment. "I haven't really thought about it too much. I think I always assumed I would have kids—we're Catholic, after all—but I haven't really thought about it. I'll need a wife, I suppose. I guess

I better get right on that, huh?"

Something about his reply struck Finn as off somehow. He frowned and was about to probe, but thought better of it. Instead, he snorted. "Yeah, you should get crackin' on that. Any prospects?"

Hugh smirked. "Wouldn't you like to know?"

"I really would."

They turned their attention back to their dinner and beer, eschewing their previous serious conversation for lighter topics, such as the latest MLB scores and what their younger brothers were up to. By the time the waiter dropped the check off, Finn was nicely buzzed—likely Hugh's intention all along—and they had solved nearly all the world's problems.

Hugh dropped him off close to ten o'clock, making sure he got safely inside before driving away. Finn was deeply asleep, dreaming he was in a prizefight—getting his ass kicked—when he fought his way to the surface and realized it was CJ batting him repeatedly across the face and meowing loudly.

"CJ? What the hell? Knock it off!" He sat up and scrubbed his hands across his face. "What are you doing here? Why aren't you with Mel?" As he said her name, his heart skipped a beat. Why was CJ here? He swung his legs over the side of the bed as the thought crossed his mind: CJ would never be here if there wasn't something wrong. The cat ran to the bedroom door and back to Finn, then repeated her movements, looking up at him imploringly, meowing madly. Her message was clear: Follow me!

Finn hurriedly pulled on a pair of sweatpants,

grabbed his crutches, keys, and cell phone, and followed, completely forgetting that Cara was in the guest bedroom. The cat ran ahead, but doubled back to check that he followed. Finn moved as fast as he could on his damned crutches, his heart pounding with fear, as he chased the cat. He smelled the smoke as he opened his front door.

The cat led him to Mel's house; Finn could see the flames engulfing her garage as he approached. He reached for his cell and quickly called it in, but knew he wasn't about to wait for the fire department to show up. Mel was in there and he would get her out—or die trying. His heart stuttered in horror as he fumbled for the keys he'd grabbed— why, he'd never know—and tried one after another blindly until he inserted the correct one into her front door lock. *Oh. God! He had to get to her! Goddamn these crutches for slowing him down!* "Mel! Where are you?" He screamed the words repeatedly at the top of his lungs, but there was no reply. Why didn't she answer? The door finally opened and he stumbled inside, the smoke swirling around him in greeting. Her bedroom was down the hall, away from the fire he now saw was raging in the kitchen and garage area. "Mel!" He had to find her! His eyes were streaming tears as he coughed, choked by the smoke. Visibility in the hallway was already limited and Finn found himself confused as he searched for Mel's room.

Her bedroom door was shut; he wrenched it open, expecting to find her cowering behind her bed. Instead, she lay inert, on her back, clearly unconscious—or worse. With trembling fingers, he reached to check for a pulse on her neck, almost collapsing with relief when he felt a weak, thready blip under his fingertips. He spared no words to try and wake her, but simply threw aside his crutches, prepared to lift her into his arms and damn the consequences to his ankle. The adrenaline raging through his body would have to compensate for his disability.

"Move aside! You'll damage yourself. I can get her!" It was crotchety Mr. Taylor, up and walking. Wasn't he crippled and in a wheelchair? Finn didn't care at the moment, simply thankful for his aid. The older man scooped the unconscious Mel into his arms, shoved Finn out of the way, and led the way down the hall to the front door. The hallway was now full of smoke, making it nearly impossible to find their way. Finn knew if they didn't get outside soon, none of them would make it. *Please, God, let us make it!*

They made it to the living room, past the now-smoking sofa, when he heard the yells of the firefighters and saw their headlamps glowing eerily. One of them took Mel, while two others each grabbed on to Finn and Mr. Taylor, guiding them out to the front lawn. Paramedics swarmed them, placing Mel on a stretcher and forcing the two men to sit. Finn tried to fight them off as they placed an oxygen mask over his face, but was unsuccessful. He watched as they intubated Mel and packed her in the back of an ambulance, speeding away within seconds.

"I don't need to go to the hospital!" He pulled his mask away to argue.

"Finn!" Cara ran up to him, barefooted and in her pajamas. "Oh my God! Where's Mel? Is she okay?"

"They just took her—" he broke off, coughing. The paramedic replaced his mask as she explained the deadly dangers of smoke inhalation and how she strongly recommended both he and Mr. Taylor allow them to transport them to the hospital. Finn finally relented when he was assured he would be taken to the same hospital as Mel and Cara could ride in the ambulance with him.

***

Mel

Why is it so hard to wake up? She tried to force her way into full consciousness, but she had to swim through thick molasses. Her throat was on fire and she was choking, dying. She struggled against the sticky darkness, but couldn't get there. She let herself sink back below the surface. Blackness.

***

"Melanie? Can you hear me? Open your eyes, Melanie. That's it. I'm Dr. Chaudhri. I need you to stay awake now, all right?"

Melanie pried her eyelids open and glimpsed a dark-complexioned woman leaning over her. It was so hard to keep her eyes open. *Let me sleep!* She tried to say the words, but she choked. Her eyes drifted closed again.

163

"Don't try to speak, Melanie. You have a breathing tube in your throat. I know it's uncomfortable, but I can remove it if you'll wake up a bit more. There's a good girl."

She managed to open one of her eyes. The doctor—what was her name?—straightened and turned to check a machine of some sort. Melanie pried the other open and darted them around, trying to gain an idea of where she was and what had happened. She realized she was in a hospital room, of course, but why? She struggled to remember, but came up with nothing. Had she been in a car accident?

"Are you ready to get that nasty tube out of your throat?" The next few minutes were unpleasant as the doctor removed the tape from around her mouth and told her to cough as she extracted the tube from her throat. Melanie gagged and felt the saliva drip down her chin. "There now. That's better, isn't it?" The doctor placed the tube apparatus on a tray and wiped Melanie's chin. She pressed a button on the bed and raised her into a more upright position, then arranged an oxygen tube under Melanie's nose.

"Unh." Melanie was trying to say 'yes,' but her tongue felt thick and useless.

"Shh. Don't try to speak quite yet. Let's try some ice chips. It will help with that sore throat." The nurse Melanie hadn't noticed stepped up to the other side of the bed and held a spoon to her lips.

Melanie opened her mouth and accepted the small spoonful of icy deliciousness. "Mmmm." The cool liquid slid down her parched throat. The nurse gave her a few more tiny spoonfuls as she and the doctor conversed in incomprehensible medical-ese.

"Melanie, I'd like to ask you a few questions, all right? I know you can't talk very well yet, so just nod or shake your head. Do you understand?" When Melanie nodded, the doctor launched into her mini-inquisition.

By the time the doctor finished, Melanie was exhausted and wanted nothing more than to close her eyes. She'd answered all the questions, letting the doctor know she remembered nothing and had no idea what had happened. The doctor had asked several questions about her alcohol consumption the night before and what drugs she had taken. Melanie made it as clear as possible that she'd had wine but taken no drugs. The doctor asked several times, in several different ways, about sleeping pills. She listed off five or so different types, but Melanie shook her head each time. She didn't understand why the doctor kept asking and felt tears of frustration leaking from her eyes. She reached to wipe them away, but the pulse oximeter on her forefinger prevented her. She still had no idea why she was in the hospital or what was wrong with her.

"Here, sweetie." The nurse wiped her eyes with a tissue.

"All right," Dr. Chaudhri said in her lovely lilting voice. "I'll leave you to rest. I'm sure you'd like to see your fiancé. He's probably going to break down the door if I don't let him back in." She smiled and patted Melanie's hand before leaving her bedside.

Fiancé? *What in the—?*

"Mel? Hey." Finn appeared in the doorway, a

crooked grin on his face. He hobbled to her bedside and leaned over to kiss her forehead. "I told them we're engaged so I could stay with you in ICU," he whispered in her ear.

The doctor left and the nurse placed the Styrofoam cup of ice chips on the rolling bedside tray. "See if you can get her to eat a bit more before she falls asleep, okay? I'll check back in a little while."

"Sure. Thanks." Finn took a seat in the chair the nurse kindly scooted closer to the bed. He waited until she closed the door before reaching for Melanie's hand. "God, sweetheart! Are you okay? You scared at least ten years off my life. When I found you lying there in your bed, not moving...I thought you...never mind. You're safe now and the doctor says you'll be okay in a few days." He rubbed his thumb across her knuckles. "Listen, I know you're probably still pissed at me, and I promise I'll let you chew my ass real good as soon as we get home, okay? For now, please let me be here with you. I need to be here, Mel. I love you." He picked up her hand from the coverlet and kissed it.

She tried to remember why she was mad at him, but nothing came to her. She absolutely couldn't keep her eyes open even one second longer, but fell asleep smiling slightly, comforted to have him beside her.

***

The room was nearly dark the next time she

opened her eyes. Her throat was painfully dry and her lips felt cracked as she attempted to lick them with a tongue made of sandpaper. She turned her head, looking for Finn, but didn't see him. Panic was her first instinct, but the door opened at that moment and he entered.

"I'm here. I step out for five minutes to grab a cup of crappy coffee and you go and wake up." He bent over and kissed her softly. "Let me get you some more ice chips. The nurse might even bring you some water." He pressed the call button and the nurse appeared swiftly.

Within a few minutes she was sipping the best water she'd ever tasted in her life through a straw. "Finn." At least that's what she tried to say. All that came out was a sort of growl. She sipped more water then tried again. "What happened to me?" Her whisper was barely comprehensible. "Accident?"

"No, sweetheart. There was a fire at your house last night. CJ woke me up and I got down to your place as fast as I could. You were in bed and wouldn't wake up."

"How did you get me out?" Her voice was slightly stronger this time. "You didn't carry me, did you?"

He chuckled. "I was about to, but Mr. Taylor showed up and carried you out."

"What?"

"Well, it turns out he's not crippled or anything. He only sits in the wheelchair to remember his wife. I guess she was confined to it for the past few years of her life and he feels closer to her there. It's kind of sad." He took the cup from her hand and set it on the tray table.

"It's beautiful." Mel was silent for a moment while she thought about what he was telling her. "How bad a fire? Why am I here? Did I get burned?" She tried to take an inventory of her physical condition, but beyond the sore throat and a killer headache, she felt fine.

"You're fine, hon." He reached to straighten her oxygen tube, tucking it behind her ear. "You're here because of smoke inhalation and because you wouldn't wake up. There are no burns or other injuries. You and Cara must have really tied one on, huh?"

As he spoke, it started coming back to her: the fight with him and the evening with Cara, drinking way too much wine. She barely remembered getting into bed and falling asleep; she remembered nothing of the fire he was telling her about. "How bad was it?"

He sighed, apparently reluctant to tell her. "Pretty bad. Your garage and kitchen got the worst, but the living room was also damaged. We'll know more later."

"What about Fluff?" She suddenly remembered the elderly dog. *Oh, God, please don't let him—*

"He's fine, Mel. The little idiot was running around the backyard, barking his head off. Cara's got him at my house. Now calm down or they're gonna kick me out. You might get to move to a regular room later if your breathing looks good. How are you feeling?"

"I think I'm okay. I'm confused and my throat

hurts."

He reached for the water cup and let her sip. "Maybe I can talk to the nurse and score a popsicle for you." He kissed the top of her head, then straightened and replaced the water cup on the tray. He grabbed his crutches and headed to the door. "Be right back."

He brought her a cherry popsicle. It tasted amazing and soothed her throat, but she couldn't finish it, so Finn did while she fell asleep again for a short nap. She was woken when the nurse and an assistant arrived to move her upstairs to a regular room. Cara and her mother arrived shortly after she was settled.

"I'm mad at you!" Cara leaned over to hug her. "You scared the living shit out of me!"

"Cara!" Moira scolded her daughter lightly, then went around to the other side of the bed and patted Melanie's hand. "Melanie, dear, I'm so glad you're all right. We were all so worried. Finn hasn't left the hospital. I'm going to take him home for a few hours so he can clean up and get some sleep. He still smells like smoke."

"But I'll stay to entertain you, Mel, don't worry." Cara took over the chair Finn vacated.

"I'll be fine." Melanie was embarrassed by their concern. "You don't need to stay."

"No way." Finn leaned over to kiss her. "Either Cara stays or I do."

She looked up into his handsome, but exhausted face. She knew he needed sleep, so she gave in with a huff. "Fine, but I don't need a babysitter."

"Stop whining, Mel," Cara said with a laugh.

"The DeLucas don't leave someone they love in the hospital by themselves. You need an advocate to make sure they take good care of you."

"I'll be back in a few hours, love." He kissed her again, then left with his mother.

Cara waited until the door closed behind them. "I told you so." The expression on her face was superbly smug.

"What?"

"I told you so." At Mel's blank look, Cara explained. "You had absolutely no reason to freak out about Tatiana. Nobody could pry Finn away from your side once he was released from the emergency room—"

"Why was he in the emergency room? Was he hurt? Did he—"

"Calm down! He's fine. They put him on oxygen for a few hours to make sure his lungs were okay. Smoke inhalation can sneak up on you. Your neighbor was admitted and intubated, like you." She anticipated Mel's next outburst. "And he's doing fine and is actually down the hall. I stopped in to see him right before I saw you. They took his breathing tube out a couple hours ago and he'll get to go home tomorrow, probably, like you."

"Why do I have to stay overnight? Am I not doing as well as I thought?"

"You're doing fine, Mel, but you were in ICU and they couldn't wake you up. Finn said they're doing blood tests. Did you take sleeping pills after I left?"

Melanie frowned as she remembered the doctor asking her the same thing. "I don't take sleeping pills, Cara. I never have. I didn't take anything last night, I swear!"

"Okay, sweetie. I believe you. We'll talk to the doctor. I don't know what's going on, but we'll figure it out."

Both women were quiet for a few minutes. Mel's mind was spinning out of control and she struggled to find something to focus on. Finally she blurted, "Finn told the doctors we're engaged so he could stay with me. And I think he said he loves me, but I was falling asleep, so I'm not sure."

"Well, I guess you're going to have to judge by his actions, huh? At least until he gets back. So, what does it tell you that he followed a mangy cat into a burning house to rescue you? He refused treatment from the paramedics until he was promised he would be taken to the same hospital as you, and then lied about being your fiancé when they told him only family members could visit in ICU. So, yeah, I'd say he loves you. Now what are you going to do about it, Mel?"

"You're a little scary sometimes, Cara."

The other woman smiled. "That's what my students say. It's a valuable tool in the classroom. I'm waiting…"

"Fine." Mel played for time by reaching for the water on her tray table. "What I'm going to do about it is love him back. At least I'm going to try."

"Good answer." Cara handed her the cup of water.

Chapter Thirteen

Finn

He took a long, hot shower as soon as his mother dropped him off. After a bit of fussing about him not getting enough rest, she'd promised someone would pick him up in a few hours to take him back to the hospital. The shower felt incredible and he let the scalding water stream down his body, washing away the lingering smell of smoke as well as the tension of the last twelve hours. He'd meant to shave as soon as he finished drying, but utter exhaustion caught up with him; he fell into bed, pausing only to tell Siri to wake him in two hours.

He'd barely closed his eyes when Seamus woke him, shaking his shoulder. "Finn! Man, your phone's been beeping for almost ten minutes."

Finn sat up, rubbing a hand over his face while reaching for his phone to silence the alarm. "Sorry. God, I swear I just shut my eyes." He tossed the phone on his bed and searched for his crutches. "Be a pal, Seamus, and put some coffee on. I need to shave." He continued mumbling as his brother left the bedroom. Soon the life-giving aroma of coffee reached him as he shaved and dressed. He grabbed his crutches and hobbled out to the kitchen.

Seamus placed a steaming mug of black coffee on the table before pouring one for himself and sitting across from Finn. "You want me to make some eggs or something?"

Finn sipped the scalding beverage and shook his head. "This is fine, thanks. You're my favorite brother, by the way."

Seamus laughed and added several spoonfuls of sugar to his own coffee. "Sure I am. Until Hugh or Tony shows up with a six-pack, that is."

"Yeah, well, whatever. Coffee is what I needed now." He took another sip. "Any news on the cause of the fire?" He'd called his brother earlier that morning, as soon as they let him out of the emergency room, and asked him to see what he could find out. Seamus' unit hadn't been called to the scene, but Finn knew his brother could ask around.

"Nothing official yet, but it looks like the fire started in the garage. I know you were worried Mel left the stove on or something, but it doesn't look like it. They've called in the arson investigation team, which means they saw evidence of an accelerant of some sort. The tricky part will be figuring out if it was a natural accelerant—garages are typically full of stuff like paint thinner and other chemicals—or a purposefully set fire. It'll be weeks before we know for sure."

"Goddammit." Finn ran his hands through his

hair. "How am I supposed to keep her safe if I don't even know what the hell is going on?"

"Hey." Seamus stood and reached for the coffee pot. "Nobody is gonna get to Mel. They'll have to go through all the DeLucas first. And Cara alone is enough to terrify anyone."

Finn chuckled reluctantly. "Yeah, true." He waved the coffee away. "I can't lose her, Seamus."

"You won't."

Seamus drove him back to the hospital and went up with him to visit Mel and take Cara home. "Hey, Mel. When do you get to bust out of this popsicle stand?" He handed her the stuffed rabbit he'd bought for her in the hospital gift shop. She was sitting in an easy chair next to Cara, with a hospital blanket draped over her lap.

"Probably tomorrow. This is adorable, Seamus. Thanks."

"All right. Get out of the way so I can kiss my girlfriend." Finn sorely missed having full use of his hands so he could shove his brother aside. "Hey, beautiful." He managed to bend down and kiss her upturned face without falling on top of her. He was beyond ready to get rid of these crutches.

"Hi." She smiled crookedly and he hoped it meant he was forgiven.

"Seamus brought you the stuffed bunny, but I brought something much more useful." He held his hand out to Seamus for the tiny carton of lemon sorbet he'd found for her in the gift shop.

"Oooh, yes! Thank you, Finn. All I got for lunch was some broth. I'm starving." She found the small wooden spoonlet and dug in. "Mmm."

174

Finn smiled indulgently. "I figured it would feel good on your sore throat. Did Cara bring you the robe?"

She pulled the soft pink bathrobe closer. "Yes, and the nurse was nice enough to undo my IV so I could put it on. I was freezing. Cara also brought me these fluffy socks." She wiggled a small foot from under the blanket. Finn admired the way it arched elegantly, and drooled a bit at the glimpse of milky thigh he was treated to. He noticed his brother enjoying the view, as well, and glared.

Seamus smirked and turned to his sister. "You ready? I've got a softball game this evening and a ton of stuff to do before then."

They left, but Cara promised she'd stop by in the morning. Finn took the seat she'd vacated. "I miss softball," he mused absently.

"You play?" She offered him a bite of the sorbet.

He took it as he nodded. "We all play on a city league together—Hugh, Seamus, Tony, and me, I mean. Hopefully I can get back to it next spring." He felt her soft hand clasp his and squeeze lightly.

"Finn, I'm sorry."

He smiled and shrugged. "Thanks, but it's okay. It's just a game."

"Not about the softball. About the fight. I shouldn't have freaked out and I should have opened the door. I'm so sorry. I'm not very good at this girlfriend thing."

"Sweetheart, you're doing fine with it. And I don't really think what happened qualifies as a true fight; there wasn't nearly enough yelling for that. I'm afraid if you want a real fight, next time you are

175

going to have to open the door and let me in." He smiled to let her know he wasn't holding a grudge. He knew she'd had a bad experience in her past, although he didn't know the details; she'd tell him when she was ready and he was trying hard not to push her.

"I saw Tatiana on the news—I guess it was the night before last; I've completely lost track of time. Then the next day, she was on your porch and you were kissing her—"

"She kissed me, an important point of clarification. God, I'm sorry you saw that. She stopped by to return her key and clear the air. That's all. Mel, she and I were together for a long time— more than a year. We needed some closure. It was a goodbye kiss. Neither one of us wants to get back together, I promise. I'm with you now, and I—" He broke off, unsure suddenly.

"What?" She was still clasping his hand, looking intently into his face.

He knew it was time; it was their moment. He took a deep breath and—

"Well, you're looking much better this afternoon, Melanie." Dr. Chaudhri, accompanied by a nurse, breezed into the room.

Or not. He couldn't catch a break.

"Let's check your lungs." The doctor put her stethoscope in her ears and asked Mel to breathe deeply, then had her try to make the ball go up in the little plastic breathing machine they'd given her. "Very good, Melanie. Your lungs sound clear, but I want you to stay on the oxygen until tomorrow. I know you're probably hungry, so you can order solid food for dinner. Your fiancé can order a meal as well, with a credit card, and you can have dinner together here, if you like. Will you be staying the night?" She directed the last question at Finn.

"Absolutely."

Dr. Chaudhri smiled. "I'll have some pillows and blankets brought in. The bench seat over there folds down to make a bed."

"When can I go home?" Mel asked.

"I think tomorrow afternoon, if you sleep well tonight and your chest still sounds clear in the morning." The doctor pulled a stool up next to Mel's chair and took her pulse. She told the nurse the number to write on the chart, then cleared her throat. "Melanie, your blood test results came back and the tox screen showed that, in addition to alcohol, you also had a high level of benzodiazepine—a sedative commonly found in sleeping pills—in your blood stream. At the level you ingested and mixed with the alcohol, well, you're very lucky to be alive. The fire may have saved your life. If you had slept until morning, you may not have woken up."

"Oh, my God," Mel whispered. "I swear I didn't take anything. I've never taken sleeping pills in my life."

"Are you sure? Did you take anything at all before you went to bed?"

"No, I didn't. I mean, I don't remember—Finn?"

"Okay, sweetheart. It's okay. We'll figure it out, I promise." He addressed Dr. Chaudhri. "Thank you, Doctor. Can we talk about this tomorrow? I'll try to make sure she gets some rest." Finn stood to see the doctor out while the nurse moved around the room, replacing an IV bag and pushing buttons on some of the other machines Mel was still connected to. When they were finally alone again, the tender moment from before the doctor came in had long passed. Mel was obviously freaked out by what the doctor had said and he had no clue what to say. He was sure she was telling the truth, but how did that explain the sedatives in her tox screen? Finn found the menu card and let Mel choose what she wanted for dinner, then called to place their order, hoping it would serve as a distraction.

"Finn, what's going on? Why is this happening?"

He could hear the trembling in her voice and it cut through his heart. "Hey, shh. It's going to be okay, I promise. We'll figure this out." He leaned over to drop a kiss on her head.

"I'm not going to be able to stay at my house for a while, am I?" She frowned at him as she spoke.

"No, sweetheart. I'm sorry, but it's going to be quite a while before you can return. Seamus told me they've called in an arson investigation team. It appears the fire started in your garage and there's evidence of an accelerant."

"Someone did this on purpose? Why? What have I ever done? Who hates me that much?"

Finn swore to himself he would see the haunted look leave her eyes if it was the last thing he did. "They don't know for sure. It could have been an accident of some sort." He heard the disbelief in his words even as he spoke them.

"I'll need to find a hotel, I guess. I don't even have any clothes to wear home tomorrow." The

178

tears he had seen building ever since the doctor came in finally spilled over. She wiped them away impatiently. "What am I going to do?"

"Mel." He sat next to her again and took her hand. "Listen. When you decided to take up with me, you got more than you bargained for. My family is a part of who I am, and we help each other out. That extends to you now. Please try not to worry. Cara, Izzy, and my mom will find you some clothes to wear until we can get to yours. And I want you to stay with me. Please, Mel. I'll do nothing but worry if you're at a hotel. You can stay in the guest bedroom—you and Fluff."

She frowned again. "I don't want to be a bother. This shouldn't be your problem."

He chuckled and brought her hand to his mouth, kissing her fingers. "Of course it should. That's how this whole boyfriend/girlfriend thing works."

She smiled crookedly, seeming to sense his need to cheer her up. "Okay. Thank you, Finn. What about CJ? She usually sleeps with me."

He knew; he'd never been jealous of a cat before. "Of course she can stay whenever and wherever she wants. I owe that silly cat everything."

***

Mel

I'm going to love him back. That's what she'd told Cara, but she really had no idea what it meant. What did it look like to love someone back? Assuming, of course, that he loved her in the first place. Argh! Why was this so hard? Wasn't love supposed to be fun and easy? How in the world was she supposed to *love him back?* She glanced across the darkened hospital room to where he was trying to sleep on the narrow and obviously uncomfortable bench/bed. She'd heard him tossing and turning for the last hour as he attempted to find a comfortable position for his large frame. She smiled as she remembered what else Cara had said: *"Well, I guess you're going to have to judge him by his actions."* He'd charged into a burning house for her. He'd barely left her side at the hospital, including giving up a much needed night's sleep for her. He was opening his home to her so she wouldn't have to stay in a hotel. If he didn't love her, why would he go to all the trouble? Maybe she didn't need to hear the words, at least not yet. They'd only known each other for a little over a month, after all. There was no need to rush, was there?

She wondered how long it would be before she could return to her own home. She dreaded the nightmare of insurance and construction in her future. Thoughts like these filled her mind as she stared at the ceiling; sleep had decided to elude her, at least for the time being. She wished she could turn on the television, but she didn't want to risk waking Finn. She didn't even have her Kindle; it and all her belongings were currently being held hostage to the nascent arson investigation and she had no idea when she would be able to have access to them. She thanked God her computer had been in her bedroom rather than the kitchen or living room. She backed up all her work to a Dropbox, of course, but it would be a hassle to replace her loyal laptop. Since she could do nothing about her current situation, she whiled away several hours plotting the next few chapters in her current work-in-progress, the sequel to *Taking Chances*. She'd hit a snag in the romance and found the enforced quiet time helpful in sorting it out. She finally fell asleep somewhere near 3:00 a.m. The hospital was the worst place to try to rest, however. No sooner had she fallen asleep than the night nurse came in to check her vitals. Finn didn't wake up, so Mel was less annoyed than she might have been; she fell asleep again soon after the nurse left.

They had nearly finished breakfast the next morning when Dr. Chaudhri returned. "Your lungs still sound clear, Melanie. How are you feeling?" She looped her stethoscope back around her neck and checked Mel's pulse.

"I'm feeling like I want to go home." She tried to keep the whine out of her voice, but feared she wasn't terribly successful. She felt ridiculous lying in the hospital bed when there was nothing wrong with her.

"Of course. Do you have a place to stay? I understand your house is not presently habitable because of the fire."

"She's staying with me," Finn said from across the room.

"Excellent. Well, I see no reason for you to stay here. I'll get the discharge paperwork started. You should be able to leave in a few hours. Plan to take it easy for a few days—no aerobic workouts, okay? That means take it easy with sex, as well."

Mel felt the heat rising from her neck and knew she was blushing furiously. Hearing Finn chuckle didn't help at all. On the other hand, she couldn't remember the last time she'd had an aerobic workout, at least on purpose. "No problem. Thank you, Dr. Chaudhri."

The doctor left and Finn came to sit next to her on the bed. "Well, there goes my nefarious plan for seducing you the minute we get home. I'll call and arrange transportation for us. God, it's going to be good to be home. Especially with you there."

"That was an extremely nice thing to say, Mr. DeLuca."

"It was, wasn't it? I think I deserve a kiss." His bright blue eyes twinkled in amusement.

"Most definitely. Come here." She beckoned him closer with a forefinger. He leaned down, placing his large hand on the pillow next to her head, and set his lips against hers. The doctor had finally removed the oxygen tube from under her nose, so there was nothing in the way. He kissed her softly and attempted to draw away, but she was having none of that. She slipped her hands over his shoulders and pulled him closer as she coaxed his lips apart. He smiled against her mouth and happily complied, slipping his arms behind her back to pull her against his hard chest. He deepened the kiss, wresting control from her for the moment.

"I'm pretty sure they frown on this sort of thing in a hospital." Cara breezed in and plopped a tote bag on the bed. "At least shut the door, lovebirds."

Mel felt herself blushing for the second time in a five-minute span.

Finn rolled his eyes, but kissed her quickly again before sitting up and turning toward his sister. "You got here quick. I only called a couple minutes ago. It's going to be a while before she's released."

"I was on my way already. I'm not staying. I just stopped by with some clothes for Mel to wear home. They're from Izzy because you two are about the same height. Mom is at your house, Finn, getting everything clean and ready for you, and I'm on my way to pick up a few things to tide you over until you can get to your own stuff. Any requests?"

"Thanks, Cara. I figured I'd have to wear my smoky-smelling nightgown home. I really appreciate this. If you could pick me up some panties and a bra, maybe? This is so weird to not have any of my own clothes available. I'll pay you back as soon as I can."

"Don't feel like you need a bra on my account," Finn said innocently.

"Don't be a lech," Cara replied with a laugh. "What sizes?" She pulled out her phone and opened the notes app.

"Um, medium for the panties, and 34B, sadly, for the bra."

"Nothing sad about it," murmured Finn.

"Don't worry, Mel. I know how to hook a sista up. I'll see you at Finn's later. Bye!"

Mel took the bag of clothes into the bathroom, where she took a shower to wash the lingering smell of smoke from her hair and skin. She was thrilled to discover Cara and Izzy had included a wide-toothed comb, toothbrush, and toothpaste, and a small bag of basic makeup, including mascara and lip gloss.

She came out of the bathroom feeling nearly human again, although her hair was still wet. It was so long it took hours to air dry. "Finn, could we visit Mr. Taylor before we leave? Is he still here?"

Finn went to find out from the nurses, and then they walked down the hall together to visit their neighbor.

He was sitting up in bed, watching a game show on television, which he clicked off when they knocked.

"Hi, Mr. Taylor. I wanted to come say thank you for saving my life." Melanie approached his bed and placed her hand gently over the back of his, relieved when he turned it over and squeezed hers in return. She was never quite sure how her grumpy neighbor would respond. "How are you feeling?"

"Oh, I'm fine. I'm old, so they decided to keep me overnight. Your young whippersnapper there got to leave the emergency room after a couple hours, but them damn doctors said they needed to shove a tube down my throat and breathe for me for a while."

"Yeah, me too." Mel sat in the chair next to his bed. "I'm sorry you had to go through that."

"Aww, don't matter none. It was worth it, I reckon. That stray cat woke me up, same as you." He jerked his chin at Finn.

"When do you get to go home?"

"Sometime today, I suppose. My sister is down signing papers and whatnot. Medicare is a goddamn nightmare."

"Is there anything we can do to help?" She knew he'd most likely refuse, but she needed to offer.

184

"No. My sister is gonna to drive me home. I might get there before you folks." He was silent for a moment. "Suppose it would be all right if you came to visit me once in a while. You got a place to stay, little missy?"

"She's staying with me." Finn stepped forward and put his hand on her shoulder.

The older man gave Finn a rather piercing look. "Oh, it's like that, huh?"

"Yeah, it's like that."

Mel stared between the two men, nonplussed by the sudden tension in the room. Somewhere along the way she seemed to have acquired a father figure. Since she owed Mr. Taylor her life, she decided to be flattered by his concern. "Don't worry. I can run a lot faster than him right now. Plus, I'm staying in his guest room."

Both men chuckled and the tension was broken. "You take care of her, young man. You hear me?"

"Yes, sir. I promise. You can come over and check on her any time you want. Consider it an open invitation. We'd like to have you over for dinner soon."

"Well, that sounds pretty good. Now you kids skedaddle so I can get my britches on." The gruff old man they knew was back.

"Okay, Mr. Taylor." Mel leaned forward and kissed him on his cheek. "We'll see you at home."

"My name's Carl."

"And my name's Mel." She squeezed his hand lightly, then allowed Finn to usher her out of the room.

Chapter Fourteen

Finn

Home had never looked so good. Tony had drawn the short straw, apparently, and had arrived to pick them up shortly after the nurse came in with the discharge paperwork. He drove their mother's Lexus and seemed amused to act as chauffeur while Finn sat in the back with Mel curled up against him. They were both feeling the effects of too little sleep for the past two nights and Finn had high hopes of spending several hours napping as soon as they got home. He should have known better.

His mother was setting the table for lunch—six places. There was definitely a dark side to being part of a large family and this was a perfect example. He would give a lot to be an orphan right about now. Guilt pecked at him as he ate the delicious spinach salad with strawberries and grilled chicken his mom had lovingly prepared to welcome Mel home. Cara had returned from her shopping trip in time for lunch, with multiple shopping bags from the mall, including an intriguing pink and black bag from Victoria's Secret. He wondered if he'd ever be allowed to view the contents, preferably on Mel.

"I brought a few more things from Izzy. I put them on the bed in the guest room for you, Mel."

"Thanks so much, both of you. You too, Tony. You've all been so wonderful. I can't begin to tell you how much it means to me."

"It's our pleasure. I just can't imagine what you've been through. When I think—"

"Mom," Finn interrupted before she dissolved into tears. She was tough as nails when she needed to be, but tender-hearted in the extreme whenever anything happened to one of her babies—even though Tony, the youngest of those babies, was twenty-two, and seated across the table from her, scarfing down the last of the cheesecake she'd brought for dessert. The boy could eat. The fact that his mother's tenderness extended to Finn's current girlfriend was telling; she'd never seemed terribly attached to any of the previous ones. But Mel was different, a fact his entire family had picked up on. Well good, because if he had his way, she'd be around for a long, long time.

"Hey, Mel," Tony said around a large bite of cheesecake. "Seamus told me to tell you he was able to get your laptop out of your house. It's in the guest bedroom."

"Please thank him for me. That's a huge relief. At least I can work now while I wait for my house to be habitable again."

"You can thank him yourself tomorrow. Dad

187

wants everyone over for another barbecue."

"If Mel feels up to it, we'll see." Finn noticed she was mostly pushing her dessert around on her plate; she'd only eaten about half her salad, as well. Exhaustion was clearly catching up with her. "Listen," he addressed his family members. "Mel and I haven't had much sleep in the past two days, so we're going to take a nap now." He saw relief spread across her features.

"Yeah, yeah. Don't let the door hit us in the ass on our way out, huh?"

"Antonio Cristoforo!" Moira's exclamation was appalled, yet resigned. She turned to Finn and Mel. "You two go on and get some sleep. Cara and I will do the dishes quietly and then leave you alone. Tony, you clear the table and then take your noisy self away."

Finn heaved himself up and grabbed his crutches before following Mel down the hall to the bedrooms. He could hear Tony grumbling as they left.

"I can be silent as the grave, Ma. Geez! Just cuz I'm the youngest..." His words faded as they retreated further down the hallway.

Mel's soft laughter sounded tired as she reached for the knob of the guest bedroom door. "I love your family, Finn. I'll see you in a couple hours, okay?"

"My family obviously loves you too. Hey." He reached to touch her arm while balancing on his crutches. "Come to my room and let's take a nap together. I need to hold you. I promise no funny business; I'm way too tired to even think about it."

She looked up into his eyes, surprised, but then smiled crookedly. "That sounds nice."

He ushered her into his bedroom and shut the door behind them. Someone had thoughtfully made his bed. He'd only stretched the truth a bit: he was never too tired to *think* about sex, but he didn't think he was capable of actually acting on his desires right now. Maybe later. He leaned his crutches against the wall and sat on the bed to remove his boot before stretching out and patting the spot beside him. "Come here."

Mel hesitantly reclined next to him with at least two feet between them. He smiled tiredly and reached for her, pulling her to spoon against him. He had just enough energy left to reach down for the light afghan at the foot of the bed and pull it up over them. He tucked Mel's head under his chin and wrapped his arm around her. *Yes.* He was asleep within seconds.

***

The room was deeply shadowed when he awoke. A quick glance at the bedside clock informed him it was nearly 5:00 p.m. He was facing the opposite direction from when he fell asleep and Fluff was now curled against his stomach, snoring softly, and serving as a poor substitute for the woman he'd fallen asleep holding. He wondered where Mel was until he realized the warmth against his back was her; they had ended up butt-to-butt. He carefully turned over and slipped his arm around her waist. He inhaled the warm scent of her: shampoo, a lingering antiseptic smell from the hospital, and her own unique fragrance, which always drove him wild. He sternly told himself not to get carried away; he refused to rush her into anything. Instead he simply enjoyed the feel of her in his arms. He could get used to this; in fact, he had every intention of keeping her here—in his house and in his bed— from now on. She stirred and he knew she was awake.

"Hey."

"Hey yourself." She turned over and faced him. "That was a great nap."

"Best ever." He leaned in and kissed her quickly. "Sorry about the nap breath."

She smiled. "No problem. I'm sure I've got the 'zacklies.'"

"The what?"

"The 'zacklies.' It's when your breath smells exactly like chicken shit."

He burst out laughing. "Oh my God! I've never heard that before."

"Yeah, well, my Aunt Karen was full of earthy little sayings like that."

He brushed her hair behind her ear, noting the sudden sadness in her eyes at the mention of her beloved aunt. He realized she must be feeling very lonely and vulnerable right now; even more reason to not take advantage of her. But lying next to her in bed was becoming too much of a temptation, so he kissed her on the nose and reluctantly sat up. "I don't know about you, but I'm starving. How does grilled cheese sound? If the gods are smiling on us, we may even be able to scare up a couple beers."

"Sounds amazing. I was too tired to eat much at lunch, so I'm starving too. Beer sounds great—I'm avoiding red wine for a while. At least a few days."

"Come on, Princess." He held his hand out to her while balancing on one crutch. "I make a mean grilled cheese."

They were in luck: his mom had stocked his fridge. He made a mental note to get her an extra-special Christmas present and give her an unexpected hug the next time he saw her.

Twenty minutes later, they had sandwiches and their second bottle of beer each while they cruised through Netflix looking for something to watch. They settled on an action thriller and settled back to relax. Halfway through the movie, Mel paused it and took the plates to the kitchen, returning with more beer.

"Can we talk for a few minutes, Finn?" Mel handed him a beer and sat, angling herself toward him.

He clicked the movie off. "Of course, sweetheart. What's wrong?" What could he have done? The grilled cheese did an unpleasant flip in his stomach.

She bit her lip and shrugged. "Nothing's wrong. I just think I should tell you some stuff about me, about why I freaked out when I saw you and Tatiana. When I talked to Cara the other night, she seemed to think it would help if I talked to you and explained."

"Okay, but only if you want to. You don't have to explain yourself, though." He took a long pull on his beer, trying to disguise his eagerness. Maybe they could finally move past whatever had hurt her and caused her to withdraw from life.

She smiled crookedly at him. "Thanks, but I think it's for the best. You need to know about my past if we have any chance of making this relationship work." She paused and took a deep, fortifying breath. "Okay, here goes: when I was freshman in college, I met a guy who was really popular and good-looking. He asked me out and we dated for about a year. I was really shy and had never dated before, so I didn't really know what to expect. To make a long story short, he pressured me into a sexual relationship way before I was ready. I later found out he'd been cheating on me the entire time. I've had a hard time trusting myself to date anyone since. I guess it's made me kind of wary about men." She took a long drink from her beer when she finished.

Wary? I'll say. God, he'd like to get his hands on that bastard! He'd known it had to be something like this. Poor Mel! "I'm so sorry, sweetheart." He took her beer and set it on the table before gathering her in his arms. "You haven't dated anyone in the years since?"

She shook her head against his chest. "Some first dates, like I told you a while ago, but that's it. There hasn't been anyone I've cared about enough to take the risk of getting closer. Until you, Finn. You kind of slipped past my defenses when I wasn't looking and I—"

He frowned as she broke off and looked away. "What? You can tell me anything, Mel."

"I think I'm falling in love with you, Finn, but I

don't know—"

He grinned and swooped in to kiss her. He'd meant it to be fairly swift, but her mouth was a force to be reckoned with, and he could not make himself pull away. He forgot his own name when he was kissing her. Her lips opened beneath his and his tongue stole inside to taste and tangle with hers. Long moments later he remembered he had something important to say to her and pulled away reluctantly. "I do know. I'm head over heels in love with you, Melanie Blythe. I know we haven't known each other long, but it doesn't matter. I love you." He willed her to believe him, to understand what he was trying to say to her.

She smiled the most beautiful smile he'd ever seen in his life and lifted her face to kiss him. He leaned back so he was resting against the cushions and pulled her on top of him. Patience became difficult to remember as they kissed slowly, luxuriously, and he allowed himself to touch and run his hands over areas he'd previously considered off-limits. Nothing seemed forbidden tonight. He knew he needed to pace himself because he wasn't sure how far she was willing to go, and he certainly didn't want her to feel like he was expecting anything simply because they'd declared their love for each other. He dared to run his hand under her t-shirt and over her bra, encouraged when she arched into his palm. He nearly leaped off the couch when she ran her hand under his shirt. He let her explore for a few moments before stilling her busy hands.

"Sweetheart," he panted. "I need to stop. I'm going to have a hard time getting to sleep tonight if

I don't." He cringed at his suggestive choice of words.

She bit that luscious lip again and looked up at him through her sooty eyelashes. "I don't want to stop, Finn. I love you and I want to be with you."

He tried to swallow past a throat suddenly bone-dry. "Mel, are you sure? We can wait, love. I don't mind." Of course he did, but he would do anything for her, including sentencing himself to a long, cold shower before bed.

"Make love to me, Finn," she whispered against his lips.

Chapter Fifteen

Mel

She'd never woken up in a man's arms or bed before. Evan had always insisted she leave almost immediately after they had sex, not caring if she had to walk across a dark campus by herself. *Jerk. What did I ever see in him? Why did I waste so many first times on a guy like that?* Her first time with Finn had been amazing and so special. Finn had cuddled with her afterward and they had laughed about not exactly following the doctor's orders. He'd whispered in her ear about how beautiful she was and how much he loved her. Then they'd made love again. She lay curled in his arms, marveling about making love compared to having sex. *Worlds apart.*

She'd been extremely nervous, but it turned out he was too. He told her he wasn't sure he'd be able to make it good for her because of his limited mobility, and was afraid she'd have to do most of the work. They'd managed well enough, however. He'd devoted himself to exploring her curves and learning what she liked, while he encouraged her to do the same. His single-minded goal seemed to be to please her, which he had done—twice. It was a beautiful, intimate exchange, and she couldn't believe how close she felt to him. By the time he reached into his nightstand drawer for protection, nervousness was the last thing on her mind. He'd gently pulled her atop him and guided himself inside. She'd never made love that way before, but found it quite to her liking, giving her a greater sense of control than she'd ever experienced. He'd refused to let her look away, which made it even more intense. He'd grasped her hips, keeping her steady as she moved, allowing her to find her pleasure before he took over, thrusting faster and faster until he too, groaned in ecstasy. She'd collapsed against him and he turned them until they lay on their sides, breathing heavily as the sweat dried on their bodies.

His warm body was now curled around her from behind and the steady brush of his crisp chest hair against her back told her he was still asleep. The ceiling fan swept the cool morning air across the parts of their bodies not covered by the sheet, so she was grateful for his warmth. She still wasn't used to the way the nights cooled off so drastically here in the desert southwest. She carefully and slowly turned over to be able to look at him and yet not wake him. His achingly handsome face was relaxed in sleep, his jaw sprouting scratchy black whiskers. Faint lines surrounded his mouth and etched from the corners of his eyes, but they weren't nearly as pronounced as they had been when they'd first met.

His cheeks had filled out some as well as the pain from his injuries faded and his appetite returned. She couldn't begin to imagine all he'd gone through in the past few months, but she felt a pang in her stomach at the thought of him lying unconscious in a hospital bed. She wondered if he'd felt the same way when he saw her after the fire.

"You're staring." His words were a mumble and his eyes were still closed.

"Sorry. I can't help it. I woke up in bed next to this amazingly sexy man and I can't seem to get my fill of looking at him."

He chuckled self-consciously and opened his cobalt eyes. "What a coincidence. I woke up in bed with an amazingly sexy and beautiful woman." He brushed a brown tress out of her face and ran his thumb over her lips. "Last night was incredible, Mel. You pretty much destroyed me."

She grinned. "Really? Is that a bad thing?"

"Not even close." He leaned forward to nibble along her jaw up to her ear, making her shiver with delight. "I can't get enough of you.

"Finn," she murmured, reaching up to run her hands through his shaggy black hair.

"Yes, love?" His lips continued their journey until he reached her earlobe. He took it gently between his teeth, then soothed it with his tongue. He pulled away after a moment and tucked her close, running his calloused palms up and down her back. "Sorry. I'll try to control myself. I know it's been a long time for you and I don't want you to be sore."

God, she loved this man. "I'm fine. I can't get

enough of you, either. It's never been like this for me, this…good." His body shook against hers as he laughed.

"Stop, sweetheart. My ego is about to explode. I won't be fit to live with." He kissed the top of her head. "All right. Stop trying to seduce me again, witch. I hear your stomach growling, so let's forage for some breakfast. I have a physical therapy appointment later this morning I'm hoping you'll drive me to, and then I think I need a haircut. I'm supposed to start back to work in a few days, and I guess I should try to look professional."

She fixed breakfast while he showered and shaved. She set a plate of eggs and toast in front of him before he pulled her on his lap and kissed her thoroughly, his hand sneaking up under the Journey t-shirt he'd given her to wear this morning. "Your eggs are getting cold," she finally murmured against his lips.

"Spoilsport." He grinned and playfully shoved her off his lap. "You are too tempting. That's my new favorite shirt, by the way."

"It's super-soft and I love that it smells like you."

"Consider it yours. I would love to see what Cara brought you from Victoria's Secret, however." He wiggled his eyebrows up and down suggestively.

"I hope she brought underwear. This is my only pair." She filled her own plate and sat across from him.

"I love the thought of you running around commando." He smiled at her oh-so-innocently as he ate.

198

"I will if you will."

"You're a sassy minx, you know that?" They ate in silence for a few moments. "Seriously, Mel. Are you okay? I'm afraid I was too rough last night."

"I'm perfectly fine." There was a slight soreness between her legs, but she found she was rather proud of it. "How is your leg? I'm afraid we weren't careful enough. I don't want your therapist to yell at you."

"He'd be more likely to high-five me, actually." At her look of consternation, he backtracked quickly. "Not that I'm planning to bring it up, of course. That could be construed as bragging."

"What am I going to do with you?" She carried their empty plates to the sink and refilled their coffee cups.

"I've got a few ideas. You could start by letting me watch you take a shower."

She laughed and bent to kiss his hair, still damp from his shower. "You're incorrigible."

An hour later, she was seated in the waiting room, waiting for Finn to finish his bi-weekly PT appointment. She'd grabbed her laptop on the way out and was rereading the last few scenes she'd written; it had been several days and a house fire since she'd even looked at it. She found her mind wandering, however, back to the fire. What had caused it? And now there was an arson investigation? The thought had a frisson of fear creeping down her neck. Was it possible? Was it personal? More importantly, was it related to the disturbing things happening to her: the dishes moved, the doors left open, the feeling of being followed. She'd begun to believe she had imagined those things, but now she wasn't so sure. Why in the world would someone target her? She was a complete nobody!

"Hey, Mel." Finn came through the office door, followed by an attractive man wearing athletic clothing. "I'm done for the day. This is Jon, my physical therapist. He wanted to meet you."

"Hello, Jon. Nice to meet you." She stood to shake his hand.

"I had to see if Finn was telling the truth about having a real, live girlfriend. Nice to meet you too. I gave him some instructions on how to not undo all the work I've done on that leg while having crazy monkey sex."

"Oh, my God," Mel murmured as she felt the heat rise in her face.

Finn punched him on the upper arm. "Shut up. I told you I'd talk to her."

"Is he okay? We didn't...I mean..." Her words faded as her embarrassment took over.

"I'm kidding. He's doing great, but he does need to stay on bottom for a while." The therapist laughed as Finn grimaced. "I estimate about three more weeks on the crutches and then we can try a walking boot for a couple months. Hopefully you guys can wait that long to get more adventurous."

"All right, Mel. Let's get out of here before he shames either of us any further. Remember, Jon, vengeance is a bitch." The therapist's laughter followed them outside.

She waited until they were in the Jeep to lay into him. "Seriously, Finn?"

"I'm so sorry about that, sweetheart. Jon's a good guy, but a bit of a clown. I swear I didn't parade our sex life in front of him to brag. I simply asked a few…logistical questions to make sure I don't do any damage to my ankle."

She couldn't help chuckling. "All right. I believe you. It took me by surprise, that's all." She followed his directions to the barbershop and waited while he got his hair cut, amused by the fuss the barber made over him.

"It's good to see you up and around! Your brothers and your dad have been keeping me up to date, of course, but I've been worried. The missus and I have lit candles for you every week at mass."

"I appreciate it, Harold. It's been a long road and I've got a ways to go yet."

"Well, it looks like you still managed to find a pretty girl along the way. You don't let something as minor as a coma and a few months in a wheelchair slow you down, huh?" The barber smirked at Finn as he gestured to where Mel was sitting; she could, of course, hear everything.

Finn smiled and winked at her from his perch in the barber's chair. "I wasn't about to let this one get away. She's a keeper."

She waited until they were back in the Jeep. "A keeper, huh?" She missed the boyish look his shaggy hair had provided, but at the same time, loved the sexy new look with his shorter hair.

He leaned across the divider between the front seats and kissed her. "Definitely a keeper. Thanks for running me around today. Let's grab some lunch, okay? Don't forget we have dinner at my parent's tonight."

"I'm looking forward to it. And lunch sounds great."

***

Finn

He couldn't keep his eyes off her. She was standing across his parents' backyard with his two sisters, laughing and sipping a glass of white wine. He still couldn't believe the events of the last twenty-four hours. How in the world was he lucky enough to be with such an amazing woman? You could have knocked him over with a feather the evening before, when she'd returned from the kitchen and wanted to talk. She'd finally told him about her past—he would dearly love to meet college boy in a dark alley someday—and then she'd said she thought she might be falling in love with him. He told her that he loved her and then tried in vain to control himself as they made out on his couch. He'd made himself pull away, which was probably the most difficult thing he'd ever done in his life. But just when he'd resigned himself to a long, cold shower and a sleepless night, she'd spoken. *"Make love to me, Finn."* Those words had changed his life because now that he'd had her, he was determined to keep her.

"Is there any way I could get you to stop ogling your girlfriend? I'm gonna have to stab myself in the eyeball if you don't." Seamus opened a beer as he pulled up a chair next to Finn.

"Shut up. I'm not ogling her. Did you bring me one of those?"

"You are so ogling her. Here." He handed him a beer. "Don't get me wrong—I like Mel. I like her a lot. But you're practically undressing her with your eyes, bro. Knock it off. There are children present." As he spoke, their niece ran up and launched herself into his lap.

"Uncle Seamus! Play with me!"

"Who is this bossy little girl? Finn, you got any idea who this is?" He bounced her wildly on his knee as she giggled.

"I don't know who she is." Finn took a long pull on his beer. "My niece, Janey, would never be so bossy."

"Uncle Finn! It *is* me! I'm not bossy!"

"Oh yeah? What happened to saying the magic word when you want someone to play with you?"

"Please, please, please play with me?"

"Well, what do you know? It *is* Janey, after all," Seamus said, feigning shock. "What do you want to play, munchkin?"

"Piggyback! Take me for a ride! Please!" She seemed to remember the magic word at the last minute, perhaps reminded by Finn clearing his throat.

Seamus obliged, telling Finn to watch his beer until he got back.

"I brought you some chips and salsa." Mel placed the paper plate in front of him.

He smiled and took her hand, pulling her across his lap. "Thanks. That's earned you a kiss." He wondered how she would react to a little PDA in front of his family.

She didn't seem to mind, but he kept it brief, mindful of their audience.

"Well, well, well." Cara plopped down across from them and helped herself to the chips and salsa. "It seems my little gift from Victoria's Secret did the trick."

He enjoyed the blush on Mel's cheeks, but scowled at his sister. As Mel scooted off his lap, he made a mental note to ask her to check the bag Cara had left in the guest room. That could be a lot of fun.

"Finn?" Mel squeezed his hand. He'd missed a question apparently, judging by the smirk on his sister's face.

"Sorry. What was the question? My mind was wandering."

Cara laughed out loud at this. "I'll bet I know where."

"Be nice, Cara, or you'll never hear anything about it," Mel said, sounding amused.

"Okay, okay. All my romance is vicarious these days, so I can't afford to lose out on a juicy story. Anyway, I asked if you two want to do dinner and movie later this week. Izzy is whining about needing a night out without the kiddo—"

"I don't whine." Izzy joined them, calm as usual. She was the unflappable one, her words and actions nearly always measured. Her unexpected pregnancy and the mystery of Janey's father was the shining exception. "I would appreciate an evening with adults, however, and it doesn't seem like we're going to be able to separate you two lovebirds quite yet. Cara and I are willing to put up with you if it means we can have some time with Mel."

"Oh, I see how it is," Finn said with a laugh. "I'm in if Mel is."

"Sure. Sounds fun."

He was gratified by how his family accepted her; it had certainly not always been this smooth when he brought home a girl. Izzy and Cara in particular had never warmed up to any of them like they had to Mel. He had the distinct feeling he was rather superfluous as far as they were concerned. His parents had always been pleasant to past female friends, but he watched as Mel joked with his father and helped his mother with the dishes and saw they were already closer to her than to any of his previous girlfriends.

He yawned; he was feeling the effects of their interrupted sleep the night before and knew she must be as well. He checked his watch and saw it was getting close to nine o'clock. Janey was asleep on his lap, effectively trapping him in his chair since he couldn't get up without his crutches.

"I guess I wore her out, huh?" Seamus chuckled and sat next to him. "You want me to take her?"

"Nah. I'm good for now. I'm going to try to get Mel out of here pretty soon, as soon as she's done in the kitchen. We're both pretty tired."

"I'm not even going to ask."

"Good. I'm not going to tell. Where's Sloane tonight?" He'd been glad when Seamus showed up alone; his girlfriend tended to cause tension at family gatherings.

"She's out of town for work. Listen, we need to

talk about the investigation."

Hugh and Tony appeared, extra beers in hand. "Did you tell him about the yard?" Tony handed Seamus a bottle while Hugh did the same for Finn.

"Tell me what?" He sat up so fast Janey whimpered and stirred. Hugh set his beer aside and took her, gently rocking until she fell back asleep.

"A message appeared in Mel's yard. The arson team noticed it this afternoon," Seamus said reluctantly.

"What kind of message?" He couldn't imagine what his brother was talking about.

"It looks like someone used gasoline on her grass to spell out **'Die Bitch.'** The investigation is ongoing, but this makes it pretty clear the fire was set on purpose."

Finn cursed and grabbed his crutches. "I need to call Chris." He stepped away to a quiet area of the yard and called his partner, arranging to meet with her the next day. "Listen," he said as he returned to his brothers. "I don't want Mel to know about this tonight. Chris is coming over tomorrow and we'll tell her then. I'll reach out to the arson investigation team and see if we can get on the same page."

"Finn, it's going to be all right." Tony slung an arm around his neck.

"You don't know that, Tony. *Fuck.*" He whispered the word this time, cognizant of his niece's presence.

"We're not about to let anything happen to her, Finn." Hugh continued to rock Janey as he spoke. "Go home. You need some sleep, and you'll be able to deal with this better tomorrow."

He could hear them joking about how he wasn't likely to get much sleep any time soon with Mel living in his house. He shook his head and hobbled away to find her.

***

Three a.m. The bedside clock cast an eerie glow over Mel's bare shoulder as he leaned to softly brush his lips across her smooth skin, so as not to wake her. She'd been adorably shy when they returned from the barbecue earlier, apparently not sure if she should presume that he wanted her to share his bed again. Silly girl. He'd wanted nothing more than to sweep her into his arms and carry her to his bedroom, but he'd had to settle for a gentle tug on her hand and kissing her senseless. Then he'd slowly stripped away every article of her clothing, kissing and tasting as he went. It had been fairly challenging for someone on crutches, but he was nothing if not persistent. She'd gotten into the spirit and figured out how to distract him, finally tossing the crutches aside and pushing him back onto the bed and showing him her shyness only went so far.

He was glad she was able to sleep, but his mind was too full to allow him any rest. Plus, his ankle was throbbing because he'd forgotten to take his ibuprofen before bed. He knew he'd never be able to get to sleep with the pain, so he eased away from her as quietly and carefully as possible. He sat on the edge of the bed and searched the floor for a crutch so he could make his way to the bathroom.

CJ raised her head from the armchair she'd decided was her sole property and purred softly as he went by. Fluff was snoring in the new bed Mel had bought him that afternoon.

He paused at the threshold of the bathroom and stared at the woman in his bed. She'd rolled over when he moved and was now facing him, the sheet covering the beautiful body he was thrilled to be discovering. *God, she's so amazing.* He remembered the discussion he'd had with Hugh weeks ago about how when he met the right woman he wouldn't spend time agonizing over whether or not to ask her to move in. He'd just know. Well, as much as he hated to admit it, his brother had been right. He knew. Mel was his...destiny...love...everything. He never wanted her to leave, and if he thought she'd say yes, he'd propose tomorrow. But first he needed to make sure she was safe from whoever was trying to hurt her. He straightened, a steely determination creeping down his spine—almost a physical manifestation of his absolute resolution to protect her, no matter the cost. He would not lose her.

Chapter Sixteen

Melanie

She turned the bacon in the skillet and poured the first of the pancakes on the griddle, humming softly as she worked. She'd woken early, assisted by CJ, and managed to exit the bed without waking Finn. After feeding the cat and dog, she'd decided to make a nice breakfast and found the ingredients readily enough.

"Now this is a sight I could get used to." Finn's deep voice from the doorway startled her into dropping the spatula into one of the pancakes.

"This one will be yours." She picked the spatula out of the goopy batter and rinsed it.

He clumped across the kitchen and stepped behind her, wrapping his arms around her waist. "Small price to pay for seeing this in my kitchen." He kissed her neck as he slid a hand up under her t-shirt.

"Mmm." She leaned back into his embrace, allowing him access to all the delicious warm parts

209

her shirt hid. "I suggest we continue this in the bedroom after breakfast."

"Excellent idea, Ms. Blythe. However, when I finally get off these crutches, I fully plan to make love to you right here in this kitchen. I've been entertaining fantasies about it for quite a while."

"I would love to hear about those fantasies sometime, but maybe not when the bacon's about to burn." She laughed and kissed his scruffy neck before slipping away to tend the breakfast.

"Knock, knock." Chris, Finn's partner whom Mel had briefly met, knocked on the screen door and entered the kitchen. "Hope I'm not interrupting." Her voice brimmed with amusement.

"Here." Mel handed Finn the spatula with a look of chagrin. "I need to put some pants on."

Finn found her in the bedroom, pulling on her yoga pants. "Sorry about that, sweetheart." He pulled a t-shirt over his own head as he spoke. "I guess I need to let people know it's not okay to let themselves in without checking anymore."

"How many people have keys to your house?"

"Well, my parents, my brothers and sisters, and my partner. I got the one back from Tatiana. I know it sounds like a lot, but when I was in the wheelchair it was really helpful. I'm sorry, Mel. Chris is not one to judge, so don't worry about it."

"I'm fine. I was just a bit surprised. Is she watching the pancakes and bacon?"

"She is. I asked her to stop by this morning, but I thought it would be a bit later. Now we have a breakfast guest." He grabbed her as she tried to slip by. "Are we okay?"

She reached up and kissed him briefly. "Of course. I'll remember not to run around in my undies from now on, however."

"That's a damn shame, sweetheart." His murmured words followed her to the kitchen.

Chris had set the platters of bacon and pancakes on the table, so Mel poured coffee for the three of them and they sat to eat. She gained a new appreciation of Finn's partner over breakfast and enjoyed watching the two of them tease each other. She had finally regained her appetite and helped herself to extra bacon and pancakes, mentally promising to work out later. *Mmmm, bacon.*

"So, Mel, we need to talk to you." Chris waited until the plates were cleared and they each had a refill of coffee.

Uh oh. Judging by the serious looks on their faces, Mel was not going to enjoy the conversation. "Okay. What's up?"

Finn reached for her hand. "Sweetheart, we're opening a police investigation into who might be targeting you."

"So, the arson investigation is finished? The fire was set?" Her heart pounded as she squeezed his hand.

"No. They're still investigating, but something happened that makes it pretty clear it was arson."

"What? God, just tell me, Finn!"

"A derogatory remark appeared in your lawn. It appears someone used gasoline to kill the grass—" Chris didn't have a chance to finish before Mel was out of her seat and racing through the kitchen door.

"Mel, wait!"

211

But she didn't even pause. When Finn and Chris caught up to her she was standing in front of her house, staring at the crooked words burned into her lawn: ***Die Bitch***. A chill washed over her entire body and she began shivering uncontrollably. Who could possibly hate her so much? She'd never, as far as she knew, had an enemy, and she had no idea what she had done to deserve one now.

"Okay, sweetheart." Finn balanced on his crutches as he put an arm around her shoulders and attempted to steer her back to his house. "Let's go talk about this. We have some questions for you. Come on."

She allowed herself to be ushered toward his house, away from the vile words and burned-out shell of what used to be her garage and kitchen. *Oh, God.* Seated again at Finn's kitchen table, she accepted the cup of strong tea with lots of sugar Chris prepared for her. Her hand trembled as she lifted the mug to her lips.

"Who would do this?" Her words came out as a whisper, although she hadn't intended them to.

"That's what we need to figure out, Mel." Chris opened a small notebook as she spoke. "Do you have any ideas about who this could be? Do you have any enemies? Maybe someone from your past who would want to harm you?"

Mel stared into her tea at the sugar coating the bottom of the cup and shook her head slowly. "No. I don't think I've ever had an enemy. I've never really had a lot of friends, either."

"What about your fans, sweetheart? Have you received any hate mail or anything like that?" Finn

212

asked.

She looked up at him, a blank expression on her face. "Fans? Hate mail? What are you talking about?"

"For your writing. Your books."

She laughed, albeit a bit hysterically. "You seriously overestimate my fame. I have one book and very little feedback from readers."

"Who handles that sort of thing? Do you have a publicist or something?" Chris scratched a few words in her notebook.

Mel shook her head again, sure she would be dizzy soon. "Nothing like that. Seriously, I have a website and a few social media outlets, and that's it. My publisher handles the bulk of marketing. Nobody knows me, really. It couldn't possibly be someone who's read my book. It's a romance, for heaven's sake! Why would anyone hate me for that? Romance novels are supposed to make people happy."

"Well, it won't hurt to check it out. If you could write down the web addresses on this sheet of paper, it would help a lot." Chris tore a sheet from her notebook and slid it across the table.

"What about other authors, Mel? Can you think of anyone who might be jealous of your success? Maybe someone who didn't get published?"

"I only know a few other authors from my publisher, and only online. I've never met any of them. They're all so nice…" Her stomach heaved and she stood quickly. She barely made it to the bathroom before she lost her breakfast into the toilet, sobbing as the dry-heaves followed her active vomiting.

"Okay, sweetheart. It's okay." Finn held back her hair with one hand and rubbed her back with the other.

"Where are your crutches?" She managed to fit the words in between heaves.

"Let's worry about you right now. A short walk down the hall won't kill me." He continued to rub her back. "Get it all out. That's it."

"Oh, God. Why did I eat so much bacon?" Another toe-clenching heave. She finally finished and collapsed against the side of the bathtub.

Finn handed her a wet washcloth. "I'm sorry, hon."

She wiped her face and neck with the cool cloth. "It's not your fault, Finn. Not at all." She accepted his hand and let him pull her up. As she rinsed her mouth at the sink, her thoughts raced in a new direction. It wasn't his fault. No part of this was his fault, yet he was caught in the middle, possibly in harm's way because someone wanted her dead. He could have died trying to rescue her from the fire. Who was to say he wouldn't be hurt if there was another attempt on her life? "I have to leave," she whispered as she pushed her way past him.

"What?" He clumped behind her to his bedroom.

She turned to look at him and frowned; he was going to injure his ankle if he wasn't careful. She slipped past him again—he threw his hands up in frustration—and grabbed his crutches from the kitchen before returning to the bedroom. "I have to leave, of course. Someone is trying to kill me, Finn, and I can't risk something happening to you because I love you." She explained her reasoning while she dressed. Then she went to the closet for her suitcase and finally realized she didn't have a suitcase or even more than a few articles of clothing at Finn's house. Her own things were still unavailable to her because of the arson investigation. She might be able to access them later in the week, but everything would undoubtedly reek of smoke. No problem. She would simply pack up everything into her aunt's car and—she crumpled to the floor as she realized the extent of her problem. "I don't even have a car."

"Mel, sweetheart, it's—"

"I don't even have a fucking car because someone fucking set my house on fire!" She was sobbing again, edging toward a hysteria she wasn't sure she could control. "I have to leave! I can't stay! You're not safe! And what if little Janey got hurt?"

"What's going on, Finn?" Chris appeared at the bedroom door.

"Give us a minute, please, Chris. She's freaking out."

"I'm freaking out because someone is trying to fucking ruin my life!" she screamed.

Finn lifted her gently by the arm and pulled her against his chest. "Shh. I'm not going to let anything happen to you and I don't want you to leave. I need you here."

Mel heard the door click as Chris left them alone. "Finn, I can't. I have to go."

"You can't run from this, Mel. If someone is trying to hurt you, it doesn't matter where you go." He led her to the bed and scooped her into his lap, cuddling her like a small child, his t-shirt absorbing her tears.

"But I can't keep you safe. I can't stand the thought of you—" She couldn't get the words out and clutched his shirt as she sobbed.

"All right. Shh. I'm here." He crooned platitudes as he rocked her. She finally quieted and allowed him to tuck her back into bed—clothes and all—for a nap.

Exhaustion from the emotions of the morning and the bout in the bathroom swamped her as her head hit the pillow; thoughts and worries swirled away as she fell asleep, still shuddering occasionally with a hiccup.

When she awoke, the light creeping through the window shades told her it was late afternoon. Good grief! She'd slept most of the day. Her mouth tasted the like the hind end of a week-old roadkill, so she brushed her teeth and splashed her face with cold water. Her rumbling stomach urged her to the kitchen.

"Hey there, sleepyhead." Cara turned the television off and followed in her wake. "You feeling better?"

"I guess. I'm starving." She foraged in the fridge for sandwich fixings. "You want one?" She waved the packet of lunchmeat in Cara's direction.

"No thanks. I've got a dinner date in a couple hours."

"Really? Who's the lucky guy?" She set her plate at the table and poured herself a glass of juice to go with it.

"He's a guy I met last week at the gym." She

shrugged. "Wouldn't milk be better with that?"

"I don't drink milk. It's gross." She paused to take a bite of her sandwich. "Did you know all this stuff about the investigation? About the words in my yard?"

"Not until Finn called me a few hours ago. Seamus found out right before the barbecue yesterday and told Finn and the rest of the boys while we were inside doing the dishes. Finn waited to tell you until this morning. Try not to be mad at him."

"Hmm, maybe. Where is he?" She stood to root in the pantry for some chips. To hell with healthy food right now.

"He went into the precinct with Chris to get started on the investigation."

"And you got stuck babysitting, huh?"

Cara snagged a few chips from Mel's plate. "I don't mind. You're my friend. Finn said you freaked out a little bit and he didn't want to leave you by yourself."

Mel laughed wryly around a bite of sandwich. "It was more than a little bit."

Cara grinned. "Yeah, Finn said you have quite a mouth on you. He also said you think you should leave. I'm really hoping a little sleep got that idea out of your head."

"I don't want to leave, Cara. I'm in love with Finn, but I don't want him to get hurt."

"Mel, sweetie, you've only known him for a few weeks, and he's been in a wheelchair and on crutches the entire time. That's not the real Finn. He's a cop, Mel, and a damn good one. He's more

217

than capable of looking out for himself and taking care of you. He and Chris will get to the bottom of this, but he won't be able to focus on his job if he's trying to follow you wherever you think you need to run."

"I'm scared." She pushed the remnants of her sandwich away, her appetite gone again.

"I know. We're all here for you, Mel."

***

Finn

"I don't suppose I could get you to sit down and stop pacing?" Chris continued flipping through files, not even looking up as she spoke. "It's pretty distracting with all that clumping."

"Sorry." He leaned his crutches against the table and lowered himself into a chair. "Your sympathy for my disability warms my heart."

"Whatever. Are you gonna help or just sit there and mope?" She shoved a stack of files in front of him. "These are all the recent arson cases in the metro area."

Although he knew searching through the files was almost certainly a waste of time, he nevertheless dug in. It hadn't taken long to look at Mel's social media accounts, where nothing even vaguely threatening appeared. He would ask her print to out all her emails the next day and he and Chris would begin the arduous process of sorting through them, looking for any red flags. He stared blankly at the pages in the file he'd opened, the words nothing more than a blur. He hadn't wanted to leave her, but once she'd fallen asleep he'd fretted and worried until Chris snapped at him to call one of his sisters to come stay with Mel so he could go to the precinct with her and do something useful. He'd been itching to get back to work, but now all wanted was to be home. The precinct, where he'd spent so much of his time over the past six years, was no longer the focus of his life. That place was now occupied by Melanie.

"She's fine, Finn. She had a shock and freaked out, but Cara's with her. She'll wake up and feel like her old self, don't worry. She's a strong person, you know."

"I know, I just...*shit*." He shoved the file away and ran his hands through his hair.

Chris stood and left the table. A moment later she returned and placed a mug of coffee in front of him.

"Thanks." He took a sip and grimaced. "Ugh. The coffee didn't improve in my absence."

Chris smiled and resumed her seat. "Nope. It's good to have you back, Finn. I hate that it's under these circumstances, but I've missed you."

All right. It was time to get his head out of his ass and get to work. "Yeah, yeah. Enough of this sappy crap." He took another sip of coffee, grimaced again, and pulled the file back toward him. "Let's figure out who the little shithead is who's terrorizing my girlfriend."

By the time they finished for the day, they'd identified two persons of interest based on the information found in the files. Chris would spend time tracking them down over the next few days and pull them in for questioning while Finn pulled desk duty, most likely weeding through all of Mel's emails. The thought of invading her privacy in that manner didn't sit well with him, but he would do it to protect her.

***

It was nearly seven o'clock when he let himself into the house later that evening. He entered quietly in case Mel was still resting. Instead, the enticing aroma of roast beef met him, as well as the lilting sound of her laughter in response to something his sister said.

"Mel?" He shut and locked the door carefully before making his way to the kitchen.

"Hi!" She set down the knife she was using to chop a tomato, wiped her hands, and met him halfway. She reached up on tiptoe and pulled his head down for a lingering kiss.

He enjoyed the kiss for a moment, but then pulled back to look into her eyes. "You look better. Are you feeling better?"

She ducked her head, embarrassed. "Yeah. I'm so sorry about this morning. I guess I royally freaked out."

"Nah."

She raised her eyebrows, disbelieving.

"Well, maybe a little bit." He held up his thumb and forefinger, a small space between them. "Teensy."

She chuckled and kissed him again. This time he

sank into it, pulling her tightly against him, needing her closer, needing to know she was here, safe in his arms.

"Don't mind me," Cara said as she slipped past them to put the salad in the refrigerator.

"I never do." But he reluctantly raised his head. "Thanks for coming over. You staying for dinner?"

"Sadly, no. I have a date. You'll have to do without me. I'm sure you can find something to talk about." She hugged Mel and Finn. "Toodles."

"Wait! Who's the guy?"

"He's new. His name is Jake and we met at the gym. That's all the info I have, so back off, big brother." She winked at him and then shut the door behind her.

"You're cute when you get all protective." Mel smirked at him sassily as she set the table.

"I don't think my sisters would agree with you. Hey, come back to the bedroom with me."

"Super tempting, but I don't want my roast to burn. Raincheck?"

He laughed and rolled his eyes. "That's not what I meant, although I wouldn't be opposed. I need to put my gun away and I want to show you how to get in the safe."

"Oh, Finn, that's totally unnecessary. I don't like guns."

"You don't have to like them, but you do need to know where it is and how to get to it in case I'm not here when you need it. Come on." His tone brooked no refusal.

"Ugh!" She visibly dragged her feet as she followed. "If you're not here, then won't your gun most likely be with you?"

"I have more than one, Mel. I only carry my service weapon with me. My personal handgun is also in the safe." He showed her the safe in the back of his closet and made her memorize the code and practice opening it several times. "Do you know how to shoot a gun?"

"Not really. My stepdad tried to teach me, but he gave up pretty quick. Apparently I was a terrible student."

He leaned down to kiss the tip of her nose. "Well, we'll just give it another try this weekend, okay? I'm a patient teacher." When she tried to object, he silenced her with a kiss. "Saturday."

"Fine. Can we go eat dinner now?"

"Yes. It smells amazing and I'm starving. Thanks for cooking for me, Mel."

"Of course. How about we don't talk about all this stalker stuff for the rest of the evening? Please? I need to be normal for one night. After dinner we can relax on the couch and watch something innocuous. Maybe puppy videos."

She did make him watch a few puppy videos and they spent a fun half-hour showing each other their favorite YouTube dog videos. Then they shared a bottle of crisp, cool Sauvignon Blanc—she was off red wine for the foreseeable future—while he introduced her to the Jason Bourne movies, which she had somehow inexplicably missed. His stomach was pleasantly full from the delicious pot roast she'd prepared. He'd skipped lunch, so he was an appreciative diner and she was a wonderful cook. *Oh, man. If I hadn't been totally in love with her before this, that pot roast would have sealed the deal. I'm gonna dream about that gravy.* He reached for her hand and raised it to his lips.

"What?" She smiled at him from her side of the couch.

"Nothing, except you're too far away. Come here." He tugged her next to him.

She snuggled into his side and pulled the afghan over her bare feet. "You're working tomorrow?"

"Only if you're okay staying here by yourself. I can see if Cara can come over again."

"No. I'm perfectly fine staying here alone. I have tons of work to do, so please don't worry about me."

He turned toward her, cupping her face in his hands. "That's my job now. Mel, I know you're used to being independent, and I swear I'm not trying to smother you. This is different, hon, and I need to make sure you're safe. I've arranged to have a unit drive by every half-hour for at least the next few days. I don't want you to be scared."

Her smile was a bit wobbly. "I'm really trying not to be. It's not terribly productive, is it?"

"We're gonna get through this, Mel. I swear we are. I will keep you safe." He kissed her and tucked her back against his side. "Please tell me you've given up the idea of leaving. You had me worried earlier. I need to know you're not going to pack up and leave while I'm at work tomorrow."

"I promise. I know I can't stick my tail between my legs and run from this. Besides," she said as she turned back to him, climbing on his lap. "I like it here." She leaned in to kiss him, spearing her hands through his short locks. "I love you, Finn DeLuca." She whispered the words in his ear, then darted her tongue out to trace the sworls.

"Urgh." He had lost the power of speech as her tongue ignited his blood. His hands came up to clasp her hips, anchoring her firmly against him as he let her explore.

She nibbled and licked her way down his neck to the vee at the top of his shirt. She calmly began unbuttoning, kissing as she exposed his chest. She reached the last button and spread it wide, splaying her hands across his muscled torso. Then she took away his ability to breathe as she sat back and pulled her own t-shirt over her head and reached back to unhook her bra. "Now would be a really bad time for one of your relatives to walk in."

He couldn't begin to answer. He simply grinned and reached for her.

Chapter Seventeen

Mel

It took two weeks, but Mel was finally cleared to retrieve her personal items from her house. The arson investigation team had ruled the fire was intentionally set using gasoline as an accelerant and had cleared out, taking their crime scene tape with them. They had let her know she couldn't occupy the house yet, however, so she was still staying with Finn. He had let her know he wanted her to stay exactly where she was—in his house, in his bed— and she wanted that too, but she wanted it to be their choice, not something forced upon them by circumstances. She loved him and knew he loved her, but they were in a holding pattern of sorts because of the ongoing police investigation. Finn wasn't allowed to be officially assigned to the case, but unofficially he was working on the mundane aspects like searching through Mel's email and comments left on her website, while Chris handled the more active parts of the investigation. She had tracked down and questioned several suspects in other similar arson cases, but all their alibis had checked out. Finn was frustrated and worried, but tried hard to keep his bad mood from her. She was worried, of course, but refused to let it ruin her time with him. She still had to pinch herself to believe he loved her and she wasn't going to waste time worrying about someone trying to kill her. At least that's what she managed in her stronger moments; the fear would catch her by surprise when she wasn't paying attention and she would have a mini panic attack. She tried to keep these from Finn, but he seemed to be able to read her mind sometimes. When she woke before dawn, heart pounding out of her chest, chills shaking her body, he pulled her against his warmth and whispered soothing nonsense in her ear until she fell back asleep.

She grabbed the stack of boxes she'd found in Finn's garage and her house keys. It was time to pack up what personal belongings she wanted, including her clothes, and move them to Finn's house. He had cleared half his closet for her and all but one bathroom drawer. It was exciting to be formally moving in with him, but she wished it were more of a conscious choice by both of them. Oh, well. It wasn't like she could do anything about it right at the present. At least there had been no further episodes from her stalker or whatever the police were calling it. She'd offered to move out now that the danger seemed to be past, but Finn hadn't taken the suggestion well.

"Mel, we don't know the danger is gone. If you don't want to live here, I'll find you somewhere safe, but you can't go off on your own." He'd been pacing, as well as he could with crutches, while he ranted.

"Finn, I don't want to leave, but I don't want either of us to be forced into this situation. We'll end up resenting each other."

"Mel, no offense, but that's bullshit. I love you and I want you here. Please stop worrying about this." Then he'd found a way to both distract her and convince her he wanted her there.

She grimaced as she walked past the *"Die Bitch"* etched in her yard. She had racked her brain for anyone she might have offended in some way, but to be honest, she never really interacted with people enough to engender violent feelings one way or another. Finn had insisted she give him all the details she could on her college mistake/boyfriend, Evan, so he could rule him out as a suspect. She highly doubted he'd ever felt strongly enough to even waste a moment's thought on her. What was she going to do about that giant burned-out patch in the yard? Maybe it would be a good spot to plant a tree. Maybe she'd call a landscaper and see about xeriscaping. No, she liked green grass too much to fill her yard with rocks and desert plants.

The stale stench of smoke and wet, sour fabric hit her as she let herself in through the front door. Ugh! It was so much worse than she expected. She would make this as fast as possible. The living room was a disaster: scorched drapes and sodden furniture. Her feet made a nasty squelching sound on the carpet as she crossed the room to the hallway. She glanced around and into the kitchen, which had sustained the worst of the damage, at least as far as the house was concerned. She had glimpsed the garage as she entered. It was nothing but a burned-out shell with the charred remains of her aunt's car inside. Hugh had assured her they would be able to rebuild and even offered to draw up some plans for an addition while they were at it.

It didn't take more than an hour to box up what she needed; all the clothes would need a good washing or two before she could hope to wear them. She gathered a few more things: her Kindle, a photo album, some books, and prepared to lug them back to Finn's house. Everything smelled strongly of smoke and she wondered if she'd ever be able to get it out.

"Yoo hoo! Melanie? Are you here?"

Oh, great. She set down her box and trudged back to the front door. "Hi, Lena. How are you?" She knew she should be polite to her annoying neighbor, but a visit was the last thing on Mel's mind right now.

"I saw you go inside and thought I'd come over and see if you needed any help." The blonde woman slid past Melanie and into the living room. "Oh, wow! This is awful!"

"Yeah. Listen, I really can't visit right now, so—"

"Oh, I know. I'm just here to help. I can carry boxes for you."

Well, that was nice and Melanie instantly regretted her reluctance to talk to her neighbor. "Thanks, Lena. That would be great, actually." She led the way back to her bedroom where the boxes were stacked. They each grabbed one and trooped back to Finn's house. It took four trips to bring everything over and Mel was grateful for the help. "That's the last of it. Thanks again." They stacked the boxes in the guest room. "How about some iced tea?"

"That would be lovely, thanks."

They sat in the kitchen and cooled off with the tea and some cookies Mel had made the day before. Lena was chatty and, although she was grateful for the help, Mel wanted to get rid of her. It had been emotionally taxing to see what had happened to her home and she needed to be by herself to process. She'd always been that way, needing more time to herself than anyone she knew. She'd spent hours in her room when she was a child, by herself, never bored. Her mother learned early on that sending her there wasn't an effective punishment; it was much better to make her stay with people. She'd do nearly anything to get away—even become the compliant daughter her mother required.

"I can't believe what happened to your house! That's so awful! You're so lucky you got out. Do you know how it started? The fire department has been over there an awful lot lately."

Mel sighed; of course the neighbors were concerned and curious. She might as well get the explanation over with now. If she told Lena, she probably wouldn't have to explain it to any of the others since she'd be sure to spread the news. "It was arson, actually. They've discovered the fire was set using gasoline."

Lena looked shocked. "Oh my goodness!

Someone tried to burn your house down? Do you think they knew you were inside?"

Mel had no intention of talking about the sleeping pills in her bloodstream. That was something she was still having a difficult time wrapping her mind around, so she hedged. "Well, it makes sense they knew I was inside because it was in the middle of the night. Where else would I be? Plus, you did see the lovely message in my yard, didn't you?"

"Yes, I guess that does make it pretty clear." Lena took another sip of her tea. "Well, I'm so glad you're okay. What happened? How did you get out?"

Mel stood, wishing to bring this conversation to an end as quickly as possible. "CJ—the cat, you know—actually woke Finn and Mr. Taylor and led them to my house. I was unconscious, probably from the smoke."

"The cat? Really? How extraordinary. I've heard of dogs doing that, but never a cat."

Mel shrugged as she smiled tightly and gestured to Lena's glass. "Would you like more?"

Lena shook her head and smiled. "I can see you're exhausted, so I'll get out of your hair. Do you mind if I use the bathroom? Too much tea." Lena laughed self-consciously.

"Of course. Down the hall, first door on the right." She was relieved the other woman had caught her social cues. She cleared the table and stacked the glasses and plates in the dishwasher while she waited for Lena to finish in the bathroom and leave. She still needed to make a call to the insurance company and run to the grocery store. She was making her mental list of chores when Lena returned.

"This is a really nice house. I like the layout much better than mine."

Melanie simply smiled; she was socially tapped out for a while. She saw Lena to the door, locked it carefully as per Finn's directives, and retreated to their bedroom for a brief nap. She woke an hour later, refreshed and ready to face people again. She made her call to the insurance company, then backed Finn's Jeep out of the garage and made a quick trip to the grocery store. She wanted to prepare something special for dinner, hoping to distract him from his worries about her safety. He was an amazing man and she loved him to distraction, but she found she preferred when he wasn't stressed and cranky. He was also fairly predictable: a good meal always had a positive effect on his mood. On second thought, she decided to swing by the mall and pick up something fun from Victoria's Secret. He had seemed to enjoy the last silky nightie Cara had given her and she was sure he'd be appreciative of another. Besides, she had discovered she felt pretty when she slept in something sexy rather than her usual t-shirt.

By the time Finn hobbled through the door later that evening, she had a chicken roasting in the oven alongside red potatoes, which were crisping nicely. She reached up to kiss him quickly, then poured two glasses of wine and carried them to the living room. He sat beside her, groaning as he removed his heavy boot and propped his foot on a pillow.

"Come here," he growled and pulled her on his lap. "Have I mentioned how much I love coming home to you?"

"Not in nearly twenty-four hours, so go ahead. I'm all ears."

He chuckled. "I love having you here," he mumbled against her lips.

She allowed herself to sink into the kiss, but pulled back after a moment. "We only have ten minutes before I need to pull the chicken out of the oven."

"Challenge accepted." He flashed a cocky grin and reached for her again. "I can do a lot in ten minutes."

***

Finn

What in the world am I going to do with her? He knew he'd been cranky and irritable for the past two weeks, but instead of riding his ass about it, she greeted him with wine and the best roast chicken he'd ever eaten. The potatoes she'd served with it were perfectly crispy and buttery and he'd gorged himself before falling asleep on the couch while they watched television. She'd let him sleep, then surprised him at bedtime with a sexy new nightie. Wow. He didn't deserve her and he'd better start pulling his weight in this relationship or he'd lose her. He pulled her close and kissed her hair before he dragged himself out of bed and grabbed his crutches. If all went as planned, he would ditch them later that week and move to a walking boot. He would never take his mobility for granted again.

"What time is it?" Mel asked sleepily.

"It's not yet six. Go back to sleep, love." He leaned over to pull the sheet over her shoulders. "I'll make coffee." He smiled as she snuggled back into her pillow. She wasn't much of a morning person. He made the coffee, then fixed himself a few pieces of toast. Chris would be by to pick him up in an hour or so; while he waited, he drank coffee and brooded about the investigation. He had examined every single email she'd received, especially those sent through her website, and had found mainly messages from fans and advertisements for author-related services. There was nothing even vaguely threatening. Tracking down the college boyfriend had proved more challenging than he'd expected, and it was really starting to piss him off. The other detectives who officially had the case were swamped with a high-profile investigation that was hot at the moment, so they were happy to have Finn do the background research for Mel's case. Chris was busy questioning all the arson witnesses and possible suspects they'd identified, but while she'd closed two other cases, none of the suspects looked good for the fire at Mel's house. Argh! He scrubbed his hands over his face, frustrated beyond belief.

"Mmm, that coffee smells amazing." Mel padded into the kitchen, wrapped in her fuzzy robe, her silky nightie regrettably hidden from his view. She poured a mug and leaned against the counter.

"Sorry I woke you up." He stood and took his

plate to the sink. He'd been doing the one crutch thing for a while around the house—with permission from his physical therapist—and was glad to be able to carry his own dishes for a change. "You want some toast or something?"

She smiled at him over the rim of her mug. "Maybe later." She sipped in silence for a few moments. "When's your birthday?"

He frowned at her slightly. "Odd question first thing in the morning. October twelfth. When's yours?"

"July seventh."

He stared at her. "That's tomorrow."

"Yeah." She nodded and continued sipping her coffee.

"Thanks for the heads up, Mel." His words were infused with sarcasm.

"Sorry. I actually forgot in all the chaos we've been dealing with around here. It struck me when I woke up." She turned and inserted a piece of bread into the toaster.

"What do you want to do? I can make reservations somewhere."

"Oh, you don't need to fuss. I can fix something here. I just wanted someone to know." There was a lingering sense of loneliness in her tone.

He crossed the kitchen and put his arms around her, pulling her back against his body. "It's not a bother, and we need to celebrate. It's your twenty-fifth birthday, a quarter of a century." He kissed her hair before returning to his seat. "I guess we really don't know that much about each other yet. It's strange."

She brought her toast and coffee to the table. "A bit. I like what I know so far, however. Tell me something new about you, something that will surprise me."

He smiled and cast about in his mind for some fact she would be surprised to discover. "I really love camping and I'm bummed I won't get to this summer."

"That doesn't surprise me. You seem like the camping type." She buttered her toast. "I've never been. It sounds like fun."

"As soon as I'm walking without these crutches or this boot, we'll take a weekend and head up to the Jemez wilderness or the Chama. You're game for staying in a tent?"

"Absolutely. I don't mind getting dirty."

"Oh, I know." He said it with a smirk and enjoyed the blush that crept across her cheeks.

***

"Finn, you've got a visitor." The receptionist handed him a stack of papers.

"Who is it?"

"One of your brothers. I think it's the oldest one. You want me to send him back?"

"Sure." He was standing outside one of their interrogation rooms, watching Chris question a rape suspect they'd been investigating for several months.

Hugh appeared several moments later. "You free for lunch? I was in the area."

"Sure, if you can wait a few minutes. I want to

see the end of this interview." He gestured toward the glass, beyond which Chris sat with a young Hispanic male.

"Listen, Miguel." Chris's voice sounded slightly tinny though the microphone as she grabbed the two small water bottles on the table at their side. "This where we are right now." She moved the bottles apart to opposite ends of the table. "But here's where we need to be." She moved the bottles next to each other. "Now I know what happened that night at the party, but I need you to tell me in your own words. You're gonna feel a lot better once you tell me. You're gonna walk outta here as soon as we're through. I'm not gonna arrest you, so you can tell me what happened. That girl was coming on to you, wasn't she?"

The young man nodded. "She was. She was all like, 'Hey, Miguel, you wanna go upstairs with me?' So I did, man, but then when things got going, she freaked out and was like, 'No, Miguel, that's enough.' Well, she got me all worked up, you know."

"Am I allowed to watch this?" Hugh asked, gesturing to the interrogation.

Finn shrugged. "Sure. You get to see Chris in action. She's one of the best I've ever seen. This little asshole will be crying in a minute. You watch. She always makes them cry."

"She teased you, didn't she, Miguel? She was asking for it, I know. So what happened next? You had sex with her, didn't you?" Chris's voice soothed, full of sympathy and understanding.

Miguel nodded, tears streaking down his face.

"I need you to tell me, Miguel. Tell me what happened."

"I was past the point of no return, you know? She knew that. You can't get a guy all worked up and then change your mind. She wanted it. She pretended she didn't, but I knew she wanted it. Yeah, we had sex. No big deal. She wasn't even good. She cried the whole time."

"She was fourteen years old, Miguel. She was a virgin." There was no longer any sympathy or understanding in Chris's voice. "All right. You can leave." She stood and ushered the young man out of the interrogation room and watched him slink down the hall. "Little fucker," she murmured. "I hope they cut your balls off in prison and shove them down your throat."

"Good work in there, as always," Finn said.

She turned and saw Hugh standing behind Finn. She dropped the file she was holding. "Oh, hi, Hugh. I didn't, um...hi." She bent to pick up the scattered papers.

"Hi, Chrissy. It's nice to see you again." Hugh helped her gather the papers while Finn watched, amused. "I came by to take Finn to lunch, but you're more than welcome to join us."

Chris took the papers and photographs from Hugh's hand and quickly stuffed them into the manila folder. "Oh. Um, no thanks. I have some surveillance this afternoon and I need to get on that. Thanks, though." She hurried away.

"Weird," Finn said. "You make her nervous, apparently."

"Huh. I guess so." He looked nonplussed. "Why

did she let that guy go? Why didn't she arrest him?"

"Oh, she will. We'll get an arrest warrant and have him in custody within a few days."

"Good. Sounds like that's where he needs to be." He turned back to his brother. "You ready? There's a new burger joint we can try."

Twenty minutes later they were seated in a bistro-style gourmet burger restaurant, orders placed, and a local brew in front of Hugh. "Mmm. This is great," he said as he took his first sip. "We'll have to come back when you're not on duty."

Finn sipped his iced tea and narrowed his eyes at his brother. "Yeah, we'll do that. Hey, I just found out Mel's birthday is tomorrow. I need a really nice place to take her."

"How about Antiquity in Old Town? It's got great atmosphere and the food's excellent."

"Great idea." Finn pulled out his phone and looked up the number. He was able to get a reservation for the next night. "Thanks. Now I need to figure out what to get her for a present. Any ideas?"

"Hmm. Probably jewelry. Something nice. You're in love with her, so maybe something with a heart. Unless she never wears jewelry. Then you're screwed."

"She wears some. Maybe I'll find a nice necklace. Good idea. Thanks."

"No problem. I was with Mel earlier, actually. We looked at her house and I gave her some ideas about what we could do. This is a great opportunity to build a two-car garage and maybe an extension. I could see a second floor above the garage easily and

I'd do it for a good price."

"That's totally up to her. It's her house." The two men were silent as the waiter delivered their meals.

"Well, I didn't know what your plans were once her house was habitable again. Are you going to ask her to stay with you and sell her house? Or is this living together a temporary arrangement?"

"We haven't really talked about it yet, but I certainly want to make it permanent. Shit." He threw his French fry down. "You were right, Hugh, although I hate to admit it out loud. When the right one comes along, you just know. I'm going to try to wait a decent amount of time, then I'm going to ask her to marry me."

"Told you so." Hugh grinned and took a huge bite of his burger. "Mel's great, and I'm happy for you. Don't wait too long."

They finished their lunch and sat enjoying another glass of tea. Hugh had opted for tea after one beer, saying he'd need a nap if he had two.

"How's the investigation going? Any idea who set the fire?"

"Not yet, and it's killing me. We've questioned a few witnesses and suspects related to other arson cases in the area, but nothing seems to be connected to Mel's case. I'm trying to track down the asshole she dated in college, but he's hard to find."

"Have you thought about looking into other relatives? Maybe there's someone who isn't happy with Mel getting the house, car, and all the money."

Finn stared at his brother. "Maybe you should be a detective. Money and sex are nearly always the prime motivations. Yeah, I got a list from her, and

I'll be checking into it this afternoon. It won't take long; there aren't many relatives to speak of. It's got to be someone who knows her and has a grudge, unless the message in the grass has nothing to do with the fire."

"Awfully coincidental timing if they're not connected," Hugh mused.

"Exactly." Finn knew it wasn't simply coincidence; the message and the fire were undoubtedly connected. His job was to figure out how.

Chapter Eighteen

Mel

She finished washing and folding the last of her clothes by noon. Finally, no more smoke smell! She put a stack of underwear in the top dresser drawer, which Finn had emptied for her. He'd had told her to make herself at home, so she had spent a few hours arranging things to her satisfaction, but careful not to move any more of his things than she must. He had been so sweet to let her move in and she didn't want to impose too much. Hugh had told her they could have her house repaired in a matter of a few months, including the addition he had proposed: a second floor with two additional bedrooms and a bathroom above a new two-car garage and a sunny little dining area off the kitchen. It would increase her square footage significantly and thus the resale value of the home. She wondered if Finn would consider selling his house so they could live in hers once it was finished. Then she realized she was thinking way too far ahead and firmly shut down those dreams. She had no idea whether he would be interested in continuing to live with her or not. She certainly hoped so, but she had no experience with knowing how a man felt about her. How could she tell? He said he loved her and told her so frequently, but did he have any hopes for a future with her? As he'd said the day before, they really knew very little about each other, especially about their hopes and dreams. She had no clue if he was interested in settling down at this point in his life. He was still pretty young, not yet thirty. He might want to be single for a few more years. Who knew? And how did she feel? Was she ready to settle down? She hadn't given much thought to it before she met Finn. Her dating life had been nearly non-existent, so it hadn't been on her radar. Her life had changed so much in such a short amount of time it was a wonder her head wasn't spinning.

She had dropped Fluff at the groomer earlier and figured she had about an hour before he would need to be picked up, a perfect amount of time to answer email and send in some design work she'd completed the day before. She was trying to decide if she was hungry enough to make a sandwich when Cara called with a last-minute lunch invitation.

"Come out and play, Mel! My summer is speeding by, and before you know it, I'll be back at work. Besides, a little birdie told me today is your birthday, so I want to take you to lunch."

She hadn't had anyone to make a fuss over her birthday in years, so she readily agreed. She called the groomer to see if she could leave Fluff a bit longer and was ready when Cara picked her up twenty minutes later.

"Izzy is meeting us there. I hope you like Thai food." The women caught up on nonessentials for several minutes while Cara drove. "How are you doing, Mel? I mean really doing? This has been a rough couple of weeks for you."

Mel thought for a moment; Cara's question had been sincere and she wanted to give an honest answer. She was quiet for so long, Cara gave her a side-long glance. "I'm thinking." She took a few more beats before answering. "I'm doing all right, all things considered. I'm still pretty freaked out and jumpy, but I'm dealing with it. It helps to not be alone all the time. It really helps. I can't tell you how much I appreciate your brother letting me stay with him."

"Yeah, well, I'm pretty sure he's not suffering any. You're good for him, Mel."

"Am I? Why?"

Cara laughed as she pulled the car into an empty spot at Thai Basil. "I don't know. Maybe because you're the type of woman who would ask why instead of basking in the compliment. You're real and I know you truly care about him."

"I love him," she said simply.

"I'm glad." Cara ushered her inside the restaurant and Izzy waved at them from a nearby table.

"Happy birthday, Mel!" Izzy stood and hugged her.

They were such a huggy family, but Mel didn't mind. She might even learn to instigate a few hugs of her own, at least with them. Cara and Izzy treated her as a friend, something she'd never had many of. She enjoyed watching their relationship, sisters but also friends, the only two girls in a large family of boys. They spent a lot of leisure time together, although both had other friends. They didn't always get along, having what Finn called frequent cat-fights, but they always made up quickly and moved on. Mel had no experience with that kind of easy relationship, and had been worried the first time she'd witnessed one of their spats. But they'd been laughing about it five minutes later and Mel had had to rethink everything she thought she knew about sisters.

They had their drinks and had placed their orders when Izzy reached under the table and pulled a slender pink gift bag out, handing it to Mel. "It's from Mom, Cara, and me."

"I didn't expect gifts," Mel objected, but she accepted the bag from Izzy.

"Birthdays only come once a year, so enjoy it," Cara said. "There's not nearly enough excuses for presents now that we're adults."

"Cara loves presents," Izzy said with a smile.

"I'm not ashamed to admit it. I love unexpected presents the best. Open it!" She was nearly dancing in her chair.

Mel laughed and reached into the bag for the tissue paper, then lifted out a bottle of white wine, a Sauvignon Blanc with a beautiful blue-green label. "Ooh, this looks wonderful."

"There's more!" Cara urged her to continue.

Mel reached in again and found a small envelope with a gift card inside for Ten Thousand Waves

Day Spa. The amount was fairly staggering, and Mel sputtered a thank-you, overcome by the thoughtfulness of Finn's family.

"We thought you and Finn could go for a romantic couples' massage. Mom and Dad have been and say it's great. It's out at the Tamaya Resort in Bernalillo," Izzy explained.

"Or you can go by yourself when you're sick of my brother," Cara added.

"Wow. This is amazing. Thank you." Mel was overcome and sniffed, feeling tears brim.

"Well, don't cry, for heaven's sake! You'll get me started and my mascara will run, so knock it off!" Cara scolded her with a laugh.

"Sorry. You caught me by surprise." Mel wondered whether they'd ever been so generous to any of Finn's other girlfriends; she had a feeling they hadn't, and wondered why she was different.

"Here, Mel. This isn't a present, but I told Hugh I'd bring them since I was having lunch with you." Izzy handed her a sample book. "It's counter top and cabinet finishes. It's nice that you at least get a kitchen update out of the fire. Do you think you and Finn will move into your house once it's finished? Hugh said you like the idea of the addition he drew up."

Mel had been wondering the same thing, but was shocked to hear it from Finn's sister. "Oh, I don't...I mean, I'm not...I have no idea." She finished lamely and took a rather large gulp of her iced tea.

Izzy smiled and covered Mel's hand with her own. "It's okay, Mel. It's all pretty new, huh? I don't mean to make you uncomfortable. It's just nice to see Finn so crazy about a girl, especially one like you. You're good for him."

"That's what Cara said earlier, but I don't know why you both think that."

"Well, it's not just us," Izzy explained patiently. "The rest of the family too. Finn has always had a regrettable tendency to choose women who were...well, not terribly gifted with kindness or compassion, let's say."

"Seamus seems to have the same tendency. I do not care for that Sloane-woman he's currently dating. She needs to go," Cara said as their food was delivered.

Izzy waited until the waitress had departed. "I completely agree. What do you think, Mel?"

"Well, I've only met her the once," she hedged.

"No excuses. Tell us what you think," commanded Cara.

"She's manipulative and a princess. I agree. She has to go."

Cara and Izzy both looked at her in surprise, then laughed. "Brava, Mel."

***

She fussed with her hair, wanting to look special for their date tonight. Finn had arrived home twenty minutes earlier and was in the shower. She gathered the top layer loosely with a sparkly hairclip, letting the remainder hang down her back. When Finn emerged from the bathroom, a towel slung low around his hips, she turned to watch, appreciating

246

his male beauty. He had a wonderful physique, well worth gazing at, with powerful shoulders and a sculpted chest that tapered to a narrow waist and hips.

"You keep that up and we'll miss our reservation." He sounded amused as he removed the towel, treating her to an uninhibited view of his firm backside as he fished in his drawer for a pair of boxers.

She giggled and turned back to the mirror. "I'm just enjoying the view."

"Well, it's yours to enjoy." He limped across the room to zip her dress, which had been hanging open, waiting for him. "I'm looking forward to unzipping this later," he murmured and kissed the spot where the ends met. "You look gorgeous, Mel."

"Thanks. I hope this dress is appropriate for where we're going." She'd bought it for an awards dinner her last year of college and hadn't worn it since. She'd been relieved to find it had escaped the smoke, bagged in plastic as it had been.

"It's perfect."

The restaurant was classy and intimate, and her eyes bulged a bit at the prices.

"Shh. This is a special occasion. Order what you want, love." He ordered a steak and a bottle of Pinot Noir for them to share. He waited for the sommelier to leave, then raised his glass. "Happy Birthday, Melanie. I love you," he said simply, then leaned over to kiss her softly. He reached into his jacket and handed her a small, flat velvet box with a gold ribbon.

She smiled and bit her lip as she opened the box to reveal a simple gold heart with a single sparkling diamond on a gold chain. "Oh, Finn. It's gorgeous and perfect." She'd never cared for large, flashy pieces and knew she'd feel comfortable wearing this. She removed it from the box and handed it to him while she held up her hair. He fastened it, kissing the back of her neck as he fastened the clasp. "I love it. Thank you, Finn. I love you too."

An amused 'ahem' broke them apart as the waiter placed their salads in front of them. The waiter redeemed himself by offering to take a picture of them with Mel's phone, however.

"All right. My turn," Finn announced when they were alone again.

"For what?"

"Tell me something about you that will surprise me."

"Oh. Hmmm, let me think." She took a sip of the delicious, rich wine while she thought. "Okay, how about this: I've never been out of the continental United States."

"Would you like to? I mean, do you like to travel?"

"I don't know. I like the thought of it. I have a passport and I'd love to get a stamp in it someday. Have you traveled outside the U.S.?"

He smiled and nodded. "Yeah, quite a bit, actually. One set of grandparents still live overseas, so we go see them every couple years. I haven't been in a while."

"That sounds amazing. You had a wonderful childhood, didn't you?"

"I did. I never realized how wonderful, of course, until I grew up. My parents would sometimes send one or two of us at a time to visit the grands, probably to get us out of their hair." He laughed as he remembered. "Hugh and I had a memorable summer in Ireland when I was fourteen and he was nineteen."

"I'm betting it involved pretty Irish girls."

"Let's just say Hugh should never have been entrusted with my safety in a foreign country. It was like a smorgasbord of girls for him."

"But not for you?" She raised her eyebrows, disbelieving.

"Well," he shrugged. "I was pretty young."

She decided to let it go, not wanting to delve too deeply into his youthful escapades. "How come Hugh isn't married? Is there a tragic love story or something? Or does he not want to settle down?"

"No, there's nothing terribly tragic; at least I don't think so. He had a long-term girlfriend and we all thought they'd get married eventually, but they broke up about a year ago. I don't know why, really. Hugh has never wanted to talk about it." He turned his attention toward his salad for a few moments. "What about you, Mel? What do you think about marriage? What about kids?"

She set her wine glass on the table carefully. "I didn't bring it up to force a conversation about marriage, Finn. I'm sorry." She felt bad for making him think she wanted him to ask.

He took her hand and raised it to his lips. "Mel, sweetheart. I'm way too clueless to pick up on stuff like that. I didn't even think of it. I just really want to know. We're living together and I know it's probably sooner than either of us was really ready for, but I like it. A lot. I'm not playing any games here. I'll be honest and come right out and tell you I want to get married, settle down, and have a few kids. I want it to be with the right woman, of course, but I think I may be looking at her. I hope that's okay, and doesn't scare you."

"It depends. How many is 'a few'?" She raised her eyebrow as she asked.

He chuckled appreciatively. "I don't know. Three or four maybe. Six is a bit much."

"I'll say. I don't know how your parents managed."

"You haven't answered my question, Mel."

"You're right. Okay. It does scare me a little bit, but only because it seems like a dream I put away a long time ago. I guess I'm afraid to hope." She couldn't meet his gaze.

"Okay, I can work with that."

***

"Finn, have you seen CJ?" Mel returned to their bedroom after escorting Fluff outside for his final potty call before bed. "She's usually here long before this."

He set aside the book he'd been reading and looked at her. "No. Last time I saw her was at breakfast. I'm sure she'll turn up. She probably met a guy."

Mel frowned, but slid into the bed next to him. "Probably. I'm a little worried, though."

"Come here. I bet I can get your mind off the cat."

Chapter Nineteen

Finn

"All right. This should do it. Let's see how it feels." Jon finished fastening the new walking boot around Finn's ankle and stood.

Finn rose and stepped out—sans crutches. "It feels great." He took a few turns around the therapy workout space, loving the freedom. "How long until I can ditch this boot?"

"One step at a time—literally." Jon laughed at his own joke. "Six weeks should suffice, as long as you don't overdo it. How's that pretty girlfriend?"

"She's amazing. She's also in the waiting room, so behave. In fact, you don't need to walk me out."

Jon laughed again. "Fine, fine. I see how it is. You don't want to take any chances she'll throw you over for me. I get it."

Finn rolled his eyes. "Yeah, that must be it. Hey, speaking of my girlfriend, am I cleared to...you know, what we talked about last time?"

"I have no idea what you mean." Jon's

expression was pure innocence.

Finn punched him on the upper arm.

"Ow! I see you haven't been neglecting your upper body workouts. Yes, you're cleared to resume having all kinds of sex in any position you like. Pay attention to your body. If something hurts, don't do it."

"Good. Don't bring this up to Mel," he warned, seeing the therapist was walking him out anyway. "I don't want you embarrassing her."

Jon smirked, but didn't say anything about sex to her. He simply told her to make sure Finn rested in the evenings after work and kept taking anti-inflammatories at bedtime.

On the way to the car, he took her hand, interlocking their fingers, and held it while they walked. "I've been wanting to do this for a long time."

She smiled up at him, that shy smile he loved and didn't see often enough. "It's nice."

"Mel, let's take a weekend away, just the two of us. We can stay in a bed-and-breakfast somewhere, maybe Colorado. How does that sound?" He wanted to find a way to erase the worry from her eyes, to help her relax and be at peace for a few days without the constant nag of the threats hanging over their heads.

"Sure. That sounds great." She squeezed his hand lightly. "Do you have time for lunch or do you need to get back to the precinct?"

"I've got time for lunch."

***

Chris was at her desk when Finn walked into the precinct an hour later. "Look at you! No more crutches, huh?"

"Finally! What are you working on?"

"I'm looking at your research for Mel's case. Good job with her relatives; they look like a dead end, huh?" She passed him the papers from the file she'd been reading.

"Yeah. There's not that many of them, and none even had a clue Karen had left her house and money to Mel. God, it must be a trip to not have a bunch of relatives. I've got more cousins than I can count." He flipped through the pages, wishing something would pop out at him.

"What about the neighbors? Where's the file?"

Finn sat at his desk, thankful for the new ease in maneuvering without his crutches, and reached into a bottom drawer. "Here. I didn't find anything worth pursuing."

She accepted the file and flipped through the pages slowly. "This guy between you and Mel, Carl Taylor? He's got a couple priors."

"Yeah, but for protests back in the sixties. I really don't think he's trying to kill Mel. He helped me save her life, if you remember. Plus, what possible motive could he have?"

"I don't know, but we'll look into those arrests all the same. Now what about this Lena Torrance across the street? Boy, that sounds like a stripper name, huh?"

Finn chuckled. Chris could be frustrating, but she was thorough, which he admired. "There's not much on her at all, which I don't like. It's like she didn't exist before moving in across the street. She told Mel she'd been through a messy divorce, so maybe she's going by her maiden name or something." He was silent for a moment, remembering how he had reacted to her the first time they'd met. There was something about her— something niggling in the back of his mind—but he couldn't quite reach it.

"Well, it probably doesn't matter since she moved in after Mel started feeling like she was being followed and after her house was broken into. All the same, I'll keep digging. I like to be—"

"Thorough. Yeah, I know." He leaned back in his seat. "I appreciate all your time and effort on this, Chris. It means a lot to me and to Mel."

She smiled and he was struck by how pretty she was; he'd never really noticed before, maybe because she was usually so stern. "No problem. I'm just glad to have my partner back. I was barely starting to get used to you when you got hit by that car. I sure wish you could remember something about it. I'd love to get the asshole who did this to you." She gestured to his ankle.

"Me too."

***

Two days later CJ still hadn't returned and he knew Mel was starting to freak out. She worried the cat had been hit by a car and lay dying somewhere. Finn figured the cat had simply found greener pastures and moved on, although he didn't mention his theory to Mel.

"Sweetheart, you had her microchipped and your phone number is on her tag. That's all we can do."

"No, Finn, it's not. I'll put an ad on craigslist today and post flyers around the neighborhood." She looked at him as if she found his lack of interest in their cat a serious character flaw.

"And I will help you put those flyers up after work today." He backpedaled quickly, wanting to remain in her good graces.

She rolled her eyes at him across the breakfast table, but smiled crookedly. "Thanks. I know I'm being silly."

"No, you're being a responsible pet owner and it's admirable and adorable." He stood and leaned down to kiss her. "I'll see you tonight."

His day seemed to crawl by; now that he was more mobile, sitting behind a desk was really starting to bug him. He wanted to be out with Chris, finding witnesses, checking out crime scenes; even boring surveillance would be better than this. Argh! He stood and walked across the crowded precinct room for a cup of what passed for coffee here, glad he could at least carry his own cup now. The only excitement today had been when Carl Taylor came in to talk to one of the detectives officially running the investigation. Finn had listened in and discovered that Carl had been quite the anti-war protestor back in the day, with several arrests and a felony conviction for assaulting an officer.

"It was 1968 and my older brother got killed over there in 'Nam. You better believe I was goddamn protesting! The cops started beating the shit out of us with bats and throwing tear gas. I was

256

one of hundreds arrested. I haven't been in trouble since, and I didn't have nothin' to do with setting that sweet little girl's house on fire! Why would I do something like that? She's been nothin' but nice to me, bringing that little dog by to visit me of a morning."

Finn frowned; he hadn't realized Mel had done that. He stared at the elderly man on the other side of the glass, intrigued by the past he referred to. It was too easy to look at the older members of society and forget they were once young. This man had an entire life story to tell, if only someone would sit still long enough to listen. It appeared Mel was one of the rare few willing to take the time to do just that.

"Mr. Taylor." The detective leaned forward, hands clasped on the tabletop. "Can you tell me how you came to be in Ms. Blythe's house the night of the fire?"

"There wasn't nothin' suspicious about it, if that's what you're thinking. That stray cat got in somehow and woke me up. It wouldn't leave me alone, and I got the message I should follow it. Don't ask me how. I just knew. I saw the fire once I got outside and figured Melanie was stuck inside, so I went in. The door was open and that cop was already there, but he couldn't lift her because of his crutches. I may be old, but I could still carry that little girl." He paused for breath, then continued. "I want to talk to that cop what lives next door. You ask me, none of this happened until she started seeing that damn cop. Seems to me he probably has more enemies than she ever could. Nothing good comes of getting too cozy with cops."

Finn thought Mr. Taylor had a point—his antipathy for police aside. It couldn't hurt to look into any recent parolees from his past cases when he was in uniform. Over the course of his career, he'd put away some truly nasty characters. Was it too much of a stretch to think one of them might be out to get revenge on him through his girlfriend? "Shit. The cranky old codger may be on to something," he muttered as he made a beeline for his computer. He spent the next several hours looking into the possibilities.

Mel had texted to let him know she was out with Cara for an impromptu girls' night, so he accepted Chris's invitation for a drink on the way home. It had been months since he'd been out for a beer after work with his fellow agents and it felt great, like he was finally getting his life back. The bar was crowded with off duty police officers, paramedics, and firemen/women, along with the usual crowd of badge bunnies trying to arrange a hook up. Chris's scowl stopped two of them in their tracks and they were left alone to enjoy their beers in peace. As Finn watched them skulk away, something nagged at the fringes of his memory, but he couldn't quite reach it. He sighed and took a large gulp of beer.

He refused a second drink, anxious to get home even though he knew Mel wasn't there. He couldn't be happier Mel and Cara were becoming close friends. It would make everything so much simpler later when he made her a permanent member of the family. He felt a huge grin creeping across his face as he let himself into the dark house. He had thought he'd be nervous about asking a woman to marry him, and he was, but he knew in his soul Mel was the one for him. If he could just get this damned investigation heading in the right direction! It was maddening, and he felt powerless to protect the woman he loved.

Mel's little dog greeted him, dancing around his feet and yipping for his dinner. *Little idiot.* He went straight to the kitchen rather than heading to his bedroom to change and put his gun away. He'd barely had a chance to feed Fluff and grab a bottle of water when a knock on the front door surprised him.

"Hi, Finn. It's Lena, remember?"

He remembered, of course. He'd been avoiding her for weeks every time she showed up to visit with Mel. "Hello, Lena. What can I do for you?"

"It's about your cat. I think she may be stuck in my crawlspace, but I can't reach her. Can you come over? I'll bet she comes to you."

Well, if he couldn't solve the case, he could at least get Mel's cat back for her. He pictured her face when she came in later and saw CJ curled up in the chair in their bedroom. Spending a few minutes with their annoying neighbor was a small price to pay. "Let's go."

He followed her inside her house, surprised to see she was still living amongst boxes with very little furniture. "Where's the access to the crawlspace?"

"It's back here in the guest bedroom." She opened the door to a bedroom and stood aside for him to enter.

He could hear weak mewls coming from inside and hurried to rescue the cat. The room was empty, save for a desk holding a computer monitor and a small pet crate in the corner. There was some kind of poor quality pornography with no sound playing on the monitor—what the hell?—and the mewls were issuing from the crate. Alarm bells began going off in his head. He was about to cross to look into the crate, sure it was CJ, when something on the monitor caught his attention and he leaned in for a closer look. The way the woman's hair rippled as she moved was too familiar. He wasn't looking at low budget pornography. He was looking at security camera video of himself and Mel having sex. He straightened, reaching for his gun, still in his hip holster. "What the fu—"

Pain exploded from the back of his head as bright, white light filled his field of vision. Then blackness engulfed him.

Chapter Twenty

Mel

It was close to eleven o'clock when Mel let herself in; she, Cara, and Izzy had had fun at dinner and the movie, and had gone out for a drink afterward. She'd planned to be home earlier, but Cara and Izzy had razzed her about spending all her time with their brother.

"Absence makes the heart grow fonder, Mel. It'll do him good to miss you," Izzy had said. "Besides, Janey is staying the night with my parents, so I don't have to be home early. You wouldn't want to be responsible for ruining my first kid-free night in over a month, would you?"

"Yeah, you need to stop pandering to Finn. Make him work for it, Mel," Cara had added, laughing a bit tipsily.

"Why do I feel like I'm in middle school and my friends are trying to make me give in to peer pressure?" But she'd acquiesced to their demands to stay out longer, of course. She'd texted Finn to tell him not to expect her until later, but he hadn't responded, which wasn't like him. She'd managed to shove aside her momentary concern and focus on having fun with her friends. She'd rarely had friends to stay out late with, and she was determined to enjoy it. *I'll deal with Finn later. Surely he isn't mad at me for staying out late?* It didn't seem like something he would do, but maybe she didn't know him as well as she thought. She pushed the worry to the back of her mind and let Cara lead her to the dance floor.

Finally home, she retrieved her key from her purse and inserted it in the lock, only to discover the front door was unlocked, which was also very unlike her safety-conscious cop boyfriend. "Finn? Honey?" She locked it behind her and set her purse on the entry table. "Finn?" All the lights were on, but he was not in sight, and the house had a silent, empty feel. Fluff scurried to greet her, but CJ was still nowhere in sight. She was surprised at how much she missed and worried about the stray cat. She walked back to the bedroom, thinking Finn might have gone to bed and left the house lights on for her. The bedroom was dark; when she flipped the lights on she saw the bed still made from that morning. "Finn?" She backtracked through the house, checking all the rooms while her stomach cramped with fear. Where could he be? *All right, calm down! He's a grown man and a cop. He can certainly take care of himself. You're nervous because of the fire and all the rest of the crap that's been happening. Finn is fine.* She made herself walk to her purse to retrieve her phone. She called, left a message when he didn't answer, then sent a series of texts, each more tense than the last.

Mel: Honey, where R U?

Mel: Are you mad at me? Please answer. I'm sorry. Let's talk.

Mel: Finn!

Each message was delivered; none were read. It appeared his phone was off and he didn't want to be reached. She slammed her phone on the entry table, halfway between worry and anger. Ugh! When she got hold of him she was going to rip him a new one! She never thought he'd be so childish simply because he was in a snit over her staying out late. Her anger lasted all of ten minutes before she realized she didn't care whether he was mad or not. She had to find him. She retrieved her phone and dialed the person she thought most likely to know his current location.

"Hugh? Hi, it's Mel. Is Finn with you?" She struggled to keep her tone calm and collected, not wanting to alarm him. "Well, do you know where he is? No, that's okay. I'm sure he's fine. Thanks." She hung up and went to sit on the sofa, wondering who else to call. She worked her way through his other brothers and his parents, glad Finn had their numbers posted on the refrigerator. She checked with Cara and Izzy, as well, although they'd been with her all evening. No one knew where he was, nor did they seem terribly concerned. She tried to adopt their attitude, with little success. Although she knew it was silly since he couldn't drive yet, she checked the garage to see if his Jeep was still there. It was, of course. God, where could he be? She sank onto the sofa, phone in hand, thinking he must be out with friends she didn't know. She had no idea what other friends he had; he'd never mentioned any others in the brief time they'd been dating. She texted—again—but there was still no answer. She wanted to start calling hospitals, but realized it was a bit precipitous and he'd definitely be embarrassed when he found out. So instead, she turned on the television and watched a couple late night talk shows. She was probably overreacting. He'd walk in soon and then they could have it out.

She jerked awake when her phone buzzed. *Finally.* But the text was from Hugh. She returned the text, telling him Finn still wasn't home; her phone rang seconds after she pressed 'send.'

"Mel, this isn't like him. Something's wrong. I'm going to call Chrissy. Stay put until we get there, okay?"

"Yeah, fine. Thanks, Hugh." She hung up and began pacing. It was now crystal clear Finn was in trouble and she was officially panicked. She had to do something, but what? She couldn't just sit—or stand—there and wait. The man she loved was missing, most likely in danger, goddamn it! She had finally found the love of her life and nobody was going to take him from her! But what could she do? *The neighbors.* She didn't care how late it was; she'd pound on their doors until they woke up and answered. She'd still be able to see when Hugh and

Chris arrived, so she wouldn't exactly be breaking her word to Hugh, either. She paused, hand on the front door knob, and turned back to the bedroom. *I should take a gun.* She didn't stop to examine the urge, but simply trusted her instincts. She punched the code and opened the gun safe, retrieving Finn's personal 9-millimeter handgun while noting his service weapon was missing. So he hadn't had time to put it back before he went...wherever. It made her feel slightly better to know he had his gun with him. She checked to make sure the one she held was loaded and the safety was engaged. *This is insane, Melanie! What are you thinking? You hate guns!* She silenced those thoughts as she realized she would do whatever it took to help Finn. She shoved the gun in the back waistband of her jeans as she'd seen Finn do when he didn't have his holster, feeling slightly ridiculous, but resolved. She was more likely to shoot her own ass off before she was able to even pull the gun on anyone. *Why am I even considering this? The likelihood of me running into anything dangerous is about a million to one. I'm simply going to wake up the neighbors and find out if they've seen Finn.* But she took the gun with her anyway.

She shut Fluff inside and jogged next door to ring the doorbell repeatedly. "Mr. Taylor? Carl? It's Mel! Please answer the door!" She saw lights go on and a shadowy figure approaching.

"What's the matter? What's wrong?" He tied the belt of a ratty terry cloth robe as he groused the words at her.

"Finn is missing, and I can't get hold of him on

his phone, and it's been hours! Have you seen him?" She hoped he could understand her rushed, frantic speech.

"I seen him get dropped off by that lady cop earlier."

"What time was that? Do you remember?" She reached to grab his arm.

"It was around seven, I guess. He must've gone somewhere else after that."

"Did you see him leave the house? Please, Carl! Did you see anything? I have to find him!"

"I'm sorry, Melanie. I was fixing my supper and I didn't see anything."

She could only nod; the tears she'd managed to keep at bay all evening were forcing their way out. "Thanks." She choked the words out and turned to leave.

"You want me to come over and wait with you?"

She shook her head. "No. His brother and partner are on their way. I'm going to go ask Lena if she saw anything. Thank you, Carl."

She wiped her eyes and sniffed; this was no time to get all weepy. It wouldn't help Finn. *Please, God, please let him just be mad at me and have gone somewhere to cool off.* She would give everything she owned if it turned out to be something as simple as a fight. She knocked on Lena's door and rang the doorbell repeatedly. She was way beyond polite societal norms. "Lena! Open up, please! It's Mel!"

***

266

Finn

My head is killing me! Where the hell am I?
These were Finn's first thoughts as he pried his
eyelids open. He tried to lift his arm to his sore
head, but quickly realized he was restrained
somehow. *Shit. Am I in the hospital again? Another
accident?* He managed to get his eyelids to
cooperate and both lift at the same time. He
cautiously looked around and realized he was lying
on carpet, his hands tied behind his back. *Nope. Not
the hospital. This is not good.* He tried to move his
legs and saw they were tied together as well. *This
keeps getting better and better. Okay, think! What
happened?* He shut his eyes again and the events
earlier in the evening slowly trickled back into his
mind. Going out for a drink with Chris. Mel not
home. Lena stopping by—Lena! That bitch! She did
this! But why? She had lured him over to her house
with a story about CJ being stuck in the crawlspace.
As he thought about CJ, he realized the air in the
room was heavy with cat pee ammonia. "CJ?" The
words came out as a croak and he had to try again.
He was rewarded with a feeble 'mew' and craned
his head around to see the pet crate in the corner.
Poor thing. He wondered if she'd been given any
food or water. Then he remembered the video. He
sat up and looked around for the desk. The video
was still playing, apparently on a loop.

"That should have been me."

He jumped, startled, and swept his head around
to see Lena leaning against the door frame. "Lena!
What the fuck is this about? Untie me!" How in the

hell did she get the jump on him? He was a trained police officer, for Christ's sake! God, this was embarrassing.

"Oh, I don't think so, Finn." She pushed away from the door and crossed the room, squatting down beside him. "Oh, this is my favorite part." She pointed at the monitor. "Oh, yeah. That's what I'm talking about. I don't think Mel was expecting that last move, do you? You've got more stamina than I would have expected, especially considering your recent health issues. Huh." She looked thoughtful.

"That's private!" He growled the words through gritted teeth. "How the hell did you get that?" He clenched his fists, wishing he could get them free. He'd never hit a woman in his life, but he'd gladly make Lena the first.

"A small motion-activated camera. I got it on Amazon. They really do have everything." She winked at him. "I hid it on the bookshelf in your bedroom a few days ago. Mel is far too trusting." Her smile didn't begin to reach her eyes. "You don't even remember me, do you?"

He was still trying to process her admission of planting a video camera in his bedroom. "Wait, what?"

"I guess I shouldn't blame you. You were pretty drunk that night. Too bad your partner pulled you away so soon. We could have had a good time."

He cast about in his memory, desperate to remember what she was talking about. The last time he'd been really drunk had been the night he'd made detective. Oh, God. "That night, about six months ago, at The Dirty Bourbon? That was you? I thought her name was Raylynn or something—"

"It's Raylene! God, you really don't remember, even when I'm staring you in the face! You think you're so much better than me, don't you?" Her eyes were wild and her face flushed with rage.

This woman is fucking insane! The badge bunny he'd been kissing and groping—to his everlasting shame—was a brunette. He searched her face, trying to picture her with dark hair. It didn't help. He hadn't really been terribly concerned with her face that night. "I'm sorry, Lena. I was drunk. I had just made detective and—"

"Shut the fuck up!" She vaulted to her feet, kicking his ankle as she stood. The pain was excruciating, even through his walking boot. "I was back at the bar the next week and you completely brushed me off! Nobody brushes me off." Now she was seething, her words hissing out between tight lips. "I say when it's over! Who the fuck do you think you are?"

Correction: dangerously fucking insane! Shit! "Hey, let's dial this down, okay? This is all a misunderstanding, Lena. I had a girlfriend when I met you. Not Mel, but another woman. I had no right to be kissing anyone but her. I screwed up and I'm sorry. It was never about you—"

"And that's supposed to make it all better, right? I'm supposed to forget it? I don't think so, Finn. You led me on, made me think we had something special."

He had no idea how she got *that* out of their brief encounter, but he did his best not to let it show in his face. He needed to try to calm her down, not fire

269

her up any more. He was usually fairly good at talking suspects down.

"Nobody pushes me away! Do you understand? I decide when it's over!" She knelt down beside him again and ran her fingers through his hair. "Oh, Finn. We could have been so good together." She leaned in and kissed him.

He felt the gorge rising in his throat and could not force himself to kiss her back. It went against everything in him simply to hold his lips still against hers.

She ended by biting him, drawing blood. She laughed as she stood. "I was so mad at you! I followed you after work and found out where you live. I watched you for weeks, trying to decide what I should do. Then you were out running one morning, listening to your music like you didn't have a care in the world. You're a selfish bastard, you know that?"

He was beginning to get the picture. His stomach clenched as he began to comprehend what she was saying. This had never been about Mel. It was about him, always. Lena was behind everything—he'd bet his last dollar on it—and it was about him. "Did you hit me with your car, Lena?"

She nodded, a faraway look on her face. "I didn't plan it. You were running, totally oblivious that I was there, right behind you. 'I could just step on the accelerator,' I thought. 'Wouldn't that show him?' So I did. I pressed down on the gas and closed my eyes when I heard the thud. I was really surprised when I heard you were still alive. I thought for sure I killed you."

"You nearly did. I was in a coma for ten days."

"Hmm. It would have been better if you'd died." She wandered around the room, her arms clasped behind her back. "Maybe I could have moved on."

"The fire. That was you, wasn't it?"

"Yes. And the words in her yard. I thought that was an especially nice touch. When I found out you were still alive and this house was for rent, I thought I'd been given another chance. I thought we were meant to be. I heard your girlfriend dumped you, and I thought we could finally be together. But that little slut, Melanie, got to you first."

His teeth clenched when she talked about Mel, but he remained silent. It wouldn't help to defend the woman he loved at this moment.

"I still don't understand how my plan failed. I put the lorazepam in the open wine bottle on her counter. Then all I had to do was keep an eye on her and wait for her to drink the rest of it. Did you know she never closes her kitchen curtains? She got a little sloppy with your sister that night and then couldn't resist one more glass before bed. I really hate it when girls can't hold their booze, don't you? I pictured her roasting in her bed and me comforting you afterward. Goddamn cat!" She exploded with her last words and crossed the room to kick poor CJ's crate repeatedly. "Well, I really screwed that one up. She moved in with you. The very last thing I wanted. Boy, it sure didn't take long before you two were screwing your brains out, huh? I'm so much better than her, Finn, but you'll never find out. I finally realized something: you're never going to pick me, are you? There will always be someone

271

else, because you're a manwhore, Finn."

He said nothing. She clearly wasn't rational, so nothing he said could possibly help.

"Well," she said briskly. "Enough of this. If I can't have you, I'm going to make sure no one can." She walked across the room and picked up a gun—his gun—from the desk. She expertly clicked off the safety and chambered a round before leveling it at his chest.

God, she had his gun too? They were going to send him back to the academy after this. If he was still around. *Shit, shit, shit.* "Lena, you don't want to do this." He strove for a calm he was far from feeling.

She smiled tightly. "Sure I do." Her smile faltered as they heard the doorbell ring repeatedly, followed by pounding and Mel's voice calling Lena. "Well, this is interesting. You say one word, make any kind of noise, and I'll kill her. Do you understand? I'll shoot her in the face."

He nodded, terror filling every corner of his soul.

Lena turned and left him on the floor of the bedroom.

Chapter Twenty-One

Mel

Where was she? Please let her be home! Mel pounded harder on the front door and rang the doorbell again. "Lena! Please!"

The porch lights flickered on and Lena opened the door slightly. "Mel? What on earth is wrong?"

"Oh, Lena! I can't find Finn, and I'm afraid something has happened! Have you seen him?"

"No, I haven't seen him all day. I'm sorry."

Mel narrowed her eyes, struck by something odd in Lena's tone. "Are you sure? Did you see him get dropped off earlier by his partner?"

Lena smiled, a tight kind of smile, which didn't reach her eyes. "I said I haven't seen him, Mel. I can't help you. I have to go."

Mel took a step back, appalled by the woman's meanness. She'd always been so nice before. Why would she act this way when Mel really needed her? She was desperate to find Finn and Lena was acting weird. The hair on the back of her neck stood up as

273

she watched her neighbor glare at her from the tiny wedge of space between the door and frame. Why didn't she open it all the way? She made it abundantly clear Mel was not welcome. It was beyond strange and Mel was suddenly certain Lena was hiding something, but a lifetime of avoiding conflict had her backing away and stepping off the porch. Lena was acting strange, but maybe she had a guy over or something and wanted to get back to him. "Fine, Lena. I can see you're busy." She turned to go, deciding she'd tell Chris about this and let her figure it out. It was probably nothing, but it felt wrong. She made it to the bottom step.

"You had to make this difficult, didn't you, Mel?"

She turned back around. Lena had opened the door and walked to the edge of the porch; she held a lethal-looking black gun in her hands, pointed straight at Mel.

"Come in, Mel. I just remembered I did see Finn. I'm sure you'd like to see him too."

Oh, God! Please don't let him be dead! Mel prayed silently as she passed Lena and walked into the house. She also prayed Lena wouldn't be able to tell she had Finn's gun stuffed into her pants. It was covered by the tunic she wore, and she desperately hoped it wasn't sticking out. She had no clue what she'd do with it, but if she got a chance, she was sure she could figure something out.

"Second bedroom on the right," Lena said. "Finn, darling, look who showed up." She pushed Mel into the room hard enough that she stumbled and fell.

"Mel! God, get out of here!" Finn yelled from where he lay.

"Oh, she's not going anywhere." Lena lounged against the doorjamb, the gun held loosely in her hand.

Mel crawled across the room to Finn, angling her body slightly behind his as she leaned over him and took his face in her hands. "Are you okay?" She noticed the blood dried near his hairline and brushed her thumb slightly over his bloody, swollen lip. "What did she do to you?"

"Mel, I'm so sorry." Finn's face creased with worry and sorrow.

"This is charming, really," Lena drawled. "But we need to move things along. I do think little Melanie is confused, so why don't you tell her what's going on, Finn? Then she can watch you die." Lena spoke as if it were a completely rational menu of events.

"Or not." Mel reached into her waistband for the gun, pulling it out as she vaulted to her feet and stepped over Finn. "I don't really give a flying fuck what's going on, Lena." She pointed the gun straight at Lena's heart as she clicked the safety off with her thumb. She had no idea how, but a steely calm descended as she held the gun; not even the slightest of tremors marred her position. "You're going to let us go."

Lena chuckled. "She's not quite as meek and mousy as I thought, Finn. I guess it should come as no surprise, seeing what a wildcat she can be in the sack." She jerked her chin toward the desk with the computer monitor.

Mel spared a quick glance toward the desk, then did a literal double-take when she saw what it was. "Is that…us? Finn?"

"Babe, it doesn't matter. Keep that gun steady, okay?"

She raised the gun, which had dipped as she stared at the video. "What's going on here? Why do you have that video?" She thought furiously, trying to put the pieces together. "You're the one who's been stalking me?" She hurled the words at Lena. Against her will, she needed to know what this was about.

"Not so much stalking *you*. It's always been about Finn. He toyed with me, you see. I don't like that. We had a good thing going until you came along, Melanie. We could have been happy together if you hadn't shown up."

What on earth was she talking about? Did she and Finn know each other? God, had they dated? Finn would have told her, wouldn't he?

"Don't listen to her, Mel. She's lying to mess with you. We didn't have anything going. I met her once, at a bar. I was drunk." Finn had managed to work himself into a sitting position.

Oh, my God. "Finn, did you and she…?" She couldn't finish the awful question.

"No! I swear we didn't!"

"Of course we did!" Lena laughed. "Well, you'll never know for sure, huh? What are you going to do, Mel? Can you shoot me before I shoot him?"

"Let us go, Lena. We can forget all about this if you just let us walk out of here." Finn's voice was soothing.

"Do you think I'm stupid?" Lena yelled, little flecks of spittle flying out of her mouth. "You'll just let me walk away? We'll forget all about this?"

"I love him, Lena. Please." Mel wasn't above begging. She couldn't see a good way for this situation to end. Lena was right: if she fired at Lena, Lena would certainly shoot Finn. There was no way to keep him safe. A giant sob bubbled up as she realized the hopelessness of their situation.

Lena smirked as she watched Mel try not to cry. "Good. I wouldn't want this to be too easy for either one of you."

Mel swallowed as she steadied the gun again. "I don't see how this ends in your favor, either. Looks to me like I may be the only one walking out of here tonight. I've been practicing a lot lately, and Finn says I'm a great shot. Want to see if I can put a bullet in your heart before you can shoot Finn?" It was a total bluff; they'd gone exactly once to the shooting range and she was terrible.

"Tell her, Finn! Tell her now or I start shooting! Tell her about us!" Lena ranted from the doorway.

"Fine," he growled. "Keep that gun steady, babe, okay? Lena likes cops. She likes to hang out in places cops hang out, hoping to hook up with them. I ran into her the night I made detective at a bar a lot of the guys in my precinct like to frequent. I got drunk and started kissing her. My partner pulled me away before it could go very far. I've never messed with badge bunnies before or since. Apparently, Lena can't take no for an answer."

"Shut up!" Lena screamed the words at him. "That's not what happened! He led me on! He owes me!"

"That's what this is all about? Are you kidding me?" She stared at the woman. "You got rejected and you're going to kill him because of it? You tried to kill me too, just because a guy rejected you?" Mel couldn't believe what she was hearing. People simply didn't do that, did they?

"Mel, sweetheart, don't antagonize her," Finn warned. "She's the one who ran me over. She will do what she says. She's not bluffing."

"That's right." Lena smiled delightedly. "I do what I say. And I don't get rejected! I do the rejecting! When I want someone, I get them. I say when we're done!"

"You're batshit crazy, Lena! That's not how the world works! You seriously need to get over yourself!"

"Mel, please," Finn begged.

"Shut up!" Lena screamed the words at Mel as she swung the gun toward her.

It was what Mel had been banking on; she'd been desperate to get Lena to move the gun away from Finn. She closed her eyes and squeezed the trigger. Nothing happened. From over her right shoulder she felt more than heard an explosion of glass and Lena dropped where she stood, blood blossoming on the right side of her chest.

Finn dove awkwardly across the room, wriggling until he could reach with his feet to kick the gun away from Lena, then placed himself between her and Mel. Seconds later, Chris burst through the bedroom doorway followed swiftly by Hugh. Chris went straight to Lena, moving the gun further away and feeling for a pulse. Then she crossed to where Mel was standing and removed Finn's nine-millimeter from her limp hand. She retrieved her cell phone from her back pocket and Mel heard her call the incident in, using some incomprehensible code. Hugh knelt behind Finn, cursing as he attempted to untie the knotted ropes Lena had used to restrain him. He reached into his pocket and Mel watched dumbly as he pulled out a pocketknife and sliced through Finn's bonds. He helped his brother stand, asking brusquely if he was okay.

"I'm fine." Finn pushed his way past Hugh and pulled Mel into his arms. He held her tightly, crooning to her softly.

She thought she might be in shock; she couldn't make her arms reach around his waist. She leaned against his chest, numb and cold. His warmth seeped into her slowly, finally bringing some feeling back to her limbs. She pressed closer, needing to be held even more closely. "Is she dead?"

She felt him shake his head. "Chris called for an ambulance. You didn't shoot her, sweetheart."

"I know. I pulled the trigger, but nothing happened. I tried to shoot her so she wouldn't shoot you. I meant to shoot her."

"You didn't chamber a round."

"Oh."

"It's okay. It's over. Let's get you out of here."

***

279

Finn

He adjusted his foot slightly, causing the ice pack to slip from the coffee table and on to the floor. "Dammit." He muttered the words so as not to wake Mel, who was curled against his side and had finally fallen asleep. CJ, freshly bathed—much against her will—was wedged between them. She had been given water during her captivity, but had returned home starving and filthy. He held another ice pack against the giant lump on the back of his head.

"I got it." Hugh walked in from the kitchen carrying a steaming mug. "Here you go, Chrissy." He handed her the mug and leaned over to replace the ice pack.

"Thanks," Finn said. "I hate to wake her. So what did they say?" He asked the last question of Chris, who had been outside speaking to their captain until a few minutes before.

"Standard paid administrative leave while they investigate. They took my gun." She sat back with a sigh and sipped the tea Hugh had prepared. "Thanks for the tea. I needed it."

"That's bullshit! You saved Mel's and Finn's lives," Hugh hissed, trying not to wake Mel. "And you're welcome."

Chris flashed a tired smile at him. "It's okay, Hugh. They have to do it. I'll be back to work soon enough. A few days off will be good for me."

"How's Lena?" Finn asked.

"Still in surgery."

They fell silent, exhausted emotionally and

physically by the events of the night. Finally, Hugh heaved himself out of his chair. "You got anything stronger than tea? I could sure use a drink."

"There's a bottle of scotch in the pantry."

Hugh disappeared, returning moments later with the half-empty bottle and three glasses. He poured two fingers for each of them and handed the glasses around. "*Sláinte.*" He offered the toast as he raised his glass.

Finn simply grunted and drank deeply. *God, what a night.* Mel stirred and woke, yawning widely. He offered her his glass, kissing her hair while she took a small sip.

She sipped cautiously and coughed as she swallowed the strong liquor. "How's your ankle?" Her voice was rough with sleep and the whiskey.

"Sore. I'll have to have it checked tomorrow. If that crazy bitch puts me back on crutches, I'm gonna be pissed." The others chuckled softly and it lightened the heavy mood, as he'd intended. They'd already worn themselves out discussing what had happened in Lena's house.

"How did you and Hugh know where we were?" Mel asked Chris.

"Your neighbor, Mr. Taylor. He was waiting for us. He watched you go into Lena's house and didn't like the looks of it. He didn't see the gun, but he thought it looked 'damned strange'—his words, not mine."

"Thank God for him. That's twice he's saved our lives," Finn said.

"I should bake him some cookies or something." Mel frowned. "Cookies seem like a pretty poor exchange for saving our lives. Maybe I'll make brownies."

They all laughed. "What time is it, anyway?" Finn asked.

Hugh checked his watch. "Nearly five. You gonna call Mom and Dad?"

Finn sighed. "Yeah, but I'll wait a half hour and let them sleep a little longer. I don't want them to see it on the morning news before they hear it from me, though. Shit. Mom's going to fuss."

"Oh, yeah," Hugh agreed and sipped his whiskey.

***

'Fuss' was a mild word for how Moira DeLuca reacted to the news of her second son's nighttime adventures. She arrived 4.6 minutes after Finn pressed 'end' on his cell phone. The trip from their house to Finn's normally took at least seven minutes. She examined his ankle and head carefully, then refilled the ice pack and wrapped it around his foot with a towel. Then she tried to nag him into going to the emergency room until he told her the paramedics had checked him out and declared he did not need stitches. Still muttering to herself about the incompetence of said paramedics and the intractability of her children, Finn in particular, she swept into the kitchen and prepared a breakfast feast for all, including the officers still investigating across the street. The rest of the family turned up within the hour.

Big Tony pulled his son into a giant bear hug and

Finn had to swallow against the sudden swelling in his throat. "It's okay, Dad. I'm fine."

"This was a hell of a thing to wake up to, son. I need a minute." He kept hold of Finn for another full minute, then turned to Mel and held his arms open. "We're a hugging family, so just get used to it."

Cara and Izzy were horrified Mel had had to go through everything alone, and griped at her for a full ten minutes about not letting them know what was really going on.

"All you asked was if I knew where Finn was," Cara moaned. "I thought you were fighting! If I'd had an inkling he was in danger I would have come over."

"Mel." Izzy took a somewhat gentler tack. "We're your friends. Let us help once in a while, okay? That's what we're here for."

"What did you think we were fighting about?" Finn asked his sisters.

"Oh, you know, because she stayed out late with us instead of running home to be with you. We told her it was ridiculous, but then you weren't home…" Cara tried to explain between bites of bacon.

"Mel, you thought I was mad at you for staying out late?" He raised his eyebrows at her, not able to believe she'd thought him capable of something so shitty.

"Well, I didn't know. I didn't think you would be mad at me for something like that, but I couldn't get hold of you. You didn't answer my texts or calls." She didn't seem able to meet his gaze.

"For God's sake," he muttered, then turned his

body to be able to look her straight in the eye. "Mel, you can stay out as late as you want. You are an adult, and it's not up to me to get mad at you for something like that. You let me know where you were so I wouldn't worry, and that's enough. I wasn't mad. I couldn't reach my cell phone."

"I know that now. At the time I was freaking out, however, and was not quite as rational as I usually am." She sniffed and sat up, seeming embarrassed. "I know you weren't mad," she finished softly.

He flashed her a crooked smile and tilted her chin up. Then he kissed her, long and hard, in front of his entire family. He was simply too tired to care. "I love you," he murmured against her lips as his youngest brother whooped in appreciation.

Mel and Finn both had to go through their stories again—both for the family and the police—then Moira insisted everyone leave them alone so they could get a few hours of sleep. He stood and held out his hand for Mel. He noticed Chris slinking out as he and Mel were ushered from the living room to their bedroom.

As they walked down the hallway, she stopped in front of the guest bedroom. "I can sleep in here."

"Why?" He was dumbfounded.

"You know, with your parents here—"

He tugged on her hand. "Don't be ridiculous. They all know we're sleeping together and no one is shocked or horrified. Come on." He pulled her into their bedroom and closed the door softly. He stripped down to his boxers and crawled into bed.

Mel stripped down to her bra and panties and crawled in beside him. "Finn?" Mel whispered from her pillow. "Is it over?"

"Yeah, sweetheart. It is." He pulled her close and spooned against her back. "Go to sleep. We'll talk about it when we wake up."

***

The house was silent when Finn next opened his eyes. *Please let them be gone.* He loved his family, but needed some quiet time with Mel to begin to process what had happened. She had been characteristically quiet since it had ended, but he knew she would need to talk about it soon. He slid from the bed as stealthily as possible, hoping to let her sleep a little longer. He limped to the kitchen, glad his ankle didn't seem to feel any worse than usual. Maybe he could avoid a trip to the doctor, after all. He was about to pour his first cup of coffee when he felt warm arms snake around his waist from behind. He turned to embrace her fully.

"Mel." He breathed in her essence, grateful beyond belief he could stand here in his kitchen and hold her. He had things he needed to say, but first he simply needed to hold her. He bent his head and laid his lips on hers, kissing her deeply, but without the urgency of passion. This kiss was about so much more than desire. This kiss was about love and commitment. And apology. "Mel, I'm sorry."

"For what?" She reached a small hand up and cupped his cheek, brushing her thumb across his scratchy whiskers.

"It was all my fault. Lena was stalking *me*, trying to kill *me*. She never would have known about you if you hadn't become involved with me."

"Finn, it doesn't matter."

"It does matter, Mel! It matters a whole hell of a lot! You were nearly killed because of me. I can't forget that!"

"So what are you saying?" She dropped her hand and backed away.

"I'm saying I'm not a safe person. I'm a cop and I deal with some really bad people. I'll always be connected with people like that. You got involved in all this because of me." He had to make her understand why she should find someone safer.

"Finn, don't be ridiculous. When you thought I was the one being stalked, you didn't hesitate to put yourself in harm's way. That's what you do when you love someone."

"Mel, I do that for living. It was my choice. You would be better—"

"Do you love me, Finn?" She grabbed his face between her palms.

"Yes, of course, but—"

She smiled and reached up to kiss him. "There's no 'but' about it. It was my choice as well. I don't regret anything about what I chose to do last night, except forgetting to chamber a round in your gun."

He sighed and rested his forehead against hers. "Don't say that, Mel. Shooting a person isn't something I ever want you to have to do."

"Me neither, but I would choose to do it again in a heartbeat if it meant I could save you. Finn, we got through this together. It's over and now we can make our own choices—together."

It wasn't over, not by a long shot if Lena lived,

but Mel didn't need to know that right now. The important thing was they were standing here together and she wasn't running away. He hadn't really thought she would, but he had to give her the chance. "Mel, I'm so proud of you. I haven't had a chance to tell you yet. You were amazing last night. I was terrified when you walked into that bedroom—I lost about ten years off my life." He would never forget the sight of her leveling his gun at Lena as long as he lived.

"Well, I really didn't think about what I was doing. I was going on pure instinct."

He felt her shiver as she remembered. "Hey, let's talk about something else, like our living arrangements. I know you've been feeling like we were forced into living together."

"I have. I love living with you, Finn, but it happened so fast and for the wrong reasons. I'd feel a lot better if I knew we had both chosen it without any outside pressures."

He tucked her head under his chin. "I get that, but I know what I want. I need to know if you want it too."

"Are you asking me to move in with you?" She leaned back to look into his face, her smile sweet and hopeful.

"No." He couldn't resist teasing her a bit. "I'm asking you to marry me, Mel."

Epilogue

Finn

"Finn? Where are you?" She slammed the door and stomped to the kitchen, where he stood at the stove, stirring marinara in a large pot.

"Hey." He greeted her hesitantly, hearing the anger in her voice. "What's up?"

"It's your family! I love them, but I'm going to kill them." She retrieved a soda from the fridge and threw herself into one of the kitchen chairs, looking tired and cranky.

"I'm guessing the wedding planning didn't go well." She'd been out with his mother and sisters all day looking at wedding venues. They'd been able to talk of nothing else since he and Mel had announced their engagement the week before. He put the lid on his pasta sauce, turned the heat down to simmer, and sat across from her. "Tell me."

She blew out a huge breath. "We drove all over town looking at venues. I'm exhausted."

"Did you like any of the places my mom dragged

you to see?"

She shrugged and toyed with her soda can. "Casa Rondeña was nice, but..." She referred to a lovely winery in Albuquerque's north valley.

"But?"

She pushed her can away and stood. "It's beautiful. So was the Balloon Museum. But it's all super expensive and fussy and you have to reserve months in advance. It's not what I want, Finn." Her voice was bordering on whiny. He knew the stress was starting to pile up for her—the wedding, the news that Lena would live and thus require a lengthy trial, the construction on her house. It was enough to drive anyone crazy. He stood and went to the cabinet for a couple wine glasses, then poured them each a glass of merlot. "Here. That soda's not going to cut it today. Now let's sit down and you can tell me what you do want for our wedding."

"Really?"

"Mel." He covered her hand with his own as she returned to her seat. "It's our wedding, not theirs. I love them too, but they don't get to make the decisions. Now tell me about your dream wedding, sweetheart. If it's within my power, I'll make it happen."

She smiled radiantly. "I don't know, actually. I've never really thought about it much. But I'm beginning to get an idea of what I don't want."

"I thought all little girls had their future weddings planned from the time they were, like eight."

"Not all of them, apparently." She took a sip of the wine. "All those venues were for big weddings.

And I don't want to wait months. I was hoping we could get married early in the fall."

"So you want a small wedding in about two months? Hmmm, sounds like we better elope to Vegas."

She laughed and stood. "That sounds amazing." She sat on his lap and looped her arms around his neck. "But we can't do that to your family."

"I thought you wanted to kill them? What happened to that? I liked the sound of it." He brushed her hair behind her ear.

She leaned against him and smiled. "Maybe I'll hold off for a while. Is there any way we can have a small wedding here in Albuquerque, Finn?"

"Of course there is." He pulled his cell phone from his back pocket and opened the calendar app. "How does…Saturday, October third sound? My parents' backyard?"

"Really? Can we do that?"

He chuckled and punched another button on his phone. "Mom? Yeah, listen. Mel and I are getting married on October third. I know, but we want to have the ceremony in your backyard. That's right. No, we don't want a big wedding. Yes, it's what Mel wants. She's right here if you don't believe me. Can you call Father Ortega and set it up? No more than twenty-five people in addition to our family, okay? Thanks, Mom. I love you too." He returned his phone to his back pocket. "Done. Anything else?"

She threw her arms around his neck and peppered his face with kisses. "You're amazing, Finn! It's perfect!"

"Amazing, huh? I would have settled for wonderful." He kissed her and pulled away, an innocent expression on his face. "Hey, I just thought of something. You're going to have lots of free time now that you don't have to plan a big wedding. I can think of a couple things to keep you busy." He slid his hand under her shirt as he spoke, making his intention abundantly clear.

"Mmm." She arched into his hand. "What about your sauce?"

"It'll wait."

The End

Acknowledgments

Writing novels is the ultimate dream for a true introvert like me, but low and behold: it doesn't happen without talking to people! Turns out I don't know everything. Huh.

Extra special thanks to Agent Wayne Harvey of the New Mexico State Police, who allowed me to interview him and pepper him with annoying emails about endless procedural questions. Any errors are, of course, my own.

Thanks also to Joshua Kragness, whose description of how it feels to have a badly broken ankle was enormously helpful!

Thanks to my brother-in-law, Linn Reece, for sharing the story of the visiting cat, which was the spark for this entire series. Thanks to Andrea for not dusting your windowsill so I could see the kitty-cat paw prints and add them to my story. LOL and I hope you're not mad I added this!

I couldn't do this without the time and attention from my incredible editor, Toni Rakestraw, and the entire Limitless Publishing team. You guys ROCK!

As always, thanks to my husband who believes in me. Thanks also to my girls, my mom, and my bestie, Carol, for listening to my near-constant prattle about my writing. You are incredibly patient.

About the Author

Amy Reece lives in New Mexico with her incredible husband and two ridiculous mutts, Greta and Sodapop. When she's not writing, she's teaching high school English and social studies or maybe wandering through a thrift store in search of the next lucky teapot for her vast collection. She is an unrepentant bookaholic and has overflowing bookshelves in nearly every room of her house. Her favorite authors include J.R.R. Tolkien, J.K. Rowling, and C.S. Lewis–must have something to do with initials! She loves to travel and is hoping to need many research trips for future writing projects.

Did you enjoy this book? If so, please, please, please leave a short, but stellar review on amazon and/or GoodReads. I would really appreciate it!

Stay tuned for Hugh and Chrissy's story, Safe Guard, coming September 2017 from Limitless Publishing.

If you want to cyber-stalk me, here are some helpful links:

Good Reads:
https://www.goodreads.com/author/show/13884337.Amy_Reece

Amazon author page:
https://www.amazon.com/Amy-Reece/e/B00WDG12RO

Facebook Fan Page:
https://www.facebook.com/areeceauthor

Twitter Fan Page:
https://twitter.com/AReeceAuthor

Website:
https://www.amyreeceauthor.com/

Blog:
https://amyreece.wordpress.com/

www.ingramcontent.com/pod-product-compliance
Lightning Source LLC
Chambersburg PA
CBHW052025240626
47153CB00006B/1960